FRANKLIN HORTON

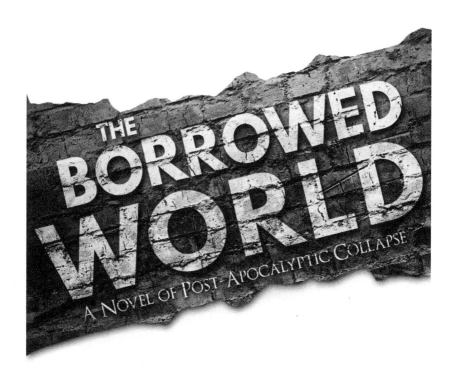

THE BORROWED WORLD

A NOVEL OF POST-APOCALYPTIC COLLAPSE

ALSO BY FRANKLIN HORTON

The Borrowed World Series

The Borrowed World

Ashes of the Unspeakable

Legion of Despair

No Time For Mourning

Valley of Vengeance

Switched On

The Ungovernable

The Locker Nine Series

Locker Nine

Grace Under Fire

Compound Fracture

Blood Bought

The Mad Mick Series

The Mad Mick

Masters of Mayhem

Brutal Business

Stand-Alone Novels

Random Acts

ABOUT THE AUTHOR

Franklin Horton lives and writes in the mountains of Southwestern Virginia. He is the author of several bestselling science fiction and thriller series. You can follow him on his website at franklinhorton.com.

While you're there please sign up for his mailing list for updates, event schedule, book recommendations, and discounts.

PREFACE

The earliest seeds of this project began during a period of my life when I had to travel frequently for work. During periods of elevated terror alerts and especially during Hurricane Katrina, I thought often about the vulnerability of a person traveling during a national disaster. It would be difficult to be prepared for all of the possible impediments that a person might encounter. As a way of passing the time during long drives, I developed "get home plans" for each trip. Given what I had in my luggage, what avenues of travel would be available to me? What would my route be? What hazards might be encountered on the route? An immediate side effect of asking myself these questions was that I began to pack better for my trips. If I was going to have to walk home, I wanted the shoes to do it in.

This is a work of fiction, though. It was not written with the intent of serving as an instructional manual on prepping or building the perfect bug-out bag. There are plenty of excellent books and forums out there already that can guide you through that process. Instead, this is a speculative novel about a person who reads "those" books and haunts "those" websites. It is about how a moderately-prepared and well-informed person might respond under a particular set of circumstances. It is intended to encourage thought and discussion.

Franklin Horton
   April 27, 2015

1

Imran ul-Haq was eating a late dinner and watching The History Channel. The veal he ate was exquisitely tender and perfectly seasoned, practically melting in his mouth. It was one of his favorite meals and The History Channel was one of his favorite channels. The show he watched was on the disintegration of America's infrastructure. He found the show to be both amusing and fascinating.

Imran was a plastic surgeon of Syrian descent who now resided in Arlington, Virginia. He couldn't help but be aware that a show this critical of the government would never be shown in his native country. During the hour-long program he learned of America's weakened bridges, failing dams, and problems with the electrical grid. He learned about the fragility of America's water supply. When the show ended he was struck with an idea he felt had practically been thrust into his hands. He couldn't help but smile at his good fortune.

At the end of the program, there was an advertisement which told viewers how to order a DVD of the show. Imran scribbled a quick note to himself, reminding him to order five copies that very evening. Four of the copies he would send overseas with no explanation necessary. When the recipients viewed the DVDs they would see them through the same lens as Imran did. A deadly idea would grow. It would blossom into a flower of death and destruction.

The surgeon recalled the attacks of September 11th. He envisioned a broader attack. Something with more men and lasting devastation. Something more visceral and less flashy. Something that would even be less complicated because the Americans had done half the work already. By allowing vital parts of their nation to weaken to this point, he suspected much devastation could be accomplished with very little work. With a few skilled men and well-placed munitions this country could be toppled like a stack of toy blocks. Imran was certain of it. The producers of the show had practically laid the plan out for him.

This was obviously not work for plastic surgeons, though. Such complex orchestrations would have to be the work of a man with the right connections and significant funding. Such a man could call upon cells of the faithful hiding in plain sight in North America and call them into action. A man on the fringes of a movement such as ISIS would be perfect. A man like his brother.

Imran went to his custom-made walnut bookcase, opened a glass door, and retrieved a mundane text on Islamic history. In Iraq, the same text sat in his brother's living room on a humbler and likely dustier shelf. Imran sat down at his computer and went to a generic webmail account that he used to communicate with his family. He started an email to his brother and typed a series of numbers.

"3-18, 28-98, 9-32 . . ."

It was a simple system. The numbers instructed his brother as to what page number to go to in the book and which word to retrieve from that page. When all the words were obtained from the book and written out in order they spelled out a message. This was referred to as a "book code" and was nearly impossible to break unless you happened to have the same copy, same edition, same printing of the book that the sender and receiver were using. When Imran completed his email, he clicked the Send button. Before rising from his desk, he went ahead and ordered those copies of the show he'd just seen on the History Channel.

His housekeeper had left him a nice chocolate cake for dessert. She was truly an amazing cook for an American woman. He placed a modest slice on a china plate and sat back down in front of the television. That show about lumberjacks was coming on and he was particularly fond of it, although they certainly used a lot of profane, heathen language. American television may one day be remembered as its finest achievement, he mused.

ALMOST SIX MONTHS had passed since Imran mailed his brother the DVDs and he was only now hearing back from him. The communication came in the form of another book code email advising him of a special family celebration taking place in Syria that he must return home for. Imran knew this message meant that the seed he'd planted had grown into something significant. He hoped it would be something very special indeed. As he had no family to be concerned about, he had his office manager clear his schedule for a month of vacation and began to pack. He hired a service to box the contents of his home and pack them in a shipping container bound for Syria. Due to trade imbalances there was very little freight leaving U.S. ports these days. Shipping all of his belongings home only cost him six hundred American dollars. That was a bargain. With his surgical skills he could easily start a new life, perhaps in some place like Dubai, a place he'd long wanted to visit. He had savings sufficient to make that happen.

On his last day in the United States Imran dealt with his financial arrangements. He had his accounts transferred to offshore banks he could access from anywhere in the world. He retained several thousand dollars in cash, which he dispersed throughout his luggage and on his person. He drove his Mercedes to the airport and left it in long-term parking where it would sit for a very long time.

Later, aboard his plane, the U.S. receded from his window. He thanked the country for his medical education and hoped that it emerged from its coming hardships a better nation than the one he was leaving. A more humble nation. A more spiritual nation.

Perhaps even a Muslim nation.

On the same day Imran fled America, an Iraqi grocer in Detroit received an encrypted email from a fellow Iraqi in Germany. He was instructed to contact four men across the United States, each the leader of a cell of men who had sworn their lives to Jihad. The men were previously unknown to the grocer and he was given a specific greeting to use with each of the men. When they heard his greeting they would know that Allah was calling for them. Each cell leader had a specific response he was to recite back to the man from Detroit. When the grocer received the correct response, the men's identities would be confirmed and they would receive their instructions.

The four cell leaders would then contact each member of their cell with further instructions. Some were to purchase handheld GPS units commonly used for backpacking or hunting. Several were to purchase ATVs and trailers for hauling them behind vehicles. One was instructed to buy a pop-up camping trailer. Two dozen men were told to purchase hunting licenses, camouflage clothing, and scoped hunting rifles in .30-06 caliber. They were instructed to practice until they were proficient with the weapons. Other men had no specific assignments other than to wait and stand ready for a call. They were all given one week to prepare themselves and pray for success.

On a Friday, two dozen ISIS-trained terrorists converged on the U.S. and crossed its borders illegally. Six crossed remote border sections in the forests of Washington State on backpacking trails used by marijuana smugglers. Several entered Texas, smuggled across the border by a drug cartel paid in cash and asking no questions. Others crossed from Windsor, Canada, into Detroit in the trunks of cars. The remainder arrived on the Florida and Georgia coasts transported by high-speed Cigarette cruisers.

Each of these groups was met by a cell member and issued a duffle bag with false identification, clothes, a handgun, extra magazines and ammunition, and a prepaid cell phone. Programmed into each phone was the number of the cell member they would be paired with for their segment of the operation. In addition, each was given a key attached to a white tag. Each white tag held a different set of GPS coordinates.

2

Bilal spoke not a word of English but that was fine. He wouldn't need it for his business there. He used his prepaid phone to contact the cell member assigned to him, a Tampa waiter.

"I'm Ali," the waiter said. "What's your name, brother?"

Bilal did not reply. He hated these amateurs.

Ali was embarrassed by the slip. He knew they were not supposed to use names but he had little training and had never been called into an operation before. He was nervous and didn't know how he was supposed to act with this terrifying man from the front lines. He realized that with his attempts at camaraderie and friendly small-talk he likely appeared inept, or worse, Westernized.

"Did you rent the house as instructed?" Bilal asked.

"I did."

"Did you gather the things that you were asked to gather?"

"I purchased everything. All has been done exactly in the manner in which I was instructed."

They spent that night at Ali's apartment and left the next morning in a recently purchased minivan. Ali had bought it used with cash he received in a FedEx package. As instructed, he had removed the seats and had the windows tinted. Using the handheld GPS unit the pair sought the coordinates written on the key tag that Bilal had been given upon his arrival. The coordinates led them to a self-storage facility and a particular block of units hidden in the dense maze of metal structures. Bilal's key fit Unit 437. He opened the lock and raised the door. Inside were several plastic trunks about four feet long and two feet wide.

"What are these things?" Ali asked.

Bilal did not answer. He despised Ali's talkative nature. He'd been allowed his whole life to speak without thinking when he should have been clouted on the head for his loose tongue. Wordlessly, he gestured at Ali to help him load the trunks into the vehicle.

"The boxes are heavy," Ali complained.

Bilal remained tight-lipped. Again, the other man felt the need to voice the obvious. He completely lacked any discipline.

When they'd closed the unit up and were back on the road, Bilal asked Ali if he'd studied the route as instructed.

"I have."

"Then take us to Baton Rouge, Louisiana," Bilal said. "To the house you rented. Do not exceed the speed limit. Use utmost caution."

"What then?" Ali asked. "What will we do when we get there?"

"When there is something you need to know, you will be told."

FOR A WEEK, Ali and Bilal stayed in their rented house in Baton Rouge. In the back bedroom was a chest freezer Ali had purchased at the Home Depot. It was around four feet long and three feet deep. Beside it was a plastic tub of water. Each hour, Bilal reached into the freezer and removed what Ali now suspected were mortar shells. There were two of them and Bilal dipped the nose end of each into the water and then replaced it in the freezer. Over the last couple of days the nose end of each shell had grown about an inch thicker with ice. When Bilal was satisfied with his work, he sent Ali to Walmart to purchase the largest marine cooler he could find. Once he'd secured the cooler he was to fill it with dry ice.

That night, as Bilal knelt in the living room floor and recited his prayers, he received a text message containing a set of numbers. Referring to a small notebook in his pocket, Bilal was able to transpose the encoded numbers until he decoded the intended message. It was another set of GPS coordinates. When he was done translating the message, Bilal went to Ali.

"It's time."

3

By 2 a.m., Bilal and Ali were concealed in a stand of trees approximately one mile from ExxonMobil's Baton Rouge Refinery. It was one of the largest oil refineries in America, capable of producing over a half million barrels of oil a day. While the shot was nearly at the limits of the 81mm mortar's range, Bilal had extensive experience with the weapon in Iraq and was more than capable of hitting such a large – and highly flammable – target as the refinery.

The weapon consisted of four manageable pieces: the cannon, the mount, the base plate, and the sighting unit. He and Ali hauled the plastic trunks into the woods beside the road. They then carried each piece to a specific site, exactly where the coordinates Bilal received earlier had instructed him to set up his weapon. When the weapon was assembled, Bilal had Ali return each plastic trunk to the vehicle while he sighted the weapon.

Bilal removed one of the ice-encrusted High Explosive mortar shells and placed it gently in the firing tube. The base of the shell slid easily into the tube. When the ice encrusted section hit the tube it was too large and would not slide further inside. This was by design and exactly as planned. The shell would hang partially exposed from the barrel, where it would stay until the ice melted.

"Genius," Ali uttered as he watched.

"We used this method in Iraq," Bilal said. "When the ice melts, the round slips down the tube and strikes the firing pin, firing the round."

"How much time do we have?" Ali asked.

"In this heat, less than an hour, I expect," Bilal replied. "Let us go. We have another to set up and not much time."

After the second mortar installation was set up, they returned to the rented house to empty the trunks and cooler from their vehicles. While Ali carried two of the trunks down the hallway, Bilal stepped up behind him with a suppressed Walther P22. He emptied two quick rounds into the back of Ali's head. As Ali slumped forward, Bilal unscrewed the suppressor and stowed it, along with the weapon, in his pocket.

Bilal watched without expression as Ali's body stiffened and spasmed, the brain dead but the body not yet aware of that fact. When the gyrations stopped, Bilal dragged Ali's body to the back bedroom and wrestled him into the chest freezer. Bilal then walked back through the house, locked the door behind him, and departed in Ali's van.

In the back of the van there remained one large plastic trunk. Inside were one dozen M72 Light Anti-tank Weapons, otherwise known as LAWs. They were compact weapons, around two feet closed, and weighing only five pounds. Their range was nearly one thousand meters. In Bilal's pocket were more GPS coordinates and a list of secondary targets. With his primary objective completed, he could proceed with taking out those other targets. He allowed himself a quick flush of pride. The night would be glorious.

As Bilal drove into the night, the ice on his mortar shell melted sufficiently that it was no longer able to resist the downward pull of gravity. The remaining ice slipped free and the shell dropped down the tube. With a loud pop, the shell struck the firing pin. The primer ignited the propelling charge and the missile arced toward the refinery. Those working at the refinery that night heard the noise and saw the arc of the shell coming toward them. A few veterans even recognized the signature sound of a mortar round and ran for their lives.

It was impossible to run far enough, though. At the end of the projectile's path the detonating nose of the mortar struck a gasoline storage tank and exploded instantly. What ensued was a massive series of explosions that would result in a tremendous loss of human life. There was damage to the refinery that would render it inoperative for at least a year, if not longer.

However, that was not the end of this long night. All of the ISIS terrorists operating that night were able to achieve their primary objectives and the majority of their secondary objectives. In operations identical to Bilal's, fuel refineries across the south were struck by 81mm mortars at ranges of one-half to one mile. The Baytown Refinery in Baytown, Texas, the nation's largest, went up in flames, as did the smaller Texas City Refinery. In Louisiana, the Lake Charles Refinery and the Beaumont Refinery were also destroyed. In the Midwest, the Whiting Refinery in Indiana was set ablaze by a twenty-seven year old Iraqi operative named Wahid. In one hour, the United States lost the capacity to refine three million barrels of oil each day.

In remote sections of Alaska, two terrorists one hundred miles apart used shaped charges on short timers to compromise the Alaskan Pipeline. Each man carried ten charges in a backpack and followed the pipeline on an ATV. They randomly placed charges and set timers to detonate in thirty minutes or less.

In Russell County, Kentucky, a thirty-two year old Syrian named Faisal used a stolen American Javelin anti-tank weapon to place a shell in a weak earthen section of the fragile Wolf Creek Dam. Before his very eyes, the earth began to crumble. Within minutes water was pouring through the dam and making its way toward Nashville. The entire city would be flooded by morning.

In the Hampton Roads-Newport News area of Virginia, an American of Iraqi descent named Hasnat drove his catering van through the Chesapeake Bay Bridge Tunnel. In the seat beside him was the ISIS operative he'd been assigned to transport around the city.

Hasnat was unsure of the nature of their operation. He only knew that the van was full of boxes and that his guest did not feel him worthy of knowing what was inside them. That was okay. He understood the importance of compartmentalization.

As the bridge turned to into a tunnel and dropped beneath the bay, Hasnat sensed a change in his guest. He suspected that he may be claustrophobic. When Hasnat turned to speak to his passenger, he saw the remote control in the man's hand and immediately understood. With only the first word of his prayers on his tongue, Hasnat's vehicle detonated and removed a seventy foot section of this marvel of engineering.

Using Javelin anti-tank weapons and 81mm mortars, explosive shells rained from fields and rooftops upon the Golden Gate Bridge, the Brooklyn Bridge, and a string of power plants. When the terrorists achieved their targets, each followed Bilal's lead and executed the cell member assigned as their escort, erasing their tracks. There were to be no loose ends remaining on American soil.

Other than the two men working the Alaskan Pipeline, each terrorist was assigned multiple secondary targets within the Eastern, Western, or Texas Interconnection Power Grids. Some had LAW rockets. Others, dressed in hunting camouflage and armed with 30-06 hunting rifles, fired into crucial and difficult to replace transformers at select power stations. As high voltage lines and crucial power stations within the grid were destroyed, the United States began to go dark. Power failed, soon followed by communication, transportation, and medical services. Law enforcement would soon fail as well, taking the peace of a nation with it.

4

I'd never been fond of staying in hotels. I'd worked for the same state agency in southwestern Virginia for over twenty years now, and I'd had to make the five-hour trip to Richmond more times than I could count. The distance always required staying in a hotel and, unlike some people, I didn't enjoy staying in hotels. However, Richmond was our state capital. Every time there was a change in the regulations governing our agency we had to send a group up to see how it was going to affect us. Richmond was where the important meetings were always held.

Six of us made the trip up yesterday and our meeting was supposed to start at 10 a.m. I hoped that it ended early and we could hit the road back toward home. In fact, getting home was the first thing I thought of when I woke from my restless sleep. I hadn't even gone to my meeting yet and already I was thinking about heading home. It was a testament to both my dislike for Richmond and my love of home.

I never slept well in hotels and the sheets there reeked of bleach to the point my eyes burned. I rolled out of my bed, my immediate plan to hit the hotel fitness room for some "me time" with the stationary bike and my iPod. When I was done, I'd head downstairs for a tasteless and disappointing continental breakfast with my colleagues. If I got in a good workout prior to my meeting I would at least feel like I'd accomplished something, unlike the feeling I got from sitting in those soul-sucking meetings.

I looked toward the bedside clock to check the time but it was blank. It took me a second to register the oddity of that in my groggy state. Then I noticed that the bathroom light I left on last night was not on either. I staggered to the dresser and retrieved my watch. It was around 5:30 a.m., my regular time to wake up. I went to the window and opened the blinds. The sky was just beginning to lighten at the horizon but it was still mostly dark out there.

I saw some vehicles moving around, but noticed that there were no security lights functioning in the parking lot. That was odd. Hotel parking lots were always lit up like football fields here in Richmond because of the crime. Then I noticed that no streetlights were illuminated. I could see one major intersection from my window and the traffic lights were not working either. I started looking around at other hotels and office buildings visible from my window. They were all dark. This had to be a power outage. I'd never been in a hotel during a power outage before, but I could only assume it would make staying in a hotel suck even worse. No elevators, no hot water, and eventually no water at all. No workout and no shitty continental breakfast, either.

I went back to the dresser and picked up my iPhone. I touched a button and the screen glowed. I opened an app and it attempted to update with the morning's news. There must have been a poor data connection because the page loaded with missing blocks of text and images. Only a red headline was visible: AMERICA, NATION UNDER ATTACK

Shit. What had I missed last night?

I closed the app, touched an icon, and dialed my wife's cell number. After a few misleading rings, I received a message that all circuits were busy. I sat down on the bed and attempted to collect my thoughts, but it was like herding cats. I was too sluggish from poor sleep.

I went to the bathroom and tried the sink. There was still some water pressure so I splashed cold water on my face in the dark. Without power there wouldn't be water up here much longer. When the city's booster pumps failed, the upper stories of buildings, like the one I was in now, would be the first to experience the loss in pressure. I grabbed a towel and dried off, feeling slightly more alert.

I carried my suitcase closer to the window and dug out some clothes. I dressed quickly since I wasn't sure at this point if I'd actually be attending my meeting or not. I remembered something I'd read once before about communicating in disasters. It was supposed to be easier to send a text message with a poor signal than to make a call. A text could go through with sporadic connectivity while a cell call required a more stable connection.

I got my phone and sat back down. I opened the messaging app and typed:

NO POWER HERE. SAW A HEADLINE ABOUT AN ATTACK. R U AND KIDS OK?

I set the phone back down and picked up my shoes. I'd brought dress shoes for my meeting but my everyday shoes were Salomon hiking boots and that's what I put on. I didn't know what the day would bring but I couldn't imagine the meeting was still on the agenda. I certainly couldn't imagine some of the higher maintenance women in our group going out in public without showers and makeup.

I surveyed the room in the dim light and tried to collect my belongings. I picked up any scattered clothes and crammed them into the bag. I went to the dresser and used the light from my phone to gather my EDC, or Every Day Carry, items. That included my billfold, change, keys, my SOG Twitch XL knife, and a little Ruger LCP .380 pistol. The LCP had an inside-the-belt holster that allowed me to carry it discreetly inside my pants, hidden by my shirt. I had a permit to carry it, although our agency policy prohibited carrying it in company vehicles or at the office. I did so anyway because I would rather have it when I needed it than die at the hands of a criminal, secure in the fact that I was dying in compliance with the agency policy manual. If bad things happened, I would survive to find another job. I would not die and have my tombstone read: Here Lies Jim, He Adhered to Policy.

I tucked the pistol away and the text alert on my phone sounded off. I saw it was my wife, breathed a sigh of relief, and read the message:

NOT SURE WHAT'S GOING ON. JUST WOKE UP. WE HAVE POWER HERE.

I quickly typed a reply:

DON'T KNOW WHAT'S HAPPENING BUT ASSUME YOU WILL LOSE POWER TOO. GET RED FOLDER OUT OF GUNSAFE AND FOLLOW INSTRUCTIONS IMMEDIATELY. TEXT ME BACK IF YOU FIGURE OUT WHAT HAPPENED. LOVE YOU AND WILL BE HOME AS SOON AS I CAN.

I hit Send. I had seen enough cell towers up close to know that many of them had propane generators for power failures. How long they stayed up varied. All it took in a network was one failure along the chain and the whole network would start to sag. The system was already overburdened and one glitch could cause a massive backup in data transmission. It was kind of like when some jerk at the office decided to print five hundred brochures on the office printer and it kept anyone else from printing for hours.

I hoped my wife got the message. I'd trained her and the kids on surviving emergencies but I never knew if they were taking me seriously. I was never sure whether they were actually listening or just humoring me. I tried to explain they may need those skills if bad things happened. I hoped they'd taken it to heart because bad things might be happening right now.

The area we lived in got its power from coal-fired plants that were only about fifteen miles away from my home. With a supply of coal, they would continue generating power for a while. The coal was all local, too. The problem I anticipated was that with demand surging the power company would be trying to send as much of that power upstream as possible. They would be under pressure to get it to the more populated areas of Northern Virginia. Under this pressure something would break. Components would overheat and fail. A transformer would pop. Something they would not be able to replace would break and then the folks at home would be in the dark too.

I got up and did a final check of the room. I gathered my jacket, my bag, and the backpack. I carried the backpack to my room last night after everyone else had gone to their rooms. I didn't want to have to explain the backpack to them because I knew taking it everywhere I traveled made me seem paranoid. Although I didn't mind the word "paranoid", I preferred to look at myself as well-informed. I knew what kind of crazy shit could happen in the world and I wanted to be as ready as I could be. The backpack was my emergency Get Home Bag, or GHB, and it went where I went. I brought it in last night because I didn't like leaving it in the car overnight. There were items in there that could save my life in an emergency. Today, might be that day.

It really wasn't paranoia, though. What changed me was seeing our nation undergo events like Hurricane Katrina and Hurricane Sandy. We as a nation just didn't have the ability we once had to step in and come to the rescue of our citizens. Maybe it was just that people were less self-sufficient than they used to be. They were more easily brought to their knees by bumps in the road. Either way, I had children and a wife that I was responsible for. With that responsibility came paranoia. I didn't want to be one of those people unable to take care of my family. I didn't want to have to take them to shelters and depend on someone else to feed us. I wanted to have a backup plan and that Get Home Bag was part of it.

I started to leave the room but was afraid to leave my stuff behind, afraid the door might not open again. I was pretty sure that the lock was battery-powered and would function even during an outage but I couldn't take a chance on being separated from my gear. I went to the door and pulled it open, leaving my gear in the door to prop it open. I stepped out into the hallway and realized how alien it was to be in a completely darkened hotel hallway. There were no exit lights and no smoke detector LEDs. There were no overhead lights and no blinking security cameras. There was no buzz and clicking from ice machines. No hum of soda machines. There was no sound of CNN or Bloomberg coming from the rooms of early-rising business travelers. No one stirred.

I stepped across the hall, using the flashlight app on my phone to light the way. I tapped on a door. Nothing. I tapped again and heard movement inside.

"Uh, who is it?" asked a groggy voice.

It was Gary Sullivan, the IT Director at our agency. He'd worked there almost as long as I had and we were pretty good friends. Mostly because he was slightly paranoid, like me. Excuse me, I mean *well-informed* like me. Having a paranoid friend made each of us feel slightly less paranoid though. That was just the kind of supportive relationship every well-prepared individual needed.

"It's Jim," I replied.

The door cracked and Gary opened it slightly. "What's going on? What time is it?"

"I think the shit hit the fan," I said. Even though I'd imagined this happening, it felt a little weird to say it.

It must have been a little weird to hear too. Gary had a blank look on his face. He shielded his eyes from the light of my phone. "Uh, what? What the heck are you talking about?"

"The power's out. The phone said something about an attack. I don't know anything yet but something is definitely going on."

Gary perked up at that. "Give me a few minutes. I'll be right out."

I retreated to my room and began to assess our situation. There were six of us here in two cars. Two men and four women. We were slightly over three hundred miles from home. We didn't know what was going on yet. There could be limited access to fuel due to the power outages. There could even be limitations on travel depending on the scale of the emergency. We were not equipped for a long journey. Above all, we were way too short on information.

It was at that moment that I remembered my trusty little iPod had a radio receiver built into it. I never used it because who the hell listens to the radio anymore? I don't. My iPod was for audio books, podcasts, and workout music.

I dug it out of my jacket pocket and stuck the ear buds in my ears. I selected the radio feature from the menu and began trying to figure it out. When I did, I scanned through channels finding mostly static. Then I landed on a station playing what sounded like an Emergency Broadcast System recording. It was the flat, monotone voice of someone reading a prepared statement. Eventually the statement began to repeat itself and included mention of the fact that it was indeed an EBS statement and to stay tuned for further updates. I continued listening to hear the message in its entirety.

"The President of the United States has declared a nationwide state of emergency in response to the widespread and devastating terror attacks that occurred overnight. We do not know yet who is responsible for the heinous actions that have shattered the peace of our nation. As it has not yet been determined if the attacks are over or if we continue to be at-risk, Americans are encouraged to stay at home and limit travel to emergency situations. Roadways should be kept clear for emergency vehicles, first responders, and those attempting to repair the damage caused during the attacks. Several major fuel refineries were destroyed and fuel may be rationed until such time as we are able to assess and take inventory of the available fuel supply. The procedure for limiting fuel sales has not been finalized yet but Americans should be aware that this is a possibility. Estimates are that over sixty-five percent of homes in the country are without power and it is unknown when service will be restored. Americans are urged to conserve water, utilize their family emergency plans and resources. They should stay tuned for further updates. Until the situation is stable, each American is encouraged to help his neighbor and we will get through this together. May God bless you and may God bless the United States of America."

When the message began to repeat itself, I turned the iPod off. There was a knock on the door. I pulled the ear buds from my ears and answered it. It was Gary.

"You ever figure out what was going on?" he asked.

"I just listened to an Emergency Broadcast System message on my iPod," I told him. "There's been some kind of terrorist attack affecting fuel supplies and the power grid. A lot of the country is without power. The fuel supply is limited and they're telling everyone to stay home until they know more."

Gary stood there for a moment absorbing that information without a reaction. He didn't appear to be a morning person. All his cylinders weren't firing yet.

"I think we need to get everyone together and get the hell out of here," he finally said. "Things could deteriorate quickly and we're a long way from home. This is the last place I want to be stuck."

"I agree. Let's get everyone together then and tell them what we know."

Gary went one way and I went the other, each of us waking up two sleeping women and thereby sharing the danger equally. They were all seasoned travelers and responded to my knocking by calling through the door rather than opening it. We each gave a condensed version of the little we knew, telling them that we needed to assemble in my room in ten minutes and get a plan together. They were not happy campers.

Gary and I were sitting in my room talking as the women began showing up. I could hear Lois Green, the head of the accounting department, complaining all the way down the hall. She would no doubt blame me for all of this. As far as she was concerned I was the root of all evil.

"What's this all about, Jim?" she demanded. "Gary said it was a national emergency and he'd tell us more when we got here. I need to know something now."

She sounded put out at being dragged from bed and not given time to prepare herself. She was a minister's wife and the two of us did not really get along. She represented a lot of the things that I disliked the most in people. She gossiped, back-stabbed, and lied while maintaining the appearance that she was above such things. I was pretty sure she thought I was the devil incarnate, but I wasn't losing sleep over it.

"We don't have a lot of information," I told her as everyone else filed in behind her. "There's obviously no power here but my wife says we still have it at home. I heard a message over the Emergency Broadcast System a few minutes ago that said there had been terrorist attack last night. The fuel supply has been affected and the power to more than half of the country is out. They're telling people to limit travel and stay off the roads."

"What do you think we should do?" Alice Watkins, the Human Resources Director, asked.

She and I got along pretty well most of the time but she was a stickler for the rules since she wrote a lot of them. She and I were part of a team that developed the policies for operating our agency. She was the one who'd written that particular policy about carrying weapons in agency vehicles that I had been breaking on a regular basis. I hoped she wasn't going to advocate for staying put just because the government told us to. If that was the case, I'd have to leave her in the parking lot. Taking orders from the government was not my cup of tea.

"I'm not interested in staying in Richmond," I said. "I think that would be a dumb and potentially dangerous move."

Gary, ever the more tactful and polite speaker, took it upon himself to act as my translator. "What Jim is trying to say is that there are a lot of risks to staying here. The government could institute Martial Law or curfews, particularly here in Richmond. The emergency broadcast said they're going to limit the fuel supply. If they do, we'll have a long walk home. It's almost like we need to get out of here before they get organized and tell us we can't."

The women absorbed this up in silence. Jim looked at the other two women in the group, Rebecca Dowdy and Randi Ward, both from the clinical side of their agency.

"Any opinions?" he asked.

"What about staying put and seeing what happens?" Randi asked. "That might be the safest move."

"I don't think it's a good idea," I repeated. "Do you remember Hurricane Katrina? Imagine that devastation on a national scale.

People are civil now and things are relatively stable but things will get much worse before they get better. Richmond in particular will have more people than supplies and things will get very bad in a few days. As stores run out of food, people will get desperate. Desperate people become violent. Meanwhile our families will be home worrying about us."

"Run out of food? Stores won't run out of food that quickly," Lois snapped at me as if I were some vile creature just making up things to annoy her.

"It's called 'Just In Time' inventory, Lois," I said. "Most stores don't keep more than three days' worth of food. If there's panic buying the stores may be empty within a day if they don't get trucks. Think about the bread aisle when a blizzard is coming. If fuel sales are limited, those trucks may never come."

Lois was ignoring me, as she often did, and was fooling with her phone. "I can't seem to get through to my husband," Lois said. "I tried to call him while we were walking down here."

I wasn't sure what was relevant about that, but Lois seemed to think that whatever passed through her head was important to the rest of us. "You might try texting," I suggested. "That will sometimes go through when a call can't."

Lois looked at me like I was personally responsible for her call not going through. "Must be nice to be an expert on everything. I guess I'll try that, though."

I rolled my eyes at her. "Try it or not. I don't care either way."

As Human Resources Director, Alice was used to mediating disagreements, often involving me. "Arguing won't get us anywhere. Are we in agreement that we want to try and get home now or do some of you want to stay?" She looked around. "Lois, stay or go?"

Lois shot me a nasty look. "Go, I guess."

I shrugged. She continued to act as if I had personally brought this down upon us. I was so glad we were in separate cars.

"Rebecca?" Alice asked.

Rebecca was a tall, dark-haired triathlete who ran our drug treatment center. She was blunt and tough as nails from working with manipulative substance abusers every day. "Go."

"Randi?" Alice asked.

Randi was short and fiery-tempered. She ran residential programs for folks with intellectual disabilities and hated meetings as much as I did. "Oh, I don't like Richmond anyway. I'm ready to get the hell out of here."

"And I'm assuming you guys both think we should go, too?" Alice asked Gary and me.

We both nodded.

"Well, I'm in agreement with everyone else," Alice said. She looked at me. "Anything else to decide or do we just get in our cars and go?"

"Well, we could ride together in one car," Gary said. "That way we wouldn't get separated."

Lois snorted. "I am not riding in a car with him," she said, pointing in my direction. "I prefer not to listen to his foul language and snide commentary."

I bit back any smart-ass comments. It would just be a waste of time. I would take the high road this time.

"Fine," I said. "Let's just ride back with who we rode up with. Grab your stuff and let's be out of here in five minutes."

While the women went to get their bags, Gary and I stood in the hall.

"That Lois," I said, shaking my head. "I don't know about her."

Gary held up a hand to silence me. "I can't be mean to her. It's like mistreating my mother."

"If your mother acts like that then she deserves mistreatment."

Gary scowled at me and changed the subject. "I don't recall you filling the car up when we got here."

"I didn't," I replied. "I usually do but I just didn't this time."

I hated leaving a car low on gas and fussed at my wife about it all the time, but I'd done the same thing. I was tired and hungry when we got here. I was ready to eat and do something besides sit in a car with my coworkers. I thought I'd take care of it when we left town.

"How much gas did we have?" he asked.

I thought back. "Um, a little more than a quarter tank."

"Not nearly enough to make it home."

I nodded. "Let's hope we can find a station with power and get more."

5

After the text from her husband, Jim's wife Ellen picked up the remote and turned on the TV in their bedroom. Some of the cable channels were out, but CNN was still broadcasting and she stopped there. The scale of devastation was almost too much to take in. Explosions and attacks had taken place across the entire country and there was little information. No one knew who was responsible or if there were still attacks occurring. She saw enough though to recognize signs of the "cascading systems failure" that Jim always warned against. The warning signs were all there. Enough services were failing that the whole fabric of society could come undone. The question was how long it would last.

Jim talked about this stuff so often that even the kids were well-versed in disaster preparation. They'd all watched programs on The Learning Channel, Discovery, and The Science Channel about how disaster scenarios could play out. By now, the entire family was aware of certain facts about disasters. Disruptions in communication led to panic, rumors, and fear. Disruptions in the fuel supply led to food shortages, interruptions in other services, and a price surge for what fuel remained available. Disruptions in power led to fear, looting, and deaths. In the winter, people froze without power. In the summer, they suffocated from a lack of air conditioning. Without power, people who relied on medical devices would likely pass away if the interruption was of any duration at all. From what little Ellen could see, she knew there could be long-term disruptions in all of these areas. Jim's worst scenarios were playing out in living color.

She got out of bed, put on her robe, and went to the gun safe in their walk-in closet. She knew the combination by heart. She had practically been forced to memorize it. Jim drilled her on the importance of being able to access weapons to protect the children in an emergency. Inside the gun safe was a red binder that Jim had shown her many times. He had never made her read it. He just made sure she knew where it was so she could get to it in an emergency.

She took the binder out of the safe, took a seat on the bed, and opened the book. Inside were neatly typed tabs and dividers. There were sections labeled Insurance Policies, Finances, and Home Information. It was the kind of stuff that a responsible husband left for his wife in case he was eaten by a bear or fell off a cliff. Toward the end of the binder were red tabs with labels that read Situation Normal, Situation Elevated, Situation Critical, and Bug Out.

Situation Normal dealt with everyday emergency preparations. These were things that Jim normally took care of but would become her responsibility if he wasn't there. They were things he felt were very important to assure their safety. It included things such as making sure they had a supply of emergency water, emergency food, and emergency fuel. Included was a schedule for rotating those items to make sure that the oldest were used first and to make sure those items were continually resupplied so that they didn't run out. There were also instructions for turning off the water and power if that became necessary. Basic stuff.

The list Jim wanted her to look for this morning was under Situation Elevated. She knew that from many, many reminders over the years. She opened that section and began reading.

In an elevated situation, there may be reason to suspect that access to resources could be compromised for the short or long-term. Stores will face an interruption in supply if fuel is limited. We have made preparations for this, but *efforts should be made to secure more of the following priority items if it can be done without substantial risk:*

1. *ADDITIONAL FOOD*
2. *ADDITIONAL FUEL*
3. *ADDITIONAL CASH*

You will carry cash to make these purchases. Be aware that panic and rioting can occur at any moment during times of fear and high emotion. You should make certain that you have your concealed weapon and permit on you for protection. Your handgun should be carried in an easily accessible manner, preferably a holster, and not buried in a glove compartment or purse. A round should be in the chamber so that the weapon can be fired quickly without having to rack the slide and chamber a round. As long as you handle the weapon in the manner that we have discussed and trained on it will not be dangerous to carry the weapon "hot". If times and conditions permit, proceed with the following:

Take cash from the emergency money in the gun safe. If the power is down credit card processing may not work. If cards can be used, do so and save the cash for later.

1. *Load all empty fuel cans into the back of the Suburban.*
2. *Go to bank and withdraw $2500 from savings in smaller denominations.*
3. *Go to the gas station and fill cans. Gas in red, diesel in yellow. Pay with a card if it will work, use cash if needed. If there is a line of panic buyers, go ahead and get in line. It will only be worse and more expensive later. Be alert that your vehicle does not get penned in. Always leave room in front of you to get out if you need to.*

4. Remove the list from the next page and buy what you can. Take the kids and have them each push a cart to allow for more purchases.
5. Be careful.

ELLEN TOOK the list from the sleeve and looked it over, then went to wake up the kids. Fifteen minutes later, she was driving down the road with two sleepy and unhappy children. Pete and Ariel were thirteen and eleven and a pretty good mix of their mom and dad's looks and personalities. Pete took more of his mom's temperament, with his soft heart and sensitivity. Ariel was a no-nonsense, spitfire of a girl. Clearly her father's daughter.

Ellen filled them in on the news of the day and the task their father had laid out for them.

"Is this the apocalypse?" Ariel asked, rolling her eyes.

"No," Ellen said. "There's just an emergency and Dad wants us to be prepared in case the stores run low."

"When is Dad coming home?" Pete asked.

Ellen composed her reply carefully. "Dad is starting home now but it may take longer than normal. Traffic could be slow because of the emergency."

Pete sat back and thought about it. Ellen could tell that this would worry him.

"Sounds like the crap hit the fan," Ariel said.

"Ariel! That's no way for a little girl to talk." In the rearview mirror, Ellen could see Pete grinning at this sister. He was always amused by the things that came out of her mouth.

Ellen got the money from the bank without incident and crossed the street to the convenience store where she frequently bought gas. She thought there would be a line already, as any sort of crisis pushed people to buy gas before they did anything else. There were a few farmers and early risers getting coffee and breakfast biscuits, but she only had to wait behind one vehicle at the pump. When it moved, she filled her tank, then the red gas cans, letting Pete lift them back into the vehicle for her. She was glad he was getting big enough to help with these kinds of things. He was as tall as she was now and a big kid. Once the red cans were all filled, she moved around to the diesel pump and did the same with the yellow cans.

Wal-Mart was about five minutes away and that was her next stop. When she pulled into the parking lot, she saw that it was no more crowded than any other morning about this time.

"I guess no one else got the memo," Ariel said.

"It's only 6:30 in the morning," Pete said. "Most people are still in bed. Smart people, anyway."

"I wish I was one of them," Ariel muttered.

Ellen parked the Suburban and they headed toward the entrance, Ellen reminding the kids of why they were there so early.

"The problem, Ariel, is that most stores don't carry more than three days' worth of inventory now. You can see that they have trucks coming in all the time. Those trucks can be delayed by power outages, fuel shortages, or damaged roads. Then the shelves empty out fast, like when it snows. What will people do for food then?"

"I guess they'll eat those old cans of beets and lima beans from the back of their cabinets," Pete said with a grin.

"Bluuck," Ariel said.

"I agree," said Ellen. "Bluck."

As Jim's binder instructed, each of them took a cart. Ellen wasn't sure Ariel could manage one if it was very full. She made a mental note to give her the paper products and other lighter items. Ariel looked at the list as Ellen read over it, trying to get a picture in her head of how to go about this.

"What are we going to do with all this junk if this isn't the end of the world, Mom?" she asked.

"It's all stuff we'll use eventually," Ellen said. "Just think of it as shopping in advance."

"I want some bananas," Pete said.

"Sorry, Bud, we're focusing on items that last a long time," she said. Then thinking better of it told him, "Go ahead. If things get hard we might not see any bananas for a while."

"Why? Where do they come from?" Ariel asked.

"South America," Ellen said. "That would be a long way to go for a banana if you had to walk."

After Pete added his bananas, Ellen went to a display of packaged nuts, trail mixes, and dehydrated fruit slices. She threw an assortment in the cart, then skipped frozen foods and picked up a few loaves of bread, some of which she would freeze when they got home. She got a half-dozen of the largest jars of peanut butter they had, several large jars of jelly, fifteen pounds of coffee, and several boxes of tea.

"I love peanut butter," Ariel said.

"We all love peanut butter," Pete chimed in. "I hope that's enough."

"I hope it is, too," Ellen said. "But if it's not, there's powdered peanut butter in the basement pantry."

"Sounds nasty," Ariel said. "You guys can have it."

"You might be singing a different tune if we go through all this," Pete warned.

They continued through the aisles, filling the carts with twenty pounds of rice, twenty pounds of beans, and two dozen different kinds of noodles. They pitched in dried soup mixes, ramen, flour, sugar, salt and other spices. They grabbed pancake mix, syrup, ketchup, tomato sauces, tuna, and dozens of other items. They bought several canned hams that had a ten-year shelf-life. They filled Ariel's cart with toilet paper, paper towels, aluminum foil, paper plates, plasticware, garbage bags, and baggies.

"I thought Dad already had all this stuff," Ariel complained. "Why do we have to buy more?"

"He does, honey," Ellen replied, "but he's concerned we'll need more and he wants us to be safe and well-taken care of. He doesn't want us to run out."

"Where are we going now?" Pete asked, fighting to push his cart due to a bad wheel that rattled as they walked through the store.

"Camping section," Ellen said.

Once there, they collected green propane cylinders, five cans of Coleman fuel, isobutane canisters for Jim's backpacking stove, and extra mantles for the propane lanterns. They picked up ten boxes of kitchen matches, several dozen cheap butane lighters, and two-dozen slow burning candles. Their carts were full at this point and they were all struggling to push them.

"Are we done yet?" Ariel asked, groaning and staggering.

"There's more on the list," Ellen said. "I think we'll go put all this in the car and then I'll come back to get the last items. It shouldn't be more than a single cart."

"Good," Ariel said. "I need to rest."

They proceeded to the checkout, where Ellen was a little self-conscious about the quantities they were buying. However this was Wal-Mart and they were used to seeing everything. The three carts didn't even raise an eyebrow. Ellen was able to pay with her debit card, preserving the cash. Once she had her two foot long receipt tucked into her purse, they struggled out the door, across the parking lot, and to their vehicle.

Ellen looked around the nearly-empty parking lot and felt like it was reasonably safe. "You guys unload this," Ellen said. "It will be faster if I go run back in now while you two are taking care of this."

Ariel groaned again and rolled her eyes, but Pete took charge. They had a system going by the time Ellen began walking back to the store. She got another cart and headed for the pharmacy section. Despite knowing that Jim already had much of this stuff, she followed his instructions to the letter and purchased more peroxide, alcohol, antibiotic ointment, bandages, and over-the-counter medications for everything from colds to diarrhea. She bought hand sanitizer, soap, large bottles of shampoo, and deodorant. Realizing she'd missed a few things, she ran back to the grocery aisle and bought three large bottles of bleach. She had to make a trip to the automotive department to pick up fuel stabilizer for all the gas they'd purchased. A few more small items and she was done.

Checking out, she was again self-conscious. Especially since she was in the same line she'd been in earlier with the same checkout girl. However there is perhaps no employee anywhere in the working world more jaded than a Wal-Mart checkout person. Not an eyebrow was raised and not a question asked.

"I'll need three propane cylinders for the grill," she told the girl.

Ellen left the store, waiting by the propane rack. Before long, a sales associate with a ring of keys came out, unlocked the cage, and removed the cylinders. Noticing that her cart was already full, the boy offered to carry them for her. He made a big show of picking them up, but she could see that he was struggling the entire way to the car. Once they got there, he set them down by the back of the vehicle.

"Thanks," she said. "I can take it from here."

"You're welcome," he said, rubbing his forearms.

When he left, Ellen opened the back door of the vehicle and called inside, "Pete, come back here and put these in the truck."

He did as he was told, struggling slightly with the heavy cylinders, and then got back in the vehicle. Ellen finished unloading her purchases, then got in the car too. Both kids were settled in their seats, sprawled out in apparent exhaustion.

"Too much work, too early," Pete groaned.

"Can I go back to bed when we get home?" Ariel whined.

"Absolutely not," Ellen said. "Someone has to help me unload all this stuff and put it away."

"Awwww," they moaned in unison.

"We all have to help out while your dad's gone."

"I hate the apocalypse," Ariel muttered, scowling and crossing her arms.

6

I don't know what Lois and Alice did in their car, but we began our drive from Richmond doing something I hadn't done in a long time – listening to AM radio. In my teenage years I began listening to the FM album rock stations of the 1970s. They'd play an entire LP of Dire Straits, Steely Dan, Eric Clapton, or The Allman Brothers. With options like that I avoided AM entirely. AM was strictly the realm of fast-talking deejays, talk radio nutcases, and preachers. FM signals travel shorter distances and we couldn't pick up a single station on that band. When we switched to AM, there were fewer stations broadcasting than you would normally find but there were some. Several were just looping the same Emergency Broadcast System message that I'd heard earlier. Some were broadcasting network news coverage of the terror attacks. The more we heard, the clearer the scale of the event became. Our level of fear and worry increased exponentially.

With communication sporadic, much of the news being reported came from social media posts. Although we couldn't see them, newscasters were describing posted images of localized disasters throughout the country. Fires, flooding, demolition of infrastructure, and power outages were widespread. Resources were stretched thin.

In some areas, localities were having difficulty prioritizing their response due to the scale of the overwhelming need. In the intensity and emotional reactions, it was like the 9/11 terror attacks all over again.

Despite the scale of the attacks, it didn't appear that there was tremendous loss of life yet. The death toll was certainly in the thousands but this attack wasn't about mass casualties. It was about inflicting long-term damage. It could take years to get things back to where they were, if that was even possible. I also knew that the death toll would rise rapidly over the coming days and weeks as the disaster began to take a toll on the medically fragile and the unprepared.

Some consultant interviewed by CNN said the power grid could collapse entirely as small power plants still generating tried to keep up with demand. They urged people to make preparations and conserve resources. That information was probably too little, too late.

"It's like they hit every weak spot we had at the same time," Gary said.

We were on I-64 getting ready to exit to I-81 near Staunton and Gary was driving. I was riding shotgun. Traffic coming out of Richmond had seemed almost normal. Maybe a little lighter than normal, like Saturday morning downtown traffic in any city. As the area we were traveling through had not been hit directly, we didn't see many emergency vehicles responding to calls. We did pass numerous convoys of military and police vehicles traveling in the opposite lane. Perhaps they'd been called to eastern Virginia to respond to events there. Maybe they were on their way to DC.

The other Impala with Alice and Lois pulled up alongside us and Lois gestured to the side of the road. They cut ahead of us and pulled over onto the shoulder. We signaled and fell in behind them. Lois came walking back to my window, on the passenger side to stay away from the passing traffic. I rolled my window down and we all looked at her expectantly.

"I need to take a potty break," she announced.

We all continued to stare at her, saying nothing. When no one responded, I pointed to the bushes alongside the road.

"Go ahead," I said. "We'll wait on you."

She looked aghast. "I will not tinkle on the side of the road like some drunken redneck. Besides, I'm hungry. I haven't had anything to eat since I got up."

Gary, fighting a smile, leaned over toward my window. "There's a travel plaza ahead, Lois. We need gas anyway. We'll stop there. I'm sure we can all use a break."

I already had my mouth open to comment when a voice came from the back.

"Don't say it, Jim," Randi said. "She already thinks you're a dick."

"Be nice, you guys," Gary warned, fighting back his own smile. "She's someone's mother."

"Yeah," I mumbled. "Satan's."

We drove about ten more miles and took the exit for the Carson Travel Plaza. It was the largest truck stop for a hundred miles. There were a lot of gas pumps, good coffee, and clean bathrooms. I'd stopped there many times while making this trip or going on vacation with my family. As we approached it, though, I realized I'd never seen it this crowded.

"What the hell?" I mumbled, seeing the line of cars stretching from the pumps back out into the road.

"There's the problem," Rebecca said, pointing to a large plywood sign propped up by the road: **FUEL SALES LIMITED TO 5 GALLONS PER VEHICLE.**

"Five gallons?" I said. "That won't get you anywhere."

"Looks like you'd have to wait an hour or two just to get your five gallons," Gary commented.

"Maybe Lois can hold it a little while longer," I wondered aloud. "This is a mess."

"She's not gonna hold it," Randi said, smiling. "She's not going to tinkle on the side of the road like a common drunk."

I laughed. Even though I didn't know Randi that well, anyone who made fun of Lois was alright in my book.

"You guys shouldn't pick on Lois," Gary said. "She's a sweet old lady."

"I think you mean sour old bitch," I muttered.

"No," Gary replied. "That's not what I mean at all. That's not even nice."

I was fine that. Who cared about being nice anyway?

Lois whipped out of the line of vehicles and drove around them. The line was just for the gas pumps and that wasn't what she needed. Despite some horn-honking and obscene gestures, she made it to the front of the store and took the only empty spot. She didn't seem to care that it was the handicapped spot directly in front of the door. She bolted from the car and into the store.

"I think she took a handicapped spot," I said, "But I ain't saying nothing. Don't want to be accused of picking on the sweet old lady."

Randi snickered in the back.

"If you guys don't mind walking, I'm going to park a little farther away," Gary said. "I don't want to get trapped in the middle of that mess."

"Fine with me," I said.

"Me too," Rebecca said. "I need to stretch my legs."

Gary pulled the car into a slightly less crowded section of the parking lot, just around the corner from the main entrance.

"I'll wait here on you guys," Randi said. "I need to smoke more than I need to pee. Besides, I don't mind to tinkle on the side of the road like a common redneck if I have to."

The rest of us headed for the front entrance and the place was a madhouse. I could hear raised voices from the line of cars waiting on the pumps. People were cursing and complaining. There was a constant stream of people going in and out of the door. My plan had been to take a leak and get a drink, maybe a candy bar, but it was apparent from the checkout line that I was not going to be making any purchases. I didn't think I was going to wait for the bathroom either since I was also willing to pee outside like a common redneck.

I stood around for a minute just checking out the vibe of the crowd. You could tell things were right at the edge of chaos. The frustration and urgency of the crowd was like an electrical charge in the air just before a lightning strike. At the register a customer was arguing with one of the clerks about the fuel purchase limit.

A red-faced man in a sleeveless Jeff Gordon t-shirt and baggy denim shorts was pointing his finger at the cashier and complaining loudly. The angry customer said he needed more gas to get home. The frustrated clerk explained they were not sure when they would be able to get more gas. They had to limit sales to make sure everyone who needed gas could get some.

"Five gallons does not fucking help me," the man said, raising his voice. "How the hell am I going to get to Tennessee on five gallons?"

"Sorry," the clerk said. "I can't do anything about it. It's company policy because of the attacks. You need to move along or I'm going to call the police."

Impatient people, already frustrated by the line, shouted at the man, urging him to pay up and move on so they could do the same. The man cursed back at crowd, giving them all the finger. I saw Lois waiting in line for the restroom with a disgusted look on her face. Alice, who'd been riding in the other car, came walking toward me.

"I was going to use the restroom but I think I'll take my chances elsewhere. I'd rather pee behind a bush than wait in this mess," she said. "I'll be in the car."

"I'll be out in a second," I said. "I'm gonna stick around to wait on Rebecca and Lois."

I was still watching the altercation at the registers when Gary touched me on the shoulder. When I looked to see what he wanted, he pointed toward the entrance. Two Virginia State Troopers had pulled in with blue lights flashing. They parked immediately behind Lois's car, blocking it and several others in. A trooper emerged from each vehicle, placing their hats carefully on their heads. The lead trooper strode through the door, followed by the second trooper carrying his 12 gauge riot gun. The gun rested on his shoulder, the way a hunter might carry it after a long day in the woods. They headed straight for the registers.

"Glad you parked away from the entrance," I told Gary.

The man who'd been arguing at the counter turned toward the

troopers, raised his hands, and stammered. "I-I was j-just leaving." He bolted for the door.

The two troopers looked at each other briefly, shrugged, and then faced the crowd. Apparently they weren't here for that guy.

"Excuse me folks," the trooper said. "By order of the Governor of Virginia all fuel sales in the Commonwealth will be temporarily halted, effective immediately. If you have filled your vehicle, you may pay and leave, but no further sales will be made. All gas and diesel fuel is reserved for authorized emergency vehicles only."

There was a moment of silence while this sank in. There were folks waiting in line for the bathroom who had not pumped gas yet. There were folks getting food who were intending to get gas, but hadn't done it either. These people immediately became very, very pissed. Limiting gas to five gallons was bad, but cutting off all sales was even worse. Interstate 81 was a major corridor and these people were from all over the country. How would they get home? What would they do? The crowd had been smoldering and the trooper had just thrown gasoline on the fire. I was just getting ready to tell Gary I was going back outside when things went south in a hurry.

An angry patron behind a rack of Terry's potato chips threw an unopened plastic soda bottle at the trooper who'd made the announcement. It bounced harmlessly off his body armor. The trooper immediately stepped toward the bottle-thrower but he took off through the store. He pushed over the rack of chips and bumped into several people as he ran.

"We need to get out of here," I told Gary.

"I'll get Rebecca and Lois," he replied, moving toward the restroom line.

Someone snatched a soup can off a shelf, threw it, and caught the second trooper in the face. A cut opened over his eye and his nose started bleeding. Another soup can came flying from the same direction but missed. The trooper raised his shotgun and fired blindly in the direction the soup cans came from. With people packed so tightly, the buckshot hit several bystanders.

An innocent woman died when she took a buckshot pellet to the forehead and dropped like a rock. Her husband, a decorated veteran of the Korean War, had lost his only daughter to a drunk driver twenty years before. With his wife dead, he had nothing left to live for. He pulled a .357 magnum revolver from his jacket pocket and fired at the shotgun-wielding trooper from a distance of less than ten feet. The trooper caught the rounds in his armor and toppled backward.

The other trooper, still chasing the man who'd hit him with a soda bottle, spun toward the gunfire. He saw the old man emptying his revolver at his fellow trooper. He drew his Sig and put two rounds in the armed man, dropping him in a heap across his wife. More guns came out and the chaos escalated. Truckers and travelers were all pulling their concealed carry weapons and trying to defend themselves as they ran for the exits. Wild rounds flew in all directions. The trooper with the shotgun tried to shake off the rounds he'd taken to the vest and fired at anyone he saw carrying a gun. More bodies fell. Some people were screaming and crying but others were shooting back.

The trooper with the Sig fired a round into the ceiling and tried to regain control of the situation. He yelled at everyone to cease fire but the situation was too far gone. Gary gripped Lois and Rebecca by the arms, rushing them toward the exit. I stood just outside the front door, trying to avoid the onrush of people and the sporadic gunfire. I stared at Lois's blocked vehicle, wondering what the hell we were going to do about it.

I turned to Gary to tell him to hurry up. Lois opened her mouth to say something to me. I knew it because she was looking me dead in the eye. I knew it was going to be something rude, too. This was all going to be my fault. As the first word formed in her mouth, a stray round caught her in the temple. Rebecca's eyes widened in shock as she was sprayed with her coworker's blood. Lois crumpled, dead before she hit the ground. Rebecca stopped in her tracks, staring at the dead woman beside her. She recoiled in horror and started screaming. Gary jerked her arm, dragging her out the door.

They joined me just outside the door and we all stared at Alice sitting in the blocked vehicle. She hadn't seen Lois fall but she knew that all hell had broken loose. There was gunfire coming from the store and people ran in all direction. She looked frozen in panic, uncertain of what to do.

I waved to Alice and she opened her door. "C'mon!" I yelled. "We have to go NOW!"

She put one leg out the car and rose up out of her open door. She looked like she wanted to discuss it but there was no time for that. I ran over and took her by the arm. "We have to get out of here. Lois is dead and this car isn't going anywhere."

"My stuff is—"

"Forget your stuff, Alice. We have to go *now*."

She looked at me like she couldn't understand me, as if the information wasn't penetrating the fear and shock racing through her brain. Suddenly, she got it. She reached into the vehicle and snatched her purse from the front seat. We ducked and ran past the front door where shots still rang out. Gary and Rebecca were already in the car with the engine running when we got there. Randi had jumped in the back seat when the shooting started and still had no idea of what was going on. I got in the front seat while Alice scooted into the back with the other two. They were unable to speak, completely traumatized by the events. Randi kept asking what happened but she wasn't getting any answers.

Gary reversed the vehicle and raced around the back of the store, hoping to avoid the chaos around front. Truck drivers ran back and forth between vehicles, some with pistols in their hands. Others were getting their rigs moving and hoping to get out of here before things got any worse. Gary cut around the slower moving rigs but got caught in a bottleneck trying to get out of the parking lot. Cars, oblivious to what was going on, were still trying to get into the plaza as others attempted to escape. There were hundreds of cars and trucks in the parking lot with too few exits.

"Come on, come on," Gary whispered, as if he could urge an opening in the traffic.

Out of nowhere, a man appeared at Gary's window and began pounding it with his fist.

"Do *not* lower that window," I ordered.

The man was screaming at Gary. "My car is out of gas! I need a ride out of here. This is a government vehicle and my damn taxes paid for it!"

Gary held up his hands and yelled back. "We don't have room! I'm sorry."

In the back, Rebecca's crying was a continuing drone. She was still in shock from seeing Lois killed beside her.

"Open this damn door!" the man screamed.

Gary tried to inch the car forward but was pinned in. He couldn't go anywhere.

The man pulled a lug wrench from his back pocket, drew back, and shattered Gary's window. Gary and I were showered with glass fragments. Gary leaned forward to brush them from his hair and face, trying to keep them out of his eyes. Without thinking, I threw open my door, drew my LCP, and pointed it at the man. He drew back the lug wrench again for what I assumed was to be a fatal blow to Gary's head.

There was no time to say anything. I fired twice.

The .380 rounds went through the man's right pectoral muscle and into his chest. He flinched, twisted, and dropped from sight. It was the first time I'd ever shot a person. Time slowed. I could hear my heart pounding like a freight train inside my head. In my peripheral vision I saw the car ahead of us finally moving. To my left I could see the car behind us, a man and woman in the front seat, staring wide-eyed in horror at what I'd done.

"Get in!" Gary yelled. "Let's go!"

I ducked into the seat, glass fragments grinding beneath me. I still had the LCP in my hand. Gary hit the gas and the tires squealed as we sped onto the road, taking onramp for I-81 south.

The women were silent. Even Rebecca's crying had stopped. Gary kept looking over at me.

"You may want to put that away," he finally said.

7

When Ellen and the kids arrived home she sent Pete for Jim's lawn mower and the garden cart he towed behind it. They set the propane tanks, Coleman fuel, gas cans, and the diesel cans out of the vehicle.

"Store the gas and diesel in the mower building," Ellen said. "Just leave them in the middle of the floor for now until I can add fuel stabilizer to the gas. Then I need you to come back for the propane cylinders, the Coleman fuel, and the camping stuff. Put it in the new storage building and make sure that it's locked when you're done. Ariel and I are going to take the groceries inside. Got it? "

Pete saluted. "Got it, Mom."

While people like Jim were called "preppers" today, he came from a long line of hillbillies that knew that hard times were always just around the corner. His father and grandfather were people who never threw anything away and tried not to own things they couldn't fix themselves. While Ellen shook her head at the various junk and scrap piles Jim maintained around the property, she never complained about them. There would have been no point in it, for one thing. Jim was his own man and probably wouldn't get rid of his personal junkyard for any amount of persuasion. But beyond that there'd been countless circumstances where he'd repaired something using material scavenged from his piles or built something he needed from scratch using those salvaged or discarded materials.

There had been some boom times in central Appalachia where they lived, but far more "bust" times. People were never that far from raising their own food, home canning, and hunting. When he'd built this house on fifty acres of overgrown farmland, Jim had taken all those things into account even though farming and hunting were not activities he actively pursued at the time. There were deer, turkeys, and squirrels on the land. He had a pond stocked with bass, trout, catfish, and bluegill. He had a garden which could easily be expanded if the need arose. There was also a spring that could provide fresh water year round. If things ever got desperate enough, there was even a cave at the back of the property that could serve as an emergency shelter.

As a weekend project, Jim had taken pallets of old cinderblocks he'd salvaged from buildings that were being torn down and walled up the entrance to the cave. After laying the blocks most of the way up, he threaded scraps of rebar and old steel fence posts down through the block cores to lock them together. He filled the voids with a wet concrete mixture to grout them solid and installed a salvaged steel door in the wall. With the door's metal frame also grouted with concrete it was a very solid entrance and would be difficult to breach. When he ran out of room for cinderblocks, he filled any irregular voids with mortar, sealing his wall tight to the rock outcropping.

It took them nearly an hour to unload and put away the purchases. As part of Jim's design, the house had a large pantry near the kitchen door that allowed them to store their food in an easily accessible location. There were also shelves in the basement for long-term food storage, bulk foods, and some of the home-canned items.

"I'm going to go lie down and watch TV," Ariel announced when they were done, her voice weak with feigned exhaustion.

Ellen reheated a cup of coffee for herself and took Jim's red binder to the porch. She sat in the porch swing and opened the book to where she'd left off:

If you still have power, you need to charge all items that can be charged in case you lose power down the road. In the mower shed are a couple of boat batteries and old car batteries. You should charge these since they can be a good source of twelve volt power in an emergency. The charger is beside them and the instructions are printed on the charger. There is also a solar charger hanging on the wall by the batteries. If the power goes out you can use this charger to charge these batteries but it takes a lot longer.

Charge all phones, entertainment devices, and the radios. The walkie talkies can use AA batteries in a pinch but you might as well charge them if you have power. Also charge the batteries to the power tools. These are on a shelf in the basement. They charge in about fifteen minutes so try to charge all of them if you can.

In the new storage building is the device I used to jump start dead batteries. It has an air compressor, a USB charger, and a radio built in. Make sure this is charged; it's the easiest way to recharge a cell phone if the power is out.

If the power does fail use duct tape to seal the chest freezers in the base-ment. They'll keep for about a week or so if you don't open them. You can extend this if you use the generator and run them for a couple of hours a day. Remember though, in an extended power outage the sound of a gener-ator running carries for long distances and can make you a target. If you do use the generator it needs to be chained up and you should cover it with a tarp when it's not running. There are rolls of black plastic in one of the outbuildings. It might not be a bad idea to cover the windows on the front of the house with this plastic to prevent anyone from seeing that the house is lit when theirs is not.

Items in the refrigerator won't last more than a day if you are opening the door at all, which is hard to avoid. If the power is out and there's no indication of when it will be coming back on, load all of the refrigerated items into boxes and take them to the spring house. There is a twelve volt cooler in the storage building that can be hooked to one of those old boat batteries. It will allow you to keep a few refrigerated items in the house for convenience. You will have to switch the battery out and recharge them using the solar charger.

SINCE THEIR PROPERTY had a spring on it Jim had insisted on building a spring house like his grandmother had. It was a cinderblock building set back into the hillside with a shallow concrete trough inside. Cold spring water flowed from a pipe in the wall and into the trough. At the other end a drain allowed the water to flow out, providing a constant level of cold running water. By setting items that needed refrigeration into the trough, they remained at a cool temperature year round. With the spring house set back into the hillside, with three walls mostly buried, the spring house didn't freeze in the winter. It made for near perfect storage in the case of a power failure. They used it for storing garden potatoes and other root vegetables mostly but it was there for refrigeration if they needed it.

Ellen's reading was interrupted by a loud shriek of frustration.

"Mom!" Ariel yelled from inside.

"What?" Ellen asked. "What's going on?"

"My TV just quit working!" Ariel yelled back.

"Well shit," Ellen said. She felt free to curse when the kids weren't standing around her.

She got up and went through the screen door into the living room. She flipped the switch on the wall. Nothing. She was starting to get worried now. She went back outside and walked around the house to the electric meter. The digital readout was blank. She knew exactly what that meant.

No power.

She couldn't help but think she may have jinxed herself by reading the power failure instructions in Jim's binder. This changed things significantly. Now she knew she would have to finish that section. There would be preparations to make before darkness fell. Without electric lights life was about to turn into an extended camping trip. She hoped she was up to it.

"Kids!" she yelled, entering the house. "We have more work to do."

8

"Y'all, that was some seriously fucked up shit," Randi said, plainspoken as always. "What the hell just happened? What happened to Lois?"

No one spoke. As the magnitude of the events settled in we dropped into a collective state of shock and numbness. The radio was still playing and I leaned forward to turn it off.

Rebecca turned to Randi and took a deep breath. Her voice shook as she spoke. "Lois is dead. She was shot while we were leaving."

"Are you sure she was dead?" Randi asked. "Maybe she was just wounded. Should we go back for her?"

"She was standing right beside me," Rebecca said, her voice rising in anger and frustration. "I saw the bullet take out part of her skull. I am wearing her blood and brains all over me."

Randi stared at Rebecca for a moment as if noticing her state for the first time. She spoke to her softly, motherly. "Honey, you do have blood all over your face."

Rebecca started crying again and scrubbed at her face with her shirt sleeve. Randi dug in her purse and removed a pack of baby wipes.

"I have grandkids," she said. "You have grandkids, you always have wipes." She removed one and began wiping the blood from Rebecca's face as if it were nothing more than chocolate.

"You don't look old enough to have grandkids," Rebecca said absently.

"I got an early start," Randi said. "Had my first child at sixteen."

No one said anything while Randi finished cleaning Rebecca's face. When she was done, she had about a half-dozen bloody wipes in her lap. She stared at them for a moment, deciding what to do with them.

"Would anyone be offended if I littered?" she asked. "I don't feel like riding home with this mess in my lap."

"Go ahead," I said. Those were the first words I'd uttered since shooting that guy in the parking lot.

"So can someone please tell me what happened?" Randi asked again. "Why did someone shoot Lois?"

Gary started telling the story and left out nothing. No one interrupted. When he was done Alice took out her cell phone and dialed a number.

"I've got to call Bill," she said. Bill was our Executive Director, the head honcho of our state agency. "I've got to let him know what happened, that Lois is dead and we had to abandon a vehicle."

"And that I had to shoot someone," I said. "You may want to mention that little detail."

"You had no choice," Randi assured me. "Did you see the way he had that tire iron drawn back? If you hadn't shot him Gary would have been toast. We'd have two dead people instead of one."

"I can't believe we left her there," Rebecca said to no one in particular. "How will her body ever get back to her family? How will they bury her?"

No one answered, all of us thinking about what she'd said. No one had an answer.

"No offense, Jim," Randi said, "but if you can carry a gun in this car then I think I should be able to smoke a damn cigarette. I need one about now." She pulled out a pack, cracked her window, and lit up. No one protested or quoted the policy manual. It seemed a small thing in light of all that had happened.

A loud dinging noise startled all of us.

"I was waiting on that," Gary said, his voice full of dread. "We're low on fuel."

Things were quiet for a moment and then the dinging started again. This was a problem that wasn't going away.

"We could try this next exit," I said. "Try a small town gas station."

"Maybe," Gary said. "It's possible they haven't heard they're not supposed to be selling gas. Or maybe they'd sell us some anyway if we pay a little extra. I can't imagine they'd be able to put cops at every single gas station in the state."

"We've got to do something," Randi said. "This car ain't going much further without gas. I've noticed a lot of cars pulled over like they're out of gas and I don't want to be one of them."

It was true. We were passing more and more cars stopped on the shoulder of the road. Some had people sitting inside or milling around outside. Others appeared abandoned. The surrounding traffic had thinned out considerably, too. There were a lot fewer moving vehicles. It was likely that the fuel restrictions were starting to have an effect. There were still convoys of National Guard and military vehicles headed north on the other side of the interstate. The occasional police car soared by with lights and siren.

Alice gave up on her phone call. "I can't get through."

"Did you try texting?" I asked.

"No, but I will," she said, thumbing a message on the screen of her phone.

This reminded me that I hadn't tried to contact my own family since leaving Richmond. I pulled out my cell and composed a quick text: *On 81. Can't buy gas anymore. Hope you guys are safe. Be home as soon as I can.*

I wanted to say more, but didn't want to worry them. How do you text your wife that you just had to kill someone in a parking lot? How do you tell her one of your colleagues got shot waiting on the restroom? I was going to have to snap out of this. I knew it was just the aftereffects of adrenaline but I'd been in a funk since shooting that guy. I knew I was only doing what I had to do but there's a physical reaction that first time and you never know how it's going to go. Maybe there was a physical reaction every time and I just didn't know it yet.

This is what I trained for when I practiced shooting, though – being able to respond automatically in times of stress and danger. You created muscle memory so your body knew what to do. I'd performed just as I had to. With the man's arm drawn back there was no time for a warning. The lug wrench was a deadly weapon and I'd responded with deadly force. There was nothing to be worried about. If things got as bad as I was afraid they might, then I'd be lucky if I only had to kill one man. That was not an encouraging thought. Was I prepared to do that?

It was at this time that I imagined my grandfather's voice in my head telling me I needed to harden the fuck up. He'd died when I was fifteen but he'd always been an icon of strength and toughness in my eyes. He'd lost his father and older siblings in the Spanish Flu epidemic. At age ten he'd become the man of the house, assuming responsibility for his mother and four younger brothers and sisters. He'd been forced by circumstance to go to work in the coal mines of West Virginia as a slate picker. He sat with other children along wooden boards placed over conveyor belts of coal. Their job was to pick chunks of slate out of the coal as it moved down the conveyor belt. It was hard, dirty work. A man with a long stick stood ready to strike them if their attention lapsed. The other consequence of not paying attention was you could get caught up in the belt. If you were lucky you lost a limb. The less fortunate were mangled to death in the structure.

There were child labor laws in place at this time meant to curtail these practices, but they were circumvented by putting the child's hours on an adult relative's paycheck. That relative would then split the money with the child's family. My grandfather kept this job until he was twelve. He was promoted to leading mules down into the mines, pulling coal carts on narrow steel tracks. This, too, was dirty, dangerous work. As a child living in an adult world, he was forced to fight his way through life early. He used his fists at the beginning, then later a knife. Later yet, he carried and used a gun.

When I turned thirteen, my grandfather, without my mother's knowledge, began recounting to me the stories of the men he'd killed and wounded over his lifetime. There were many and these experiences made him a hard man, physically and mentally. I still remember the stories of all those fights. He told me that I had to be a hard man too because there were men in the world who needed killing – men you could not turn your back on. These were men you couldn't leave alive because they'd ambush you when the odds were in their favor.

"There's an exit," Gary said. "There's no signs for hotels and fast food. That's just what we're looking for. Probably fewer people are stopping because there's not much there."

Gary eased off the exit. A sign pointed right and told us that it was three and a half miles to the nearest gas station. Gary turned in that direction, signaling his turn even though there wasn't another car in sight.

"You guys sure this is a good idea?" Rebecca asked. "The interstate seems safer."

"No," I said. "I'm not sure it's safe at all. Do you have a better idea?"

"Maybe we should just go as far as we can on the interstate," Alice said. "We can stop at an exit with a hotel and stay there until we can get help."

"I'm not sure we'd be better off," I said. "Those exits will become dangerous as more and more desperate people gather there. If no help comes, people will turn on each other. The cops are all tied up and you won't be able to depend on them for help."

Rebecca had quit crying but still absently wiped the side of her face as if some invisible remnant of blood remained there. "We survived the 9/11 attacks and things didn't get that bad then. People weren't shooting at each other. Why is everything falling apart?"

"Those attacks killed a lot of people but we didn't lose resources,"

Gary said. "This attack damaged vital resources. It could take years to recover from this. If those attacks destroyed enough transformers it could take two years to replace them. If power isn't available to manufacture more, who knows how long it could be?"

"I think you're overreacting," Alice said. "There's no need to scare people with these doom and gloom fantasies."

"We'll see what happens," I said. "I hope we *are* overreacting."

We made it less than a mile before the Impala rounded a corner and encountered a roadblock consisting of two sheriff's department cruisers parked nose-to-nose. They blocked both lanes of traffic. Gary slowed as we approached and a deputy with a Remington 870 shotgun moved from behind the barricade, eying us carefully. When we came to a stop, they stared at our local government tags. They were the same type their cruisers carried. A deputy approached cautiously.

"What can I do for you folks?" he asked.

"Just looking for some gas," Gary said in his friendliest tone. "We're on our way back home from Richmond and we're getting pretty low. I wasn't sure if we could make it to the next exit."

The deputy lowered his head a little and got a good look at each us. He lowered his gun, not perceiving a threat.

"You might not have heard," the deputy said, "but the Governor has locked down the gas supply. All available fuel is for official emergency response only."

I leaned over toward Gary, to where I could see the deputy's face. "Any chance of a tank out of professional courtesy?" I asked. "We're local government, too."

The deputy considered this. "What branch?" he asked. "Where you guys from?"

"Mental health," Alice spoke up before I could answer him. "Russell County. Far southwest."

I slapped my hand over my forehead and shook my head. I'd been prepared to say Emergency Services or county government on our way back from a meeting. Something that sounded more official –more critical to public safety. Anything but mental health. Cops didn't give a crap about mental health workers.

"Mental health?" he laughed. "Not a chance in hell."

"What difference does it make that we're mental health?" Alice asked, her eyes moving from me to the deputy.

"Do you know how many times we call you guys to get someone committed to a mental facility and you say they don't meet the criteria?" he asked. "It happens around here every day."

"Sorry," Alice said. "This isn't our area. You can't blame us for what your local agency does."

"No dice. Mental health can hoof it like the rest. You folks need to turn your car around and go the other way."

"We'll do that but, if you don't mind a question, why the roadblock?" Gary asked. "I'm just curious."

"We're getting overrun by folks trying the same things you folks are trying – looking for someone to sell you gas. When those folks couldn't find anyone who'd sell them gas they started trying to steal gas. My own mom called me and said she saw someone drive up to her house, cut off a piece of her water hose, and use it to siphon gas out of her Buick. When I got there the guy looked at me as if he wasn't doing anything wrong. He told me he was doing what he had to do. So that's what I'm doing. I'm doing what I have to do."

"You're not letting anyone else come in then?" Gary said.

"Damn right we're not," the deputy said. "Local traffic only. If I don't know you, you can fuck off. You'll find a lot of towns along the interstate are doing the same thing. I've heard talk of it on the radio."

"We'll be getting out of here then," Gary said. "Good luck."

"You folks will be the ones needing good luck," the deputy replied. "Russell County is a hell of a long way away and travel just got a lot more difficult."

With little choice, we turned the car around and headed back to the interstate. Each ding of the Low Fuel alert hit me like a blow to the stomach. What were we going to do?

"I guess we might as well try to get as far as we can," Gary said.

No one had any other comments or suggestions. We were all

getting hungry and more than a little scared. Most business trips sucked but this one was really going off the rails. We made it another fifteen miles or so before the gas tank went dry. In a curve the fuel pump sucked air and the engine missed. It smoothed out when we came out of the curve and we all started breathing again. Then the engine stuttered and the car stalled completely.

Gary put it in neutral and coasted to the side of the road. We came to a stop on a level stretch of grass beside the road. "Maybe if we leave it here they won't tow it. I'll leave a note in the window."

"What do we do now?" Rebecca asked. "Sit here and wait for help?"

"I guess we walk to the nearest hotel," Alice offered.

"If they don't have power, they might not be accepting guests," I said. "We can try, though. I'd rather be moving than sitting here."

Everyone got out of the car and stood stretching. A single semi-truck passed by and disappeared over the next hill. It was the only vehicle visible from our position. That was definitely unusual for a busy interstate like this one. Gary popped the trunk and we all stared at the luggage.

"At least I don't have to worry about carrying a suitcase," Alice said. "Mine is still in the other car." For the first time, it was hitting her that all she had with her were the things she carried in her purse.

"But you're alive," Gary reminded her.

She had nothing to say to that.

"I think we should go through our bags and lose a few things," I said. "It could be a long walk and carrying a suitcase will suck. No use hauling dead weight." I got my suitcase from the car and found a slightly more private spot to consolidate what I was taking with me.

"That's convenient," Randi said, noticing the pack in my hand for the first time. "You brought a backpack."

"I brought one, too," Gary said. "I never travel without one."

"I don't either," I said.

"Why?" Randi asked.

"Boy Scout," Gary said simply. "I like to be prepared."

"I'm just paranoid," I said.

"I can appreciate that," Randi said. "Remember, it's not paranoia if people really *are* out to get you."

Gary retrieved his backpack and suitcase then set about doing the same thing I was.

I loosened the expansion straps on my backpack to allow it to accept more cargo. From my suitcase, I took my toiletries kit but left my shampoo and shaving items behind. I'd never cared much for shaving and it certainly wasn't a priority now. I took all the spare socks and underwear I had. I grabbed a spare pair of pants, spare t-shirt, and the rain shell that I carried in case the weather turned nasty. After sealing up my pack, I closed the suitcase and returned it to the trunk. I knew I'd probably never see again.

"Did you guys thin down your load?" I asked the women.

All I saw were shaking heads. I raised an eyebrow.

"Our suitcases have wheels," Rebecca said. "Randi and I are just going to pull ours for now. If they get too heavy, we can always throw stuff out along the way."

"Is there anything from the car we might need?" Gary asked, preparing to lock up.

"Policy requires that all vehicles carry emergency kits in the trunk," Alice said.

"Policy again," I muttered, rolling my eyes.

"Sometimes policy can be a good thing," Alice replied.

I looked in the trunk and found a first-aid kit still sealed in shrink wrap. I stuffed it inside my pack. There was another plastic box about the size of a small tool kit. Inside was a flashlight. I tried it and got a weak yellow glow from the bulb. Although I had a better flashlight and a headlamp in my pack, I stuck this flashlight in there, too. If we came across some good batteries, maybe we could revive it. I also got a pair of cyalume light sticks, two highway flares, and a thin plastic poncho from the box. All of it went into the pack.

"Why are you carrying all that crap with you?" Rebecca asked. "We're heading to a hotel." She gave a nervous laugh, like I was obviously an idiot.

She was completely oblivious to how serious things were becoming. I was becoming more and more aggravated with people not getting the big picture.

"Didn't seeing Lois get shot make it clear to you that things are *not* the same anymore?" I asked. "You may think that was an exception, but I would bet you anything that chaos and violence will quickly become the rule. This is not the same world you woke up to yesterday. You might as well accept it now, otherwise the next few weeks are going to be really hard for you."

Rebecca stared back at me coldly, tears welling in her eyes.

"You don't need to talk to her like that, Jim," Alice said, her voice a little too reminiscent of a schoolteacher for my taste. "None of us are children here."

"Then quit thinking like children," I snapped. "I'm a little concerned that you all aren't grasping the seriousness of the situation."

"Just because we don't respond in the same way you do doesn't mean that we aren't aware of how serious this is," Alice said. "People have to deal with things in their own way."

"As long as they deal with them," I said. "Ignoring the circumstance is not dealing with things."

"You are such an asshole," Alice said. "Why do you have to be this way, arguing with everyone? You're this way all the time. Do you just hate people? Remember there's no 'I' in team."

"Yeah," I said, "but there is an 'I' in bitch and that's what Rebecca is acting like." I gave up at that point. There was no use continuing. I was wasting my breath. They would either wake up or not. I couldn't make them. In fact, I didn't really give a shit whether they got it or not. My only concern was getting home to my family.

As to whether I just hated people?

Maybe.

I slung my pack over my shoulder and headed off down the road. It felt good to be using my muscles and burning off some of the stress of the day. I was an avid hiker and backpacker. There was something about walking with a pack on that felt very comfortable to me. I walked ahead of the group, energized both by anger and at my relief in no longer being caged up in the car. I never was a good car traveler and hated confinement of any sort. I could hear Rebecca and Alice talking behind me. I heard the words "paranoid" and "concerned" thrown around.

To hell with them, I thought. I was heading home and I was going to make it alive. They could either go with me or not. I was not responsible for them. I'd have been much happier to not be saddled with them. Randi was okay from what I knew of her but I had little use for the other two. Let them travel for a while in their little bubble and we'd see how far they made it before it got pricked.

I knew from years of traveling this road that we were about five miles from the nearest exit. It was now around noon and the early summer sun was high overhead. It was not miserable yet but we were getting baked by the heat reflecting back off the pavement. I had some water in the pack that I wasn't going to use unless things got desperate. Same for food. I had some energy bars, some ramen and packaged macaroni, a few other items. I was sure Gary was equally supplied but neither of us had ever planned for supplying a group. Though we hadn't discussed it I expected he felt the same. There was just not enough in our packs for everyone so best to keep our supplies low key.

I pulled out my cellphone and checked for signal. One measly bar. I composed a quick text to my wife and sent it. Unsure if it went through or not, I left the phone powered on and stuck it back in its holster. If she got my message and replied, I didn't want to miss it.

After three miles, we'd passed several abandoned vehicles but no people. We were passed by an ambulance and a few semis. The semis appeared to be holding out longer since their diesel tanks had a larger capacity. It would be a little longer before they hit crisis state. The scary part was that when those trucks quit running, goods would no longer be reaching store shelves. The food supply everyone depended on would be interrupted. People who had not made preparations would start going hungry.

I'd travelled a lot of interstate highways in my life and this section was as generic as they got. Woods on both sides with occasional glimpses of open field. No houses, no signs of life, and no personality. Just open road.

At one point a convoy of armed National Guard troops passed us in the other lane. They didn't look very excited. They were probably concerned about leaving their families behind to this mess. I know I would be. I wondered how many had not shown up for duty. Once, Alice stuck her thumb out when a semi passed but the truck had not even slowed down. I started to tell her that under the circumstances it might take a more impressive display to get a trucker to stop but I bit my tongue. I didn't want to hear what policies I might be violating with my comment.

I topped a hill and approached another stalled vehicle on the shoulder ahead. I could see this one was occupied. I glanced back and saw the rest of my group was clustered together about fifty yards behind me. I raised my shirttail so I could put my hand on the grip of my Ruger LCP before carefully approaching the car.

"Hello," I called once I was close enough to be heard.

I saw movement in the vehicle as a large man struggled to get out. He was around seventy, tall, and neatly dressed. He was red-faced from the heat beating down on his car.

"Hello, young man," he said, his tired voice unable to maintain the attempt at enthusiasm. He reminded me of my dad.

"You alright?" I asked. "You look a little warm."

"Nah, I'm okay," he said. "I am a little concerned about my wife." He moved stiffly around the back of his car, heading for the passenger side. He stopped suddenly and stuck out his hand to shake. "I'm Jack, by the way. My wife there is Ruth."

I relaxed and took my hand off my weapon. I shook his hand. "I'm Jim."

I followed him around to the passenger side of the car. He leaned through the open door and spoke to someone, then straightened and turned back to me.

"My wife just had surgery yesterday at UVA Medical Center at Charlottesville," he said. "They discharged her this morning and we were on our way back to Roanoke when we ran out of gas. Every place we stopped was either out or wouldn't sell us any."

"We ran into the same thing," I explained. "We ran out of gas and we're trying to walk to the next exit now."

"I thought to do the same thing," he said. "There's no way my wife can make it, though. She's too weak. She's got stitches from the surgery and is on medication. I'm worried about her being out here in the heat too. We don't have any food or water."

I dropped my pack and dug into it. I had an 8-pack of 12 ounce water bottles that were part of my Get Home Bag. I hadn't touched them yet since things weren't desperate for us but these folks were already there. I took out two water bottles and handed them to the man.

"It's not much," I said. "But it's something."

"Oh, God bless you," he said, uncapping a bottle and hurrying to put it to his wife's lips.

I could tell she was weak. She didn't even raise her own hand to help hold the bottle. I started to ask the man what he was going to do, but it was clear that he didn't know and I didn't have any suggestions. It was a question better left unasked.

When the rest of my group topped the hill, I pointed them out to the man. "Those folks are with me. We were at a meeting in Richmond and are trying to get back home."

"How far do you have to go?" the man asked, opening his own water bottle now and taking a drink.

"All the way across the state," I said. "Russell County."

The man shook his head. "That's a long way."

"It's a long way even if you're driving," I said. "A lot longer if you're walking."

When my group was together, I explained the situation to them and Randi said she wanted to look at the lady.

"I'm a nurse," she said, heading for the passenger door.

"I didn't know that," I said to no one in particular. "Good to know."

Randi was back in a moment. "She's way too hot and her pulse is weak. He's got some blankets and a pillow in the car. I'd like to make her a bed in the shade by the car. It will get her out of that hot car. It's got to be 120 degrees in there even with the doors open. Her clothes are soaked in sweat."

"You make the bed. Gary and I will help Jack get her situated."

When we had the woman lifted out and comfortable, Alice approached me. My chest constricted with tension the moment she drew near. It was the first time we'd spoken since the earlier confrontation and I assumed she was ready to pick up where we left off.

"Are we just going to leave them here?" she asked.

"What do you propose?" I said, putting it back in her lap.

"I don't know," she said. "They'll die if we leave them here."

"To be blunt, they'll probably die anyway," I said. "At least the woman will. If things are as bad as they said on the radio, people who require medication may not be able to depend on a regular supply much longer."

Alice looked me in the eye. "That's pretty harsh. My mom is a diabetic. Are you saying she might not be able to live through this?"

I ignored the comment, not wanting to speculate on the fate of her family. "They remind me of my own parents. I'd like to help them but that lady is over two hundred pounds. I can't carry her two miles. Can you?"

Alice didn't answer. In her job she often had to handle complex situations and I knew it was eating at her. Here was a problem and she wanted to solve it. *Needed* to solve it. Even though she got on my nerves sometimes she was an excellent problem solver. Problems had just gotten a lot harder to solve, though.

"Maybe we can come back for them later or bring them something?" she suggested.

"Maybe we can," I replied. "I'd be willing to do that if we're able to stay at the next exit for the night." I wasn't sure that either of those things would happen but I didn't know what else to say.

When we prepared to leave, I shook the man's hand and told him what Alice and I talked about.

"I keep thinking someone will stop," he said. "I've tried to flag down several police cars but no one will stop."

This was a man who could not comprehend the current circumstances. He didn't have a frame of reference for a world in which the police would not stop to help a lady in need.

I patted him on the shoulder, gathered my gear, and joined my crew at the front of the car. We walked off in silence, not happy about leaving those poor folks but unable to do anything for them.

This would not be the last time we would have to leave people to their fate.

9

The kids were not excited about being recalled into duty. The day had gone downhill for them since being dragged out of bed on a summer morning, having to go to the grocery store and then carry those same groceries into the house. Now there were even more tasks? Ariel and Pete both entered the living room dragging their feet, stumbling loose-limbed with pleading looks. Ellen took one look at them and burst out laughing.

"After what I heard from your father and on the news," she said, "there's a possibility that the power won't be back on anytime soon."

Both children rolled their eyes and moaned a death rattle.

"There's work that has to be done unless you want to be caught in the dark. Your dad left me a list of what needed done and I'll need your help to do it."

Despite their drama, both children were good helpers and snapped to attention.

"Get your shoes on and then come back here. I'll tell you what I need you to do."

When the kids returned, Ellen had a ring of keys and an LED flashlight.

"The first thing Dad said we need to deal with is the freezer. We're going to duct tape the lid down and we're going to stay out of it. If we run the generator a couple of hours a day it will keep things frozen. We'll eat the food from the refrigerator first then, if the power isn't back on, we'll start eating items from the freezer."

Before the kids would go in the basement, they each went to their rooms to retrieve headlamps. Jim insisted they always have a working headlamp in their room so that they were never at the mercy of darkness. You never knew when the power would go out or when you would have to get up in the middle of the night for some reason. Once the kids had glowing headlamps, they went into the basement together.

The kids always thought the basement was a little creepy. Ellen didn't have any particular reservations about it. After all, the basement held the woodstove that kept their house nice and toasty for free. The basement was Jim's domain, though, and it was odd to be down here without him. Looking around, she saw his stuff everywhere –except for the pile of dirty laundry by the washer. She supposed that the generator would run the washer for now but what would happen when the fuel was gone? Except for an antique washboard in one of the storage buildings, they had no good backup plan for washing clothes.

While Ariel held Ellen's flashlight, Pete tore off strips of duct tape and handed them to Ellen. Ellen went around the perimeter of the freezer lid until it was sealed securely.

"There," she announced when they were done.

"Are we done now?" Ariel asked.

"No," Ellen said. "We're just getting started. Besides, it's not like you can watch television anyway. You might as well be helping me. It'll make the day go faster."

They went outside to an older storage building that was used for yard tools, mowers, chainsaws, and spare lumber. Ellen unlocked the padlock and swung the plywood double doors open. Hanging from a hook just inside the door was a thick extension cord about ten feet long. She knew it was the cord for the generator because Jim had drilled it into her head frequently. In his attention to detail, he'd also attached a plastic tag to it that labeled it "**For Generator Use**". She removed the cord from the nail and passed it to Ariel.

"Take this over by the basement door and wait on us."

"It's heavy," Ariel said, pretending to stagger under the weight.

Ellen climbed into the building. She tried lifting the wheelbarrow handles on the generator but it was extremely heavy. She couldn't get it herself so Pete climbed in to help. Together, they wheeled the beast to the door and carefully guided it down the ramp to the yard.

"That's heavy," Pete said.

"I know," Ellen agreed, wiping her forehead. "And we still have to get it over there beside the basement door."

They each took a handle, lifted, and guided the generator the forty feet or so to the back of the house. It was slightly uphill to their destination. There was a little alcove created by an addition near the entry to the basement. In this alcove was a transfer switch. When the generator was plugged into the transfer switch it allowed Jim to safely power ten priority circuits in the house without the danger of feeding power back into the grid or starting a fire.

Ellen and Pete were huffing and puffing when they finally reached the back of the house.

"We need to get more exercise," she told Pete.

"We're getting it now."

"Here's the cord, Mommy," Ariel said, reaching it to Ellen.

Ellen took the cord and plugged one end into the transfer switch and the other into the generator.

"Are we going to start it now?" Pete asked.

Ellen shook her head. "No, we'll wait four hours. Since the power just went off everything is still cold now."

"Are we done yet?" Pete asked.

"No," Ellen snapped. "You'll be done when I say you're done. I need you two to help me so quit asking if we're done all the time. You might have to work all day, and if you do, you'll just have to get over it."

Ellen didn't often have to speak to them like that. She usually had infinite patience. She was worried, though. Worried about Jim and worried if she could do this without him.

"What do you need me to do next, Mommy?" Pete asked, tears in his eyes.

Ellen hugged him, pulling Ariel into the hug, too.

"We need to find the little red box that Daddy uses to pump up your bike tires and jumpstart the mower."

"I know where that is!" Ariel exclaimed.

"Where?" Pete asked.

"In the Daddy Shack."

The Daddy Shack was the newest storage building. It was a large, organized building where Jim stored bicycles, kayaks, camping gear, and fishing supplies. He was particular about this building and that was why they called it the Daddy Shack. The three of them walked over to the shack and Ellen studied her key ring.

"It's the silver key," Ariel told her confidently.

"How do you know that?" Ellen asked.

"Because I asked him," Ariel replied. "He told me it was the silver key with the square top."

Ellen looked and found a key that fit that description. She tried it and, sure enough, it worked. "Very good, Ariel."

Ariel beamed.

Sitting just inside the door was the red box they were looking for. It was a Wagan Power Dome, a rechargeable device that could boost a car battery or pump up a tire. It also had an inverter that would allow users to operate a 110 volt device, such as a laptop. There was also a USB port that would accept USB chargers for phones or tablets. Jim sung the praises of this device every time he used it. Ellen hoped that she and the kids had paid enough attention to be able to operate it.

"Pete, go get the mower and trailer. We'll need it to haul the things we need to the house," Ellen said.

Pete walked off, always anxious for an opportunity to demonstrate his skills at operating the mower. He was proud of the fact he'd recently learned to back up a trailer, which was something Ellen certainly couldn't do. His dad had told him it was an important skill.

While Pete was gone Ariel and Ellen went on inside the building. Ellen opened a tall plastic Rubbermaid cabinet and examined the contents. Inside were cans of Coleman fuel, green one-pound propane canisters, isobutane canisters for tiny backpacking stoves, and various boxes with writing on them listing the contents. Ellen took out two propane canisters and handed them to Ariel.

"Set these by the door," she said. She moved to a plastic tote of camping supplies and removed the lid. She took out a Coleman propane lantern and handed it to Ariel, who dutifully stashed it beside the door. Ellen then removed several battery-operated camping lanterns of various sizes. She and Ariel piled them by the door as well. While Pete was backing the mower up to the door, Ellen spotted the camping stove.

"Come help me with this, Pete," she said.

She and Pete struggled to pull the camping stove off the shelf and set it on the floor. Jim had told her that food was the way to keep the kids interested in camping when they first started going. So instead of using a grill, he bought a fancy propane stove and oven combination that allowed them to cook pizzas, chicken nuggets, biscuits, and cinnamon rolls. It kept everyone happy. Though the oven was fueled by green propane canisters, she knew Jim had recently bought an attachment that allowed him to fuel it with the larger tank from the gas grill. If she could figure out how to connect the other tank, they could run the stove for longer. Jim had dozens of the small tanks but those would run out eventually if this emergency stretched on.

Ellen looked around at the impressive pile of gear, thinking of all the camping trips they'd taken. She'd never been camping before she married Jim. She wasn't even sure if she'd like it but when the children were out of diapers, Jim wanted to get them interested in the outdoors. They started with short hikes and fishing trips before working their way up to an overnight camping trip. For their first, Jim took them to a nearby state park with fishing and a swimming beach. He wisely stayed close to home in case the trip was an utter failure and they had to pack up and leave.

It wasn't, though. They had a great time and started many of the camping traditions that they still practiced, like Jim hiding an emergency bag of Oreos in the camping gear. From that first overnight, they moved to weekend trips, and eventually to trips that spanned several weeks. Just last summer they'd gone to Acadia National Park in Maine and biked, kayaked, and hiked it. Ellen thought it was the best time of her entire life. From there, they'd driven through New Hampshire and Vermont, spending another week camping at Vermont state parks. They fished and kayaked a new pond every day. Those memories just made her miss him more.

"Let's get this out of here," she said.

She and Pete struggled to get the stove into the mower trailer. They formed a human chain with Ellen in the building, Pete at the trailer, and Ariel in the middle. In this manner they loaded the one-pound propane canisters, the Power Dome, the lanterns, and other items she'd found in the camping box. When she stepped out of the building, Ellen made sure she locked all the buildings they gone in. She directed Pete to drive the mower to the back porch for unloading. The back porch was covered and screened in. She could use the camp stove there since it was well-ventilated.

When they were done shifting their load onto the back porch, they all took seats at the patio table. "I forgot something," Ellen said. "We need to hook up some batteries to that solar charger."

"What's that?" Ariel asked.

"Daddy said he had a charger in the building that you could set in the sun and it would charge a boat battery," Ellen explained.

"Oh yeah," Ariel said. "It's hanging from a nail just inside the door. The batteries are in the old building with the mower. They're under the shelves."

"How do you know all this?" Ellen asked, surprised again.

"Daddy showed me," Ariel said proudly.

"I'm glad he showed you," Ellen said. "And I'm glad you paid attention."

"I always pay attention," Ariel said.

The three of them walked back to the storage buildings and Ellen unlocked the doors again. While Pete struggled to get the three 12-

volt marine batteries from one building, Ariel and Ellen went inside the other to retrieve the solar charger. It was exactly where Ariel said it would be. Reading the simple instructions, Ellen attached the alligator clips to one of the batteries, and then laid the solar panel where it would catch optimal direct sunlight.

"It will be your job to charge these batteries, Pete," Ellen said. "We'll let this one charge all day tomorrow. Then you'll need to take off these clips and move them to the next battery, making sure you put the red clip on the post with the plus sign and the black clip on the post with the minus sign."

"Got it," he said.

"Now let's go get a drink," she said. "I'm thirsty."

Ellen led the way, filling glasses of water for all of them. Since they still had ice, she went ahead and used it, but she turned off the ice maker when she was done. Once this ice was gone, it would not refill. Without power, they still had what water remained in the pressure tank in the basement, but the well pump would not run again unless the generator was running. Water was not a big concern for them. She had hundreds of gallons stored for emergencies. They had cases of bottled water and dozens of gallon milk jugs that Jim had refilled with water. He'd also accumulated a significant number of two-liter soft drink bottles that they'd cleaned and refilled with water. Then there was the spring house on the property which provided a constant supply of clean, cool water. Jim had installed a gravity filtering system so they could turn on a tap in the house and fill bottles with filtered and immediately drinkable water.

As Ellen gathered the three plastic cups to deliver to the porch, there was a knock on the front door and Ellen jumped. She nearly dropped the cups, managing to spill water on both the floor and her shoes. They rarely had unannounced visitors on their property. Even so, Ellen would not have been so startled if not for the heightened state of stress they were under. She realized that the gun Jim told her to carry with her to the store was still in her purse, which was in her car. There were other guns, but they were put away and not immediately within reach. She had become too comfortable and forgotten the situation around them. If Jim had been there, he would have tried to lecture her about not being on top of their security.

She knew that she was going to have to go look out the window and see who this was. She also knew that things were going to have to change around here for the short-term. Until Jim came back, they would have to keep some weapons closer at hand. She could not get caught like this again. She placed the cups back on the counter and moved to the living room, stepping as quietly as possible. She leaned toward the door and placed her eye to the peephole, her heart pounding in her ear.

It was Henry, a neighbor that lived several miles down the road but owned the farm next to them. She sighed with relief and unlocked the front door. As her hand moved to the deadbolt, she realized that the door wasn't even locked. They would definitely have to be more diligent. Jim usually took care of these things for them. He kept them safe and obsessed over the little details they ignored. With him gone, she was going to have to step up to the plate and start thinking like he did.

She swung the door open and plastered a smile on her face. "Hey, Henry. How's it going?"

"Oh fine," he said. "I was just checking my cows and wanted to make sure you guys were okay. Jim told me he was going to be out of town and I noticed he wasn't back yet."

She could hear a lot of unsaid sentiments in his few words. She could tell he was thinking it might be hard for Jim to make his way back home. There was the thought that things were dangerous and Jim could be injured or killed trying to get home. She couldn't go there, though. She couldn't think that way. If anyone could make it through this, Jim could. She knew that like she knew anything.

"He got trapped in Richmond," she said. "They started home but ran into trouble getting gas. I've had trouble reaching him except for a couple of short texts that take a long time to get through. I know he's trying to get home but don't know when he'll get here."

"Things may get tough," Henry said. "Going by what they said on the news."

"We're pretty set, Henry," she said. "Jim was a little paranoid about this kind of thing already. He made preparations."

Henry smiled. "That's good to know," he said. "Just keep your eyes open...and your doors locked."

She realized that Henry had heard the door open without being unlocked. He was gently encouraging her to be more careful. "I will. Heard of any trouble locally?"

"There's trouble all over," Henry said, shaking his head. "People are starting to loot in the cities. My only worry back here where we live is that big old trailer park."

She knew the one. While Henry's farm was beside their house, his home was about two miles down the road. Halfway between them was a trailer park with about twenty older trailer homes.

"What worries you about that?" she asked.

"They're already out of water," he said. "Their water came from a single well and with no power they've got no water. I'm pretty sure that none of them have any food storage. Won't be long before they're out prowling around trying to see what they can find. Only trouble we've ever had in this community came from that trailer park. The people in there have no roots in this community. They don't feel the same way about it as the rest of us."

He was exactly right. There were several houses between her and the trailer park but they would probably eventually make it up this way. If they were looking for houses to rob there weren't very many to choose from. This was rural farmland with no subdivisions or neighborhoods.

"There's a lot of rough people living there," she commented. "If you see a police car coming in this direction, that's where they're going. Old trailers that rent for cheap to druggies and drunks."

Henry just nodded. "Yep."

"We'll keep an eye out," she said. "Thanks for checking on us."

"No problem," he said. "Jim would do the same if things were the other way around. If you need us, we use channel ten on the farm. I know Jim has some of those little walkie talkies because he's called me on them a time or two. If you've got batteries you should just keep one of those things on all the time, set to channel ten. That way we can let each other know if there's going on around here. "

"That's a good idea, Henry. I know where the radios are and I'll get one out tonight."

Henry smiled and waved, then stepped off the porch. He strode across the yard and climbed onto a big orange Kubota tractor with a hay mower attached to it. Disaster or not, a farmer had to work. When Henry pulled away, Ellen retrieved her purse from the Suburban. She removed the pistol, tucked it in her jeans pocket, and then locked her car. When she returned to the house, she closed the front door behind her and this time she made certain it was locked.

10

As we approached the off-ramp and began to walk down the exit, I could see more activity than I'd seen in a while. There were a couple of chain hotels, a few fast food restaurants, and two convenience stores with gas pumps. There were also a lot of cars and a lot of people. From the moment we started down the ramp, the shoulder was packed with a disorderly line of vehicles. There were cars stopped in the middle of the road, blocking all the lanes. There were more packed haphazardly into the parking lots of the restaurants and convenience stores. Some people sat around their vehicles like it was a tailgate party. It might have been festive if not for the undercurrent of fear and desperation. In the distance, I could see a line of several white tents with people gathered around them.

People were friendlier here, though reserved. We nodded and greeted the stranded travelers we passed. They, in turn, nodded and greeted us back. After all, we shared a common dilemma. At the bottom of the ramp, we turned right and walked past a fast food restaurant where several people were eating ice cream. A woman holding a child by the hand walked out of the restaurant parking lot. I looked at the little girl's ice cream smeared face and smiled.

She smiled back. "They're giving away ice cream," she said.

"That sounds delicious," Rebecca groaned. "I'm starving."

"What's going on at those tents?" I asked the woman.

"Some church is cooking food for stranded people."

About that time the smell of grilling burgers hit me. "That's where I'm headed."

I thanked the lady and looked at the faces of my group. No argument or discussion was needed. They were all as ravenous and thirsty as I was.

It was amazing what food did for people. All of the people we passed on the way to the tents were stranded travelers with no idea how they were getting home or what they would be going home to. With a full plate of food they were all smiles, awash in blissful ignorance. People greeted us in a friendly manner, as if this was some outdoor festival instead of a national crisis. When we finally arrived at the tents, we were met with more smiling faces.

"Lay down your burdens and eat with us," said a man with ministerial bearing and perfect dark hair. He wore shorts and a blue polo shirt, spreading an arm with great flourish toward tables laden with all manner of picnic foods. There were grilled burgers, hot dogs, and barbecue sandwiches, coleslaw, baked beans, chips, potato salad, cookies, pies, cakes, and much, much more. It was a beautiful sight.

I was not about to turn down their charity. I took a Styrofoam plate from a smiling woman and began filling it with earnest. Even as I appreciatively heaped food onto my plate, I could not help but be aware that the generosity I was seeing was an indication of very poor planning on the part of these friendly folks. They didn't understand that they might not be able to replace the food they were giving away. They probably assumed that in a day or two there would be more trucks of food showing up at their local grocery store. The power would come back on and things would return to normal.

It was possible this would be the case but not likely. I suspected it could be months before we saw things restored to normal, maybe even longer. The very food they were giving away might mean the death of their own families when the food supply dried up. Despite that awareness, it was already cooked and waiting, though, so what was I supposed to do? I was not about to voice my concerns and make them feel bad during their time of giving.

With my plate so full it was bending under the weight, I found a shady spot beneath a nearby tree and slid my pack to the ground. I went back and took two bottles of icy cold water from a cooler under the tent. I was already eating when my fellow travelers joined me.

"Make sure you save your water bottles," I reminded them. "We may need to refill these if we have to walk."

"I hope we don't have to walk," Randi said. "My feet aren't used to this. What did we just walk? Ten or twelve miles? Fifteen?"

"It felt like twenty," Alice said.

"It was a little over four," I said, my mouth full.

Randi groaned.

"I guess we'll just have to see what tomorrow brings," Alice said, digging into a hot dog.

The plastic-haired minister approached and stood over us while we ate. "I know you folks have your mouths full so I won't bother you. Much." He grinned at that. "May I ask where you folks are headed?"

Gary took a drink, cleared his throat and replied, our default spokesman in this kind of situation. He was probably the best man for it, too. He had a more agreeable disposition than I. People tended to like him. I had the opposite effect.

"We left Richmond this morning headed for Russell County," he said.

The minister gave a low whistle as he considered this. "I've never been there but I know it's a far piece. How many miles are you talking?"

"Over two hundred still to go from here," Gary said.

The minister shook his head. "Any idea how you're going to get there?"

Gary shook his head. "Don't know yet. We just left our vehicle behind a couple of hours ago. We're hoping to find a place for the night and then see what tomorrow brings."

"The last town we stopped in was not this friendly," Rebecca commented. "We appreciate the hospitality."

"I'm afraid the town itself isn't that friendly," the minister said with a little regret in his voice. "You can't see it from here, but they have a roadblock just over the hill there and they're not letting anyone into town, either. They agreed to let us try to ease the suffering of you weary travelers but that's all. They warned us that we couldn't bring anyone back to town. If not for that threat, we'd open our church as a shelter, just as the Lord would have us do."

"What's the latest news? Heard anything?" I asked between bites of baked beans.

"Pakistani terrorists have taken credit is the last I heard," the minister said. "A lot of the terrorist acts took place in remote areas so the full effect isn't known yet. The news is getting kind of spotty and there isn't much official information coming in. I think the power outages and fuel shortages are starting to interfere with collecting the news. Whatever is happening is nothing that we can't make it through. People must not lose hope."

In that last sentence I could hear that the minister believed this moment right here might be as bad as it got. I knew the local area received its fair share of ice storms and people were used to power outages. They experienced downed trees and impassable roads on a regular basis. Perhaps that was what he was expecting from this – nothing more than an ice storm's level of inconvenience. That was a mistake.

"What about the gas situation?" Gary asked.

"Not good," the minister replied. "What news you can get says they hit pipelines and refineries. They destroyed large quantities of the gas stored at those refineries. They don't know when we'll be able to start buying gas again. Some say it could be months. They're telling people to conserve what gas they have because it may be all they get for a while. Most of the folks serving food here today walked or came on bikes. We used ATVs to bring the food."

"If they're not selling gas, why aren't there are any guards at the stations we just passed?" I asked. "The last station we stopped at up the road had troopers there to make sure no gas was being sold."

"There's no gas here to guard," the minister said. "All the tanks sold out this morning. I think there's a little kerosene left and that's it."

"Are the hotels accepting guests?" Alice asked.

"I think so," he said. "There's a rumor that FEMA is supposed to charter some buses and deliver people down the interstate. One rumor is that they'll bus people closer to their homes and drop them off. Another says they'll bus them to FEMA camps to sit out the worst of this. That rumor is why people are sitting around like they don't have a care in the world. They're waiting for the buses to show up. The hotels don't have power and I'm sure the water is probably down to a trickle by now but I guess it beats sleeping in the bushes."

At the mention of FEMA, I caught Gary's eye and fought back a grin. While we were both a little paranoid, FEMA inspired severe paranoia in much of the prepper community. They were attributed with all manner of powers specifically tailored to taking our liberties. FEMA and the Department of Homeland Security were alleged to be evil incarnate.

"Are people behaving themselves?" I asked. "There are a lot of people here."

The minister considered this. "They are for now because they think buses are coming to get them. When it gets dark and there are no buses, I'm not sure how they'll act. Not everyone has the means to pay for a hotel, even if they are accepting plastic. There have also been a lot of folks purchasing alcohol from the convenience stores. They're sitting around drinking since they don't have anything else to do. We tried to discourage that by saying we wouldn't serve food to anyone who was intoxicated, but some preferred the bottle to the burger."

"Things might not be so pretty here if those buses don't show up," I said. "When people get desperate, they get ugly."

"Yes," Alice agreed. "We've seen that today already."

"You folks have seen the face of man's ugliness today?" the minister asked.

"We lost a member of our group this morning to an act of random violence. It was pretty upsetting to us," I said.

"I'm sorry if I hit a sore spot," the minister said. "I do a lot of spiritual counseling and prying is in my nature."

"That's okay," I said. "No harm done. We definitely appreciate the information and the hospitality."

"You're most welcome," the minister said. "I see more hungry folks coming so I better get back to the serving line."

"Sir?" I said. "Before you leave, can I ask one more thing?"

He turned back around. "Yes?"

"You mentioned ATVs," I said. "We passed an elderly couple about two miles north of here on the interstate. They were out of gas and the woman was in medical distress, unable to walk. Do you think that someone might be able to go pick them up and bring them back here? I'm really concerned about them but I'm not sure what to do. I don't think the lady can walk and it's a long way to carry someone."

"I'm certain that we can do that," the minister said. "We have a side-by-side ATV that holds three people and has a cargo bed. We also have a trailer attached to it."

"I'd be glad to go with you," I added. "We hated to leave them, but didn't know what else to do without a vehicle."

"Why don't you folks go see if you can secure a hotel room after you finished eating?" he said. "Come back here in about thirty minutes and I'll have someone available to pick them up if you can show us where they are."

"I appreciate that," I said.

The minister smiled, turned, and walked back to his station. Along the way he patted shoulders and greeted more hungry faces.

We decided to start with the hotel farthest from the interstate. We'd had a short discussion about it and Gary pointed out that it was likely to be the least crowded since tired travelers would probably stop at the first hotel they came to. We walked in that direction, passing the second convenience store. As the minister had mentioned, there was a lot of drinking going on in the parking lot. Most people there appeared to be part of two groups. One consisted of young rednecks in tank tops and ball caps. They were hanging around a cluster of pickup trucks with fishing poles and canoes in the beds. The other group was primarily Hispanic, chugging forty ounce beers and casting hairy eyeballs toward the rednecks. Both groups were playing music from their sound systems, running down the batteries of useless vehicles. In the battle between Lynyrd Skynyrd and Latin hip hop, it seemed like hip hop was winning.

There was some hostility there that went beyond the battling tastes in music. Who knew what insults may have been cast back and forth over the course of this drunken day? Maybe it was just shitty looks. I knew things like this didn't end well. Someone would be hurt before the night was over. Eyes from that parking lot cut toward us as we moved along down the road. We kept faces forward and walked straight to the Comfort Inn. I'd had my share of altercations for the day.

As we neared the hotel, we could see people hanging around outside the entryway. Kids played in the parking lot, made safer by the absence of moving vehicles. Some of the folks drank from water bottles, beer bottles, or red plastic cups. It was an odd environment. In its informality it was more like a backpacker's hostel in a trail town than a chain hotel by an interstate highway.

We wove through the milling people and entered the dark, humid lobby. Light entering through the large picture windows revealed a tired Pakistani woman in a sari sitting on a stool at the counter. Rather than greeting us or asking us what we needed, she stared apprehensively in our direction.

"We're looking for rooms," Alice said, taking the lead. "I'm assuming that you're open to guests?"

The woman looked us over. "Can you pay?" she asked. "No free rooms."

"We can pay," Alice responded, "As long as you still take credit cards."

The woman shook her head. "Cards no good," she said. "Cash only."

Alice was visibly frustrated by this. "Listen, this is official business. We work for a government agency," she said. "Our cards are good."

"No matter," the lady said. "Processing is down. Cash only."

"You could write the information down off our cards and bill them later," Rebecca suggested helpfully. "When the processing comes back up."

The woman's head shook rapidly and she began muttering before Rebecca was even done. "No, no, no!" she said adamantly. "Cash only or go away."

"How much are rooms?" Alice asked.

"Two hundred dollars cash for a room," the lady responded. "For twenty you can sleep in hall or lobby."

I sighed. These were rooms that were probably $58 a night before the shit hit the fan. We were being gouged.

"Does anyone have a thousand dollars cash?" Alice said quietly, turning back to us.

As usual, I could not restrain myself. "You've got to be kidding me. If I had a thousand dollars I would not spend it on a night in this hotel. There could be more pressing needs before this trip is over."

Alice frowned at me. "I guess we share," she said. "Is everyone willing to put in forty dollars each and share a room?"

Everyone coughed up forty dollars and Alice handed it to the lady across the counter. She handed Alice a plastic key card.

"Does this even work?" Alice asked, looking at the card.

"Batteries still work," the lady responded. "Card will work. Water does not work, though. You have to go outside, make pee in bushes."

"Great," Randi said. "There's probably three hundred people here and I think I saw two bushes out there."

"More bushes out back," the desk clerk offered helpfully.

I elbowed Randi. "It's a new hotel, too," I pointed out. "The bushes aren't really even that leafy."

"Great," she sighed.

"Is the kitchen serving anything?" Gary asked.

The lady nodded. "Bar open. Kitchen open. Cash only."

"Of course," Alice muttered. "Cash only. Everything is cash only."

We made our way up to the third floor in a stairwell dimly lit by small windows placed at each landing. When we entered the third floor hallway we found a scene much like the one we'd left behind that morning – a dark and strangely silent hallway. Without the HVAC system working its magic the hallway was musty. It was also clear from the smell of the hallway that not everyone was utilizing the bushes as they'd been instructed. The hallway stank of unflushed toilets and urine. Our room was stuffy but well-lit and had opening windows that allowed in a little fresh air.

We crowded into the small room with two double beds, standing around awkwardly. All of us wanted to sit down on the nearest bed but we didn't have a protocol for this. It was way too awkward.

"It's probably fine if you guys take the beds," Gary offered. "Jim and I will sleep on the floor. Work for you, Jim?"

I nodded. "Not a problem." I didn't expect to sleep well under these conditions whether I had a bed or not.

"Are you going back after those older folks?" Alice asked me. "Who all is going?"

"I don't think we all need to go," I said. "I think if Gary and I go from our group that should be enough. Then I guess the church will send someone, too."

"If you're sure," Alice said. "I don't mind going."

"It should be fine," I said. "I just need to shift a few things in my pack before we leave."

I tried to decide if I was going to take my pack with me on this little errand or leave it in the hotel room. As much as I was ready to have the heavy, sweaty thing off my back I was also afraid to leave it. What if I didn't make it back here for some reason? What if it was stolen? The idea of trying to make it home without my gear was not encouraging. I'd put too much planning into this Get Home Bag to step out of this room without it. If I was going, it was going.

I also wanted to switch pistols. While the Ruger LCP was my primary carry pistol due to its light weight and the fact that it was easily concealable, I carried a larger pistol in my Get Home Bag. It was Beretta 92 9mm with fixed sights. Although it was not the first gun I'd ever owned, it was the first gun I ever went out and bought with my own money. I'd just gotten my first full-time job and wanted a handgun.

Concealed Carry Permits were difficult to obtain at the time. You had to go before a judge and present a damn good reason for needing one. My reason for needing one was that I travelled a lot, at odd hours on lonely highways, and didn't want to be caught unprepared. I ignored the law and carried because I felt it was my right to do so. For twenty years, that gun had been my constant travel companion. It didn't have a fancy accessory rail, tritium sights, or a laser, but it was dependable and comfortable in my hand. I knew it intimately and it was the pistol I wanted on my belt.

I took a flashlight from my pack and disappeared into the bathroom. I shifted a few things around, tucking away some extra water bottles I'd brought from the church tent. I also removed my other pistol from the pack. When my cargo adjustments were complete, I had the heavier Beretta concealed in a Fobus paddle holster under my un-tucked shirt. I also had two spare magazines for the pistol in a magazine holster on my left hip. Everything was hidden but easily accessible.

When I exited the bathroom, I had the Ruger LCP in my hand. Rebecca stared at it. I looked at Randi. "You ever shoot one of these?"

She smiled. "Hell yeah. I've shot guns my entire life."

"Keep this in your pocket until we get back," I instructed her. "If there's an emergency, use it. I just reloaded it. There's no safety so when you pull it out, just point it and pull the trigger."

"I've fired guns, too," Alice said. "You could have left it with me."

I looked at her skeptically. "I was afraid you might not give it back, Alice. Policy violation, you know."

She frowned at me.

"So you brought *two* guns?" Rebecca asked. "As if it wasn't bad enough that you brought one. Why in the hell would you bring two guns on a business trip?"

"One is a pocket gun," I said. "I carry it every day."

"Hopefully not to the office," Alice commented. "We—"

"—have a policy against that," I cut in. "I know. The Beretta is the gun I carry in my pack for real emergencies, Rebecca. Emergencies like the one we're experiencing now. The events of the day should clearly demonstrate just why in the hell I would carry two guns on a business trip."

She turned away unconvinced.

"Randi, make sure you don't wave that thing around as a threat. People may try to steal it if they see it. Only pull it out if you're fully intent on killing someone. You got it?"

Randi nodded.

"You really think she'll need that thing?" Rebecca asked. "We're in a hotel room, for God's sake."

"I don't know if she'll need it or not," I said. "I want you guys to have it if you do need it, though. There's a parking lot full of drunks out there. The food and alcohol are going to run out soon and tensions are going to flare. Anything could happen."

Rebecca rolled her eyes at me and lay back on the bed. "I think I'm going to take a nap. You guys are making my head hurt. You're a little too gung-ho for me."

I couldn't hold back a smirk. "You do that. Take a nice long nap and have sweet dreams. Maybe something with unicorns and sparkles." I shouldered my pack. "Gary?"

"I'm ready."

11

Thirty minutes later we were speeding up the shoulder of the northbound lane in a Polaris Ranger with a retired insurance salesman named Emmet. It was a newer side-by-side ATV that seated four people. Behind us, we pulled a utility trailer. Although we'd not seen any traffic on the highway, we stayed to the shoulder to avoid being run down by a fast-moving semi or military convoy. This was something that would have been illegal yesterday but today was of little consequence. The world had bigger problems.

When we reached the elderly couple Emmet swung around and drove across the median. It was another action we probably wouldn't have taken yesterday. We pulled in behind the stranded car and stopped. Jack was sitting on the ground beside his wife. He was leaned back against the car and looking a little more disheveled than when I'd seen him earlier. At first I thought they might be dead, but he rose awkwardly and stretched his back. He tried to smile but appeared worried. I was glad he wasn't dead. I would have felt pretty shitty about him dying while I was enjoying my cheeseburger and baked beans.

"Howdy, friend," he said, his voice raspy. "You remembered us."

I nodded a greeting and handed him another water bottle. "Hey, Jack. You look like you need this. How's Ruth?"

"I'm not really sure if she's asleep or unconscious," he said. "She went to sleep and I haven't been able to wake her. She's still breathing, though, best I can tell."

I crouched by Ruth and placed the back of my hand against her cheek. Her skin was warm and clammy.

Emmet came up behind me and assessed the situation. "She alright? She doesn't look so good."

I shook my head. "I don't know. Let's get her back to the exit and see what they can do for her."

The three of us loaded her onto the utility trailer. The trailer had a tarp laying in it, held down by a few odd tent poles and a framing hammer. All stuff left over from the church's serving tents. We shifted a few items to make her as comfortable as possible on the tarp. After getting her settled, we stood at the front of the ATV while Jack retrieved a few items from his car.

Digging in the back seat, Jack removed his wife's purse and a suitcase. When he locked the car up, he paused for a moment, staring at it from end to end. "Not sure what the hell will happen to all these cars. Hell of a thing leaving them all out here sitting by the road. That's a lot of money to walk away from."

We had no answers for him. It was one problem in a world full of problems. Jack was headed back our way when he stopped and stared past us. Gary, Emmet, and I turned toward the trailer to see what he was staring at. From nowhere, a couple had appeared and were standing at the end of the trailer, looking down at Ruth. The girl appeared to be in her twenties, mousy, with long stringy hair that needed washing. She had sores on her face and was chewing on a fingernail with rotted teeth, staring at Ruth's inert body.

The man with her appeared to be a little older. He wore a dirty white t-shirt and his bare arms were covered with crude jailhouse tattoos – names, words, crosses. He needed a shave, and probably a bath, too. He looked us over, squinting against the sun. The girl continued staring at Ruth, not making eye contact with us. She seemed a little out of it. Her movements were off.

When we didn't offer a greeting, the man broke the ice. "We were on our way to the clinic and run out of gas."

I stared back, trying to get a read on him. I saw no weapon but it was hard to gauge a person's level of desperation. He could have been hiding a gun, a knife, or even a length of rebar. With no traffic and no access to law enforcement, any encounters people had on the highway were subject to completely random and Darwinian forces. Those who survived had to be quicker, sneakier, more paranoid, or better armed than those they ran into. That was the simple truth of it.

"We're in the same boat," I finally said. "We can't get gas, either."

Emmet spoke up from the seat of the Polaris. "One of you folks sick?"

"Sick?" the man replied, confused.

"The clinic," Emmet reminded him. "You said you were headed to the clinic."

"Oh, yeah," the man said. "Not that kind of clinic, the *methadone* clinic. We have to go twice a day. Reba here is trying to kick the OC."

"The OC?" Emmet asked warily. "What the hell is the OC?"

"Oxycontin," I said. Working at a mental health agency, I saw these kinds of people every day. Some were harmless, but some were not. Some were people wanting help, some were soulless leeches who used and abused their fellow man.

The man cast his eyes to the Polaris. "You got that thing," he said, raising a dirty finger toward it. "Would you sell us some gas from it?"

I shook my head. "Not enough gas in there to be of any help to you, buddy. It's a small tank and it's nearly empty anyway."

"I got to get to the clinic," the girl said, raising her eyes and speaking for the first time.

In her, I saw the desperation I'd seen many times before in the eyes of addicts. I wondered if she was preparing to appeal to our sympathy. To throw out some story about how pitiful she was and why we should help her. Substance abusers were masters of manipulation. It was a tool of their trade.

I spoke to her softly, trying to be calming. "The clinic may be closed for while. Have you guys seen the news? The country is under attack and things are falling apart. It may take a while to get everything going again."

"We've heard about it," the man said. "But life goes on, you know. People need what they need."

I had nothing to say to that. There was a degree of truth there.

"Can you give us a ride?" the girl asked. "It's probably just twenty-five miles or so to the clinic. We got to go soon. If we're late, they quit dosing and I can't get any until tomorrow. I can't wait that long."

"Sorry, we're not giving any rides," I said firmly. "If we take you somewhere, we're burning gas we can't replace. We came out to pick up this sick lady and we're heading back how. She needs medical care. We wish you good luck but we can't help you. The clinic probably isn't even open. I doubt they can get their methadone delivery since they can't get gas."

The girl appeared not to hear me. "What's wrong with the old lady?"

Jack, who'd worked his way from the car back to the trailer to stand at his wife's side, addressed the girl. "She had surgery. We're on our way home and she's very sick." He leaned over the side of the trailer, placing the suitcase and his wife's purse in there.

The girl's eyes lit up and fixed on Ruth's purse. "Surgery? Did they give her anything?"

"Excuse me?" Jack asked, unsure of what she meant.

"What did they give her?" the girl yelled, her voice shrill. "What medication? For the pain?"

I stepped toward the trailer. "We're not giving you any medication." I lowered a hand to my shirttail, reaching for the grip of my Beretta. I would not draw it unless things escalated but I wanted it close at hand.

In a blur of motion, the girl drew a flimsy steak knife from her pocket and jumped over the side of the trailer. She stuck the knife to Ruth's neck and screamed in my direction. "I will kill this bitch if you don't give me her fucking pain pills!"

At the other side of the trailer, Jack lunged, reaching for the knife with both hands. "No!"

Without hesitation, the girl slashed at his grasping hands, cutting him across his forearm. A trail of blood splashed across Ruth's unconscious body and Jack drew away from the knife, falling as he backpedaled. He tumbled down the shoulder into the high weeds. The girl's troubled eyes turned back to me and I caught a brief flicker of panic before a concussive blast erupted behind me. I ducked and backed away from the noise, drawing my weapon as I moved. The girl's body jerked and she slumped backward over the tailgate of the trailer, falling onto the ground.

"Reba!" the man screamed. He lunged for her but another loud gunshot froze him in his tracks.

It was Emmet who had fired. He was holding what looked like a nickel .357 Magnum in a single-hand grip and it was now pointed toward the man at the end of the trailer. "We're pulling out of here right now. You don't move until we're gone. If you move a damn muscle, I'll kill you, too."

"You killed my girlfriend, you fucking asshole!" the man bellowed.

"Any girl who'd put a knife to a sick old lady's throat ain't worth missing," Emmet replied. "Good riddance to bad rubbish." Damned if Emmett wasn't a badass, after all.

Gary and I ducked over the shoulder of the road and checked on Jack. The wound would require stitches but was mostly superficial. There were no gushing arteries. I pulled a bandana from the cargo pocket on my pants and wrapped his arm tightly.

"Let's get you into the trailer," Gary said. "We need to get out of here."

We got Jack in the trailer while Emmet kept his gun trained on the man. Once Jack was situated, Gary pulled his Glock and kept it trained on the weeping man. Emmet lowered himself into the seat and started the Polaris. When we pulled forward, the man dropped to his dead girlfriend and began talking softly to her. He shook her gently as if she'd awaken and continue their desperate walk. Gary watched him until we were out of sight, then sat down in his seat. He kept the Glock in his lap, close at hand for the remainder of the ride.

"Lowlifes," Emmet muttered. "Is this what people are acting like in times of national crisis? What happened to people pulling together? This ain't *my* fucking America."

Emmet was getting wound up but I understood completely where he was coming from. "From what we've seen, this could be the new normal," I remarked.

On the drive back, I remembered the circumstances under which my grandfather first told me about the violence he'd experienced in his life. I was a kid then, visiting him in West Virginia with my parents. I'd been hanging out with some of the kids from the hollow he lived in and we were playing basketball in the road. In those days, it was nothing for people in rural areas to place a goal beside the road so that the packed surface of the roadway could serve as the basketball court. There was not enough traffic to be concerned about and people couldn't drive very fast on those rough roads anyway.

A scuffle broke out when one of the West Virginia boys tried to take the ball from me. He was being more aggressive than I was used to and it led to a scuffle. He wanted to fight. I had no interest in fighting over basketball, a game I didn't really like anyway. I walked off with him calling me names as I left.

My grandfather, who heard about it later from a neighbor, was not happy about the way I acted. "Never show fear. Never walk off and never let anyone know you're afraid. They smell weakness and they'll never let up. The world will eat you alive."

I didn't know what to say to that. The world eating me alive was a vivid and somewhat disturbing image.

"When I was thirteen," my grandfather told me, "my sister Lou was twelve. I was working in the mines already but Lou was in school. She came home one day and was all upset, crying, and wouldn't talk to no one. I found out from one of my friends that there was this boy at school telling everyone that Lou let him touch her. You know what I'm saying right?"

I nodded that I did.

"Well, I knew my sister and I knew there was no way it was true. The boy who said this was seventeen and big as any man around these parts. I knew that if I went after him directly I'd get my ass whipped, maybe even killed. People were hard then. They'd kill you in the woods, bury you, and no one would ever hear from you again."

My grandfather, who smoked Pall Malls, lit one up at that point and his eyes shifted from me to the wooded hillside above his house. I knew he was going back there in his head. The memory was fresh enough that he could walk back inside it like a familiar room.

"So this boy, his name was Jake, walked home each day down a trail by the Tug Fork River. He got off school about the same time I got off work at the mines. I had this little pump-action Stevens .22 rifle that I used for squirrels and rabbits. I hid it in the woods in a hollow tree where I could get to it quick after I got off my shift. I would get the rifle and run to this rocky bluff that looked out over the path that Jake walked. The first day, I just fired off a shot in the air. Not even close to him. Just a shot to make him wonder who was shooting and what they were shooting at. That next day, I caught him in a different spot and I barked a tree just off the path. That got his attention."

My grandfather put his feet up on the porch rail. His voice was hypnotic in the West Virginia evening, the air a soup of musty river smell and humidity. No traffic moved on the road in front of his house. The world was still, only the two of us in its entirety.

"Each day, I'd catch him at a different spot and shoot closer than the day before. I could tell he was getting nervous from the way he walked, the way he hesitated before each step. One day I shot a hole in his lunch bucket while he was carrying it. The next, I shot the top right off of his pop bottle. He pissed his pants that time and I knew I'd made my point. I put the fear in him."

"The next day, that boy comes to the house and he apologizes to my sister. I was on the porch and never spoke a word to him, but he made eye contact with me. I knew his eyes were saying that we were square now and that I shouldn't have reason to keep shooting at him.

I never told anyone what I was doing but I guess he must have figured it out."

"Why didn't he just tell someone?" I asked him.

"He knew what we all knew then, which is that a man's problems are his own to solve. You don't put them off on other people to fix for you. If a man wrongs you, it's between you and that man. Not between you and the law and him. In the mountains, we take care of things ourselves. That boy knew that he had wronged me and he had to make it right or one of those bullets would eventually find its way into his head."

My mom only heard the last part of this conversation and she did not approve. She loved her dad, but didn't want me growing up in that way of life. She didn't care for feuds and fights and blood vendettas. That's why she moved away and never went back. Thinking of my mom made me wonder how they were doing. I was hoping that my wife and kids would check on them, maybe even bring them out to our house if they'd be willing to come.

12

When we reached our exit, Emmet pointed the ATV toward the church tents. Since we were the only thing moving under gas power at this time, we attracted a lot of attention as we passed by the crowds of stalled travelers. The convenience store drunks were still drinking, with a little more staggering and obvious drunkenness than earlier.

"You're going to have trouble out of these folks here," I told Emmet.

"No shit," he replied. "I'm expecting a fight to break out any minute. I hope they keep it among themselves and leave us out of it."

Before we reached the church tents, Emmet slowed and addressed Gary and I in a low voice. "I would like to keep that little incident on the road just between us. You all know I didn't have a choice about shooting that girl but I don't want folks second-guessing me. It's a small community here."

Gary nodded.

"Fine with me, Emmett," I said. "I'll speak with Jack when we reach the tents. I know he's grateful so I'm sure he'll respect your wishes, too."

When we reached the food tents I heard loud voices. Emmet

pulled the ATV into the shade of a massive maple tree away from the crowd. Randi, who was apparently already at the food tent, hurried toward us with a lady in tow.

"This is Bonnie," she said. "She's a nurse practitioner."

The two women approached the trailer and Bonnie immediately began providing aid to Ruth. She fired questions at Jack and he answered them to the best of his ability. He was struggling, obviously glazed over from exhaustion and perhaps a little shock. He stood cradling his injured arm and looking very tired.

I pulled Randi to the side. "What's going on over there? What's all that yelling?"

Gary and Emmet walked up about that time and were just as anxious to find out what all the noise at the food tent was about.

"There are a bunch of drunks who want food. The minister said he wasn't feeding them. They started getting all mouthy and Rebecca intervened, trying to keep the peace. You know how she is – Little Miss Mediator. Now they're all pissed at her *and* the minister. Thing are getting a little heated."

"It was only a matter of time," Emmet said. "You know those damn dopers can't sit down there all day smoking their marijuana and having to smell cooking hamburgers. Eventually something has to give."

"I think there's going to be a fight," Randi commented. "I've been in brawls before. This is how they start."

I raised an eyebrow at her. Obviously this woman had a more entertaining life than she let on at work.

Bonnie, the nurse practitioner, interrupted. She took Emmet by the arm and said in a low voice, "We're going to have to take her in to the hospital. She needs fluids immediately."

"I thought they weren't letting anyone into town?" Gary asked.

"They'll make an exception for a medical emergency, I think," Bonnie replied. "Let's move it, though. She's in a fragile state."

"I'm going to tell the deputies at the roadblock to keep an eye on this situation," Emmet told us. "We don't need a bunch of people getting hurt."

I wasn't sure that calling the cops would help anything, but these were Emmet's people here in the tents. If that's what he thought he should do, I wasn't going to tell him otherwise. We all shook hands, wished each other luck, and Emmet drove off.

Gary and I reluctantly approached the tents. It was the last place I wanted to be. Inside we found a cluster of people with an opening in the center. There, Rebecca and the minister were faced off against more than a dozen loud and angry-looking drunks. It turned out to be a combined force from the Hispanics and the rednecks who'd been drinking at the gas station. Though they might not like each other, they were unified in their desire for cheeseburgers. There was a lot of gesturing on both sides and it was hard to tell what was being said in the cacophony.

"Shit," I said to Gary. "I hate getting in the middle of something like this, but what are we supposed to do?"

He shrugged. "I'll go with you but I'm not happy about it either."

We elbowed our way through the crowd and joined the parties in the circle. "What the hell is going on?" I asked Rebecca.

"These people were being aggressive and threatening toward the minister," she said. "He refused to serve them because they are intoxicated and they're having a reaction to that."

"I will not serve people who are drunk," the minister said. "They chose drunkenness over food today. Sin over sustenance. They have to live with the consequences of their decision."

I turned to the group of angry men and shrugged. "It's his food and his decision on who to serve."

"The hell it is," said the apparent ringleader, a short man with close cropped hair. He wore a white tank top and was covered in tattoos, including several on his face. "What's stopping us from taking what we want?"

"I'll stop you," the minister said. "I'm a man of peace but our food will not be used to fuel your bodies for further sinful endeavors. If you take so much as a single wiener, you will be smote in the name of our Lord."

"You need to go back to Mexico," said an obese woman in a tight red shirt. She'd been serving food and appeared to be of some relation to the minister. "We're doing God's work and you people are nothing but takers."

The man laughed. "First off, I'm of Salvadoran descent, not Mexican. Second, I was born in California which makes me a U.S. citizen. Third, you're a fucking racist bitch."

The minister surged toward him. "You cannot talk to my wife that way!" he yelled while Rebecca and I struggled to hold him back. He was worked up into a frenzy now.

"Listen, crazy man, I'm getting tired of fooling with you," the Hispanic man told the minister. He raised his tank top and showed the handle of a gun, then lowered his shirt back down. "We want cheeseburgers and we want them now or someone is getting fucked up."

I turned the minister loose and faced the guy. I shook my head. "You have guns, we have guns. We really gonna have a war over hamburgers and hot dogs? You willing to die for that?"

"I don't plan on dying," the man replied, his eyes cold, his voice low. "The question is, are *you* prepared to die for that?"

I looked him in the eye. "I don't think anyone should die for a burger, no matter how good it is. I also think we need to work this out without guns. You turn this up a notch and there's no telling how many people will get hurt. That what you want?"

My attempt at negotiating was interrupted by sirens and a flurry of emergency vehicles pouring over the hill toward us. I saw several police cruisers, a few police SUVs, and even two armored personnel carriers with painted sheriff's department logos. The Hispanic-redneck army abandoned their quest and took off running at the sound of the sirens. The rest of us stood our ground while the vehicles rolled to a stop beside the tent.

Two of the police cruisers and a large brown SUV stopped at our tent. The rest of the force continued down to the convenience store where the drinking had been concentrated. Two deputies approached, one with a black pump shotgun, the other with an M-4 carbine. The deputies were wearing black fatigues, followed by a tall man in a regular brown sheriff uniform with a wide-brimmed brown felt hat. I decided that he must be the sheriff.

"You alright, Minister?" the sheriff asked.

The minister nodded, straightening his clothes and attempting to regain his bearing. "Just a little scuffle but the forces of righteousness prevailed."

"Emmet Cox is on his way to the hospital with that sick lady and her husband," the sheriff said. "He told us what was happening out here."

"We've fed many mouths today, Sheriff," the minister said. "The drunks only became a problem a little bit ago."

"I appreciate your efforts but I'm going to have to ask you to shut it down," the sheriff said. "I can't guarantee your safety. I have an announcement to make to the folks stuck here and when I'm done I expect you to have your stuff packed and follow us back into town. We'll maintain a presence at the roadblock tonight but we need all the townspeople back in town. We're stretched too thin to have to go out rescuing folks, no matter how well intentioned they are."

The minister nodded. He had no basis for an argument, although he seemed reluctant to give up his work feeding the hungry. "We'll be packed."

"Good," the sheriff said. "Can I ask the rest of you folks to work your way down to the exit ramps there? I have some announcements to make and then you folks can do whatever you're going to do for the night."

With that, the sheriff turned and walked back to his Blazer. The two men who'd arrived with him stuck around, presumably to encourage us travelers to promptly make our way down for the announcement.

"Well, I appreciate the hospitality," I said to the minister. "You guys stay safe and take care of yourselves."

He extended his hand and I shook it. "Oh, hold on," he said, raising a hand to me, then bolting off toward the serving line. He returned in a moment with a blue cooler and reached it toward me. "I know you missed dinner bringing those folks in. That's packed with

food. There's burgers and hot dogs, beans, slaw, all the fixings. It's
your reward for doing a good deed with that old man. I appreciate the
help with the drunks, too."

I laughed. "I was just saving that guy's ass. I thought you were
going to take him down."

The minister blushed and looked down. "I let my personal weak-
nesses get in the way of the Lord's work."

I shook his hand again and we parted ways. Our whole crew was
still wandering around and we reassembled, making our way down
toward the growing cluster of people at the foot of the off-ramp. From
a distance, we could see that the sheriff was standing on one of the
armored personnel carriers. It used to be unusual for local police
forces to have equipment like that but not anymore. It came through
a combination of Homeland Security grants and the glut of surplus
equipment from the wars in Iraq and Afghanistan.

Other deputies were breaking up the party at the convenience
store. Some belligerent and uncooperative revelers were face down
on the oily concrete, their flex-cuffed hands behind their backs. With
the hotels, businesses, and surrounding parking lots emptied there
were more people here than I would have ever expected. I estimated
the crowd to be around three hundred fifty or so. The crowd stood on
the paved roadway, some sitting on the various guardrails and
disabled vehicles. When it looked like there were no more people
streaming in, the sheriff took up a bullhorn and addressed the crowd.

"Good evening, folks," he began. "I need to make a few announcements but first I want to express that I'm sorry so many of you have
found yourselves unable to make it home due to the unfortunate
circumstances that we're experiencing right now. From the information that I'm receiving, there is extensive damage to the nation's
infrastructure and to our fuel refining and delivery systems. There is
no projection as to when things will return to normal. It's likely that
we may have to endure several months, possibly even several years, of
hardship before all the services and conveniences we were used to are
restored."

This led to a rumble in the crowd. Apparently some people had not been able to put the pieces together for themselves. Those were the people who would not be prepared for the difficulties of the coming year. Looking around me, I knew at least half of these people were likely to be dead in a year if government projections on this type of scenario were accurate. Lack of medicine and food would wreak havoc on the population in short order. Some estimates even went as far as to say that serious systems failure could result in a 90% fatality rate at the end of the first year due to starvation, violence, and illness.

"I've been on the radio with Virginia Emergency Management officials and it's clear that what is going on here at this exit is going on across the whole country. Throughout the Commonwealth of Virginia, up and down the interstate highways, people are clustered at exits and rest areas doing the same thing you folks are – trying to figure out how you're going to get home and how you're going to survive. It's clear, though, that allowing people to stay at exits is not going to work. Things will disintegrate into chaos and lawlessness, just as you folks have seen today.

"The word we're getting is that FEMA, in cooperation with state and local authorities, is establishing shelters for stranded travelers. The nearest will be about twenty-five miles away, at the junction of I-81 and I-64, near Lexington. Tomorrow morning, a convoy of chartered buses will begin picking up folks at exits and rest areas. The buses will transport you to this shelter where you can receive food, shelter, and have any emergency needs seen to. FEMA staff will assist with developing a plan for getting people back to their own regions, although you need to understand that this may take quite some time."

"If the buses pass by our town, can we get off?" a voice shouted from the crowd. It was a hairy man in a white tank top and a red Bass Pro Shops cap. "I live closer than Lexington."

"My understanding is that if the bus passes your exit, they will let you off there, although the buses will not leave the interstate to take you any further," the sheriff replied.

"What if we don't want to go to these FEMA camps?" asked

another man, a bearded trucker in a Harley Davidson t-shirt with a chain wallet.

The sheriff shook his head. "Don't go calling these FEMA camps," he said. "These are emergency shelters for stranded travelers."

"Does that mean I don't have to go?" the trucker asked.

"There was no mention of forced relocation," the sheriff said. "However, I am following suit with the actions of other law enforcement authorities up and down the interstate. I will be taking action to shut down this exit after the buses pass through here tomorrow."

There was more of a rumble as people began discussing this.

"What do you mean by closing the exit?" someone asked.

"I mean," the sheriff responded, "that it will be like closing time at the bar. You don't have to go home, but you can't stay here. My force is stretched too thin to have to deal with policing this area. Everyone here will have to leave tomorrow morning, one way or another. You can take the buses or you can leave on foot, but you cannot enter our town and I would heavily advise against setting out on foot. Word is that crime is rampant on the interstate as folks are becoming more and more desperate. There's word of murders, robberies, and sexual assault all up and down the interstate, and law enforcement is obviously unable to respond to everything. We're facing limitations of our own. It's likely that things out there will get worse before they get better."

Gary and I caught each other's eye. We'd seen that increased crime and desperation already. Obviously it was just a little taste of what was out there in the world waiting on us. It made me wonder what things would be like in a couple of weeks if they were this bad already.

"You don't leave a man many choices," the trucker spat. "Trust the government to get you home or take a chance on getting killed on the highway."

"Yep, that's about the size of it. I could put lipstick on it, but it would still be a pig," the sheriff said grimly. "Now if there are no more questions, we'll be back in the morning to coordinate with FEMA and assist anyone who needs help getting on the buses. After that, we'll expect you all to be gone. And as a warning to anyone thinking they might stay and get arrested as a way of securing shelter and meals for the duration of this crisis, we are not prepared for that. Anyone who does not cooperate will be loaded onto trucks, taken down the interstate and dumped off at a spot of our choosing. So don't try it."

With that, the sheriff handed the bullhorn to a fatigue-clad deputy and jumped down from the APC. The sheriff and his deputies loaded into their various vehicles and crept off back past their road-block, closing it behind them with vehicles.

"I thought they'd at least stay and offer some level of security for the night," Gary said.

"I guess they've got their own problems," I remarked.

"Maybe we should head back to our room and discuss our plans," Gary suggested. "Who knows how long the peace will last with those guys gone?"

"You can say that again," I commented, pointing toward the gas station parking lot where deputies had left the flex-cuffed trouble-makers. Their friends were now using knives to slice them free of their plastic handcuffs. They'd be back raising hell in no time. It could be a long night.

13

E llen stood in front of the gun safe with the children behind her. She was wearing a Petzl headlamp that Jim kept hanging nearby to better see inside the dark recesses of the safe. "You guys need to remember that we have to be safe around these guns."

"We've been shooting a lot, Mom," Pete said. "We know to be careful."

"I know all that," Ellen said. "This is different. Your dad's not here and these guns may be a bigger part of our life until he gets home. You don't touch them without permission. Do you understand?'

Pete and Ariel nodded seriously.

"There may be a time that I ask you to bring me one. How do you handle one safely?"

"Always point it in a safe direction," Ariel said. "Where there aren't any people."

"That's right," Ellen said. "What else?"

"Don't put your finger on the trigger," Pete said. "Never put your finger inside the trigger guard unless you are planning on shooting it."

"That's right, too," Ellen said. "Always treat them as if they're loaded and ready to shoot. I'm going to get a few out and we're going to put them around the house so we can get to them easily if we need to."

"Why?" Ariel asked. She was always the practical one who required an explanation. Pete took you at your word; she did not.

"Because we have to be on the lookout that no one comes to take any of our supplies," Ellen said. "People may want our generator, our food, or our gas. We may have to protect ourselves. If people come down this way – if *anyone* you don't recognize comes down our road – you come get me and you lock the doors. You don't talk to anyone. You don't answer any questions. People may get a little crazy."

"That's scary, Mom," Ariel said, scowling at Ellen. "Why are you telling me scary stuff?"

"I know, honey," Ellen said. "It *is* scary. That's why we have the guns. They are for protection if we need them. We'll be okay. I promise you."

When the kids had no other questions or comments, Ellen unlocked the combination lock to the gun safe. As the door swung open, she realized she'd not really paid a lot of attention over the years to what was in there. She recognized guns they'd shot and had all been trained on when they went shooting as a family. It did appeared that there were a lot more guns than she knew about.

She wouldn't be surprised if Jim bought guns and never told her about them. She knew he also traded different things for guns. He was always concerned about seeming too paranoid or worrying that she'd say something about the money he spent on them. She would never say anything about it, though. She understood why he bought guns. It was because he loved his family and he wanted them to be safe.

Well, that and the fact that he really, really liked guns.

Her plan was to take a few guns she was familiar with and place them at strategic locations throughout the house. She began with Jim's customized Remington 870 shotgun. It was a 12 gauge with a short barrel and a magazine extension that nearly reached the end of the barrel. It also had a collapsible M-4 style stock and a single-point sling. Jim had outfitted it with fiber optic sights that were inexpensive but collected a lot of light. They were fast to acquire and made it easy to track a moving target.

"This is a very dangerous gun," she told the children. "They're all dangerous but this one is very loud and the shot spreads out over a larger area than regular bullets do."

"Of course it does," Ariel said. "It's a shotgun."

"Yes, dear, it is," Ellen said, realizing Ariel had absorbed more of Jim's training than she thought. "Pete, I want you to take this gun and slide it behind the couch by the back door. Put these shells with it, too. Put it where we can reach it easily but no one can see it from the back door."

"Got it," Pete said.

Ellen reached back into the gun safe and removed a bandoleer containing more rounds of 00-buckshot for the weapon. She draped it over Pete's shoulder, then handed him the shotgun. He left to carry out her instructions. The next weapon Ellen removed from the gun safe was Jim's M-4. She didn't know what brand it was, but knew it was one of Jim's favorite weapons. He'd told her once they were like Barbie dolls for men because of the amount of accessories that could be put on them.

There was a thirty-round magazine inserted into the weapon but no round in the chamber. She knew this because of a yellow safety flag that protruded from the chamber. She picked up the weapon, checked the safety, and then drew back on the charging handle. While she had the chamber open, she removed the safety flag. She made sure the magazine was seated, then pressed the release button to allow the bolt to fly forward and chamber a round.

Atop the weapon was a fairly inexpensive, but very functional, Primary Arms optic that she'd purchased one Christmas for Jim. She twisted a knob and confirmed that the red dot inside the optic illuminated. She turned the red dot back off, hung the single-point sling from her shoulder, and took a few spare magazines from the shelf in the gun safe. This reminded her that there was an entire ammo can of empty magazines in the basement for this rifle. She also knew that

Jim had thousands of rounds of the 5.56 ammunition that this rifle used. She would have the children fill those empty magazines tonight. That would be a good activity that they could do by lamplight.

Ellen handed the full magazines from the gun safe to Ariel. "Carry these, sweetie."

To Ellen's surprise, Ariel did not complain about not getting to carry the weapon. They went to the front door and Ellen propped it up in the corner, where it would be within reach behind the front door.

"Put those magazines on the floor beside it," Ellen said.

Ariel stacked them carefully on the floor and they went back to the bedroom where Pete was waiting on them.

"What next?" he asked.

"The Mini-14, I think" Ellen said, looking though the contents of the safe.

Ellen withdrew the Ruger. It was a 1970s police model with Detroit Police Department stamped into the barrel. It was a mostly stock weapon with a leather sling and a thirty-round magazine. There was a stack of polymer Tapco magazines to go with the weapon. Only the magazine in the rifle was loaded. The rest would have to be filled when they did the M-4 magazines.

The safety on this weapon always confused Ellen, as it was not marked. She finally remembered how it worked, confirmed it was safe, and handed it over to Pete. "Put this on the kitchen counter. Make sure the barrel is pointed in a safe direction." She handed Ariel the spare magazines. "Put these on the bed. We'll need to fill them tonight.

Ariel carried out her duties, she and Pete returning about the same time.

"Can we get out my gun, too?" Pete said. "We may need it."

Ellen considered for a second. "I'll get it out but you have to leave it wherever we put it unless it's needed. You can't carry it around or play with it."

"Geez," he said. "I know all that, Mom. I'm not a baby."

Ellen smiled at him. "I know you're not. You both are very big and are a lot of help."

They beamed. She couldn't help but reach out and hug them tight to her. When they broke the embrace, she turned back to the gun safe and looked for Pete's gun. It was a Ruger 10/22, shorter than most of the long guns in there and took a second to spot. When she found it, she drew it out and checked the safety. There was no magazine in the gun. She drew back the action and confirmed it was empty, then handed the gun to Pete.

Digging back in the gun safe, she found a trio of the black rotary magazines that the weapon used. She handed those to Pete and then removed three clear high-capacity magazines for the same rifle. All of those magazines were empty and she knew they'd need to fill those tonight, also. Fortunately, she knew that Jim kept tens of thousands of rounds of .22 ammo because they used it so frequently while target shooting. With the four of them shooting, and with Jim owning nearly a dozen rifles and pistols of that caliber, they could easily burn through a thousand rounds in a few hours.

"Put your rifle in the kitchen," she told Pete. "We'll fill up some magazines tonight."

When she started to close the safe, Ellen saw the rack of handguns on the top shelf and decided it might be a good idea to have a few of those scattered around the house. After retrieving her own Ruger LCP from the vehicle earlier, she'd tucked it in her back pocket but she wanted to make sure guns were where she might need them. She removed a 9 mm S&W Shield, another gun that she felt familiar with. She ejected the magazine and made sure it was full. She racked the slide and chambered a round, then set the pistol aside.

She picked up a Taurus PT92, a Beretta clone, and took it through the same process, then did the same with a several other handguns. She made sure each pistol was ready to fire and placed them where she thought she may need them. She put a Springfield XD with its laser sight under her mattress, the S&W Shield in the kitchen cabinet, and the Taurus in the bathroom under the sink. Finally, she took a Ruger .22 to the Daddy Shack and placed it on a shelf just inside the door.

"What can I do now, Mommy?" Ariel asked.

Ellen checked her watch and saw it was dinnertime already. She didn't know where the day had gone. Though they had been constantly busy, she was still surprised to find it was already so late. She had ground beef in the refrigerator that needed to be eaten before it went bad.

"Would you prefer cheeseburgers or spaghetti?" she asked.

Ariel and Pete looked at each other. "Pasketti," Pete said, and Ariel nodded in agreement.

"Let's make some dinner," Ellen said. "Then we'll need to get some bullets and start filling those empty magazines."

Since they needed to run the generator for a few hours to keep the basement freezers cold, Ellen went ahead and started it before dinner. She ended up having difficulty with it even though Jim had written out instructions on a piece of wood and zip tied it to the generator. She was able to find the On switch easily enough, but it was pulling the starter rope that gave her a hard time. Jim had talked about upgrading to a generator with electric start but he'd not done it yet. She finally had Pete come out and give it a shot. He got it running on the first pull.

"You must have warmed it up for me," he told her, patting his mother on the back.

With the generator humming away, Ellen went inside and flipped the ten breakers in the transfer switch. Those breakers routed ten prioritized electrical circuits from grid electricity to generator power. It didn't allow everything in the house to run, but it could get them by. As soon as she started flipping breakers, Ellen heard the hum that indicated the water pump was filling the pressure tank. She flipped another and heard the hum of the refrigerator compressor in the kitchen.

Even though the generator would power the refrigerator as long as she ran it, she knew those foods needed to be eaten first. While the well pump ran, she couldn't run any other high wattage items or she would risk tripping the overload breaker on the generator. When she heard the click of the pressure switch turning off the pump, she knew it was safe to start running the microwave.

In the interest of emptying the refrigerator, they had a wide assortment of leftovers with their spaghetti. They had leftover macaroni and cheese, green beans, mashed potatoes, leftover pizza, and a few other odds and ends. It was not the most well-balanced meal, but if tomorrow was anything like today they would easily burn through all the calories they consumed. Depending on how long this crisis lasted, they may not always be able to eat so extravagantly.

When they finished dinner, they threw their paper plates in the garbage and stacked the emptied pots, pans, and Tupperware in the sink. Ellen made a mental note to remember to wash them while she could use the well water. The generator was not powerful enough to run the hot water heater along with everything else so she'd have to fill a pot and heat it on the gas grill.

"Pete?" Ellen called back through the house.

"Yes?" Pete said cautiously, sensing that he was going to be called into labor.

"Fill the big pasta pot with water and start heating it on the grill burner."

"Ahhh, why can't Ariel do it?" he griped, walking into the kitchen.

"First, she can't lift it," Ellen said. "Second, she's going to help wash the dishes when there's hot water. Would you prefer to do the dishes?"

"No," he said quickly. "I'll fill the water."

She patted him on the back. "Just as I suspected."

While Pete set about finding the pot, Ellen got a flashlight and headed into the basement. In one corner there was a large yellow Jobox, a massive steel locker that contractors bolted to the floor on jobsites to prevent tools from being stolen at night. It had a shielded hasp that allowed you to padlock it. Without a cutting torch, these boxes were tough to get into. Jim kept it bolted to the basement floor. He stored ammunition and a few other items in it.

Ellen retrieved a hidden key and opened the padlock. The heavy lid had gas shocks that assisted with opening it. Shining her flashlight into the box, she was amazed at the amount of ammunition Jim kept. She'd been in the box before, helping him load ammunition for shooting, but she'd never really paid attention. It was not hundreds of rounds. It was not thousands of rounds. It was tens of thousands, perhaps hundreds of thousands, of rounds. There were also more magazines for the various weapons. She picked up a plastic shoebox and found it to be full of knives of different sizes and blade configurations.

"Oh, Jim," she whispered, half out of admiration, half because she didn't know what else to say. Being in the basement, in his domain, made her miss him deeply.

She turned her light around the room and saw an empty five gallon bucket. She brought it closer and turned her attention to the stacks of ammunition. Remembering the M-4 and Mini-14, she knew that they needed more 5.56 caliber than anything else. There were large boxes and small boxes. She scanned them, then took out several from brands like Wolf, Tulammo, American Eagle, and Federal. When she had about five hundred rounds in the bucket, she switched calibers. She took a five hundred round brick of .22 for Pete's gun and stuck it in the bucket. For the pistols, she took a 250 round box of Remington UMC in 9mm and .45. For good measure, she grabbed another 50 round box of Speer .380.

She hadn't even made a dent in the supply. There were additional calibers in there that she didn't even realize they had weapons for. She had to assume Jim had a few tricks up his sleeve. At this very moment she was very comforted by that thought. Though she had women friends who were scared of guns, she'd always found them comforting. The contents of this box and the weapons upstairs would go a long way toward assuring that she and her children were not victims of desperate people.

She took the bucket upstairs, surprised at the weight of the ammunition. With the bucket bouncing off her leg, she made her way through the hall and into the bedroom where she sat the bucket down with a thud. With the generator running, Ariel had wasted no time in putting in a DVD and was lying on Ellen's bed watching a movie. Ellen had forgotten that the bedroom was wired into the transfer switch, but recalled Jim doing it so they could watch TV during a blackout.

"I'll need you to wash out those pots and pans when the water heats up," Ellen reminded her.

"Okay," Ariel replied weakly, as if exhausted by the burdens already placed upon her today.

"Good girl," Ellen said. "Now I need you two to help me fill up all these empty rifle and pistol magazines."

Ariel perked up at that. She found anything to do with guns much more entertaining than dishes.

"Go get Pete," Ellen said. "You two can watch a movie while we do this."

14

Back in our gloomy hotel room, Gary and I sat on the floor by the glass balcony door and dug into the cooler. We offered to share but the others all said that they'd eaten their fill at the tents before we got back. That being the case, we ate as much as could, not knowing where our next meal would come from. Even cold, the burgers were delicious. Maybe not worth dying for, but pretty damn close.

Ever the facilitator, Gary cleared his throat and leaned back against the patio door, speaking between bites. "Maybe we should talk about our plans for tomorrow to make sure we're all on the same page."

I kept eating. Group discussions never went well for me. They always turned into a fight when I was involved. People said it was because I was oppositional. I said it was because they were assholes.

Alice, also used to being a facilitator, jumped right in with him. "That's probably a good idea, Gary, but I don't see that there is much to discuss. Sounds like we really only have one option here, going by what that officer told us today."

"There's never just one option," I commented, knowing that I should probably keep my mouth shut but I didn't. Why didn't I just concentrate on my food? I had moved on to a hot dog with chili and coleslaw now. It was good, too.

"Of course," Rebecca said. "Mr. Difficult over there can't just agree with anything. You tell him the sky is blue and he has to offer the exceptions."

I ignored her and focused on my hot dog. I thought of responding to her with my middle finger but I could occasionally show some restraint.

"Before you're so quick to label Jim," Gary said, "I wanted to bring this up because I'm pretty sure we *won't* agree on how to proceed from here."

"Really?" Alice asked. She was looking at Gary curiously, as if he'd announced a move to the dark side. In her eyes, that meant that he agreed with me on something.

Gary looked at me, waiting on me to jump in and take over with the explanation. They were less likely to argue with him since they felt he was less antagonistic. They already thought I was disagreeable and contrary. I agreed with that assessment so I left Gary to it. I was both enjoying the food and enjoying someone else taking the contrarian position for a change. Let him lay out his arguments and see how they dealt with it. I would enjoy the show and try to keep my mouth shut unless I was shoving food into it.

"I can't speak for anyone else but I'm not comfortable with placing my trust in FEMA," Gary said. "I want to get home. I'm very worried about my family. You all know I have a houseful of daughters and granddaughters that I'm very concerned about. I think I can get myself home faster without entangling myself in FEMA's bureaucracy."

"Amen!" I said between bites of baked beans. The beans were good, too. I had the thought that churches probably actively recruited good cooks, using them to lure heathens into the fold. That was sneaky.

"So what exactly are you planning on doing?" Rebecca asked. "Walking home?" From the look on her face, the pure astonishment,

Gary might have just announced that he'd be taking a goat as his next wife.

Gary looked at me and shrugged, still looking for some backup. "Well, yeah. That's exactly what I was thinking. I'm going to walk."

"I'm not sure that's safe," Alice commented, always acting as the risk manager. Her tone was both maternal and condescending, as if she might start patting him on the back of the hand while she was making the comment.

I put down my plastic fork and took a swig of my warm bottled water. "I'm pretty sure it's not safe," I said. "There's no guarantee those camps will be safe, either. There's probably not much of anything that can absolutely be guaranteed to be safe anymore. But it's not about safety, it's about having control of your own future. I am not about to relinquish that control to the government. Hell, we work for the government. You all are know what a mess it can be."

"The government is not the enemy," Rebecca hissed, exasperated. "You conspiracy theorists wear me out with your crazy bullshit."

"In some cases the government is most definitely the enemy," I shot back. "That's not exactly what I'm talking about though. I'm talking about *capability*. I am pretty sure I am capable of getting myself home in a couple of weeks, on my own, by walking. I've backpacked extensively. I am *not* sure FEMA is capable of getting us home efficiently. We may sit in those FEMA camps for months while they attempt to work out the logistics of getting people home. Remember, once you're there and safe you become less of a priority for them. Getting you to the camp is more important to them than getting you home."

"You don't know that," Alice said.

"No, we don't know that for sure" Gary interjected, "however, experience and history suggest it. I'm not trusting my life – and my family's safety – to them, either. How would this work if our own agency was in charge of these camps? With fuel being limited we would conduct a survey to figure out the route where we could drop the most people off while using the least fuel. That process of surveying and determining a route could take a week or two, especially if the situation is constantly changing with new people showing up. You know this is just going to turn into some kind of mess. The task will be so daunting, and resources so limited, that nothing will get done."

"You could always go and see what it's about," Rebecca said. "Then you could leave later if you wanted to. You'd at least be about twenty-five miles further down the road. That's twenty-five miles you wouldn't have to walk."

"No way," I said. "I'm not turning my weapons over to them, which they would probably require prior to getting on their buses. Also, I bet residents of the camps will not be free to come and go as they please. That would make the camp too difficult to secure. My guess is the camps will be fenced and guarded with limited traffic in and out."

"That's pretty paranoid," Rebecca said.

Gary shook his head. "In this case, I don't think so. I've read those government reports on disaster response. Some of us have been on those local task forces. We know how they'll respond. Jim and I are of a like mind on this. I think we'll try our luck on foot."

Alice turned to Rebecca sitting beside her on the bed. "So I guess you and I are taking the bus out of here tomorrow?"

Rebecca nodded. "Damn right. I think you guys are nuts for trying to walk home."

"Randi?" Alice said. "You haven't said anything. I'm assuming you're going with us, too? Are the girls sticking together?"

Randi was standing in the patio door, smoking a cigarette and blowing her smoke outside. She was slow to respond, appearing to think it over.

"No offense, Alice, but I think I'm going with the guys."

"*Really?*" Rebecca asked, clearly shocked.

"Oh hell yeah," Randi said. "I would go nuts sitting around a shelter worrying about my grandkids. At least this way I'm doing something. And like they said, I'll be in control of my fate."

"I think you're crazy, too," Rebecca said bluntly, staring at Randi.

"Well, I think you're a fucking snarky bitch and I've about had all of your condescending attitude that I'm going to take," Randi fired back. "You've never shown me the first bit of respect in all the years that I've known you and I'm over it. You open your mouth to me again and I'm going to slap your soul right out of it."

The exchange was so funny I nearly spat chocolate cake out my nose.

"Let's not argue, ladies," Alice said, quickly intervening. "There's too much going on for us to waste time fighting with each other."

Rebecca was staring at Randi. Randi met her eye, grinning with amusement. I had no doubt that Randi would slap the shit out of Rebecca without hesitation if she opened her mouth again. Rebecca seemed to realize this also.

"Randi, we'll be glad to have you," I said. "We'll need to do some planning tonight to get ourselves ready. We'll also need to consolidate your luggage down to something easier to carry."

She sighed. "You mean I have to leave the expensive, heavy stuff behind, right? Like shampoo? Curling iron?"

I nodded.

"I don't have luggage, Randi," Alice said. "Anything you want to leave in your bag, you can give me to me and I'll take it with me. I'll get it back to you whenever we get back to work."

"I appreciate that," Randi said. "Thanks."

fter sunset that evening, there was a lot of noise and yelling coming through the open patio door. Music blared from a car stereo and I was glad I wasn't outside. It sounded like trouble was brewing. Since there was no law tonight and people would be forced to move on tomorrow, this night would likely present a good opportunity for folks intent on getting into trouble.

Gary and I sat on the floor, Randi beside us. Despite my recommendation that they not do so, Rebecca and Alice had taken a walk. They were determined to find some type of restroom facility, or at least a more private bush than the one the desk clerk had directed them to earlier. Their desire to stay out late was probably driven by my warning to stay in. What the hell did I know, right?

"Is your Bug Out Bag fully stocked?" I asked Gary.

"Yes, it is. I built it off the list you gave me so it should be like yours, except for a few personal preferences."

"What the hell is a Bug Out Bag?" Randi asked. "Ya'll need to speak English around me."

"A Bug Out Bag is basically a survival kit for an event where you might have to get the hell out of dodge." I answered. "Mine, and I guess Gary's, are primarily designed to get us back home in the event of an emergency. Some people refer to those as a Get Home Bag."

She stared at me like I was crazy. "You take that damn thing everywhere you go?"

"Not everywhere," I replied. "Just if I travel any distance from home. There are a lot of people out there, me included, who feel that it's just a matter of time until the shit hits the fan and we needed to be better prepared."

"Are you, like, some doomsday survivalists or something?" She was not the least bit accusing or condescending, just curious. She leaned forward and whispered. "Are you guys in a militia, too?"

"No, we're not in a militia," Gary chuckled. "Jim and I just started talking about this at the same time. It was after Hurricane Katrina. I never thought that people in our country could just be abandoned like that for days to fend for themselves. When I saw the footage of those people in that convention center, I swore I would never be one of them. Jim and I talked about it at lunch every day. We started reading books, following websites, and found there were a lot of people like us who felt the same way."

"Ya'll care if I smoke?" Randi asked, holding up a cigarette.

We both shook our heads.

"Anyway, we both carry roughly the same basic items with a few extras thrown in. We have some food, water, a means of shelter, a way to start fire, and spare clothes. We also carry at least one firearm and spare ammo," I said. "Tonight, I'm going to repack my bag and get things ready for tomorrow. I'm also going to do a little recon through the hotel and see if I can pick up anything that might help with our journey."

"I didn't bring any of the kind of stuff you guys brought," she said. "I just brought girl shit. Plus a pocketknife. My daddy always said a girl should have a knife in case she needed to cut somebody."

"Your daddy was right," I said.

"How am I going to carry my stuff?" Randi asked. "Any ideas?"

"I thought about that earlier," Gary said, getting up and taking a pillow from the bed. "I thought we could make a drawstring pack out of a pillowcase."

Gary shook the pillow free of the case. He drew a Kershaw folding knife from his pocket and put a slit in the wide hem near the opening of the pillow case. "Hand me some cord."

I pulled out a roll of 550 paracord from my pack and started to cut some off but had trouble making myself do it. I looked around the room and saw the cord hanging from the blinds on the patio door. I decided to use it instead and save mine for later. I drew the blinds to the position that left the most slack in the cord and then cut it free. That left me with about fifteen feet of strong white cord around the same diameter as the paracord. I handed it to Gary.

Gary threaded the cord through the hem of the pillowcase, creating a drawstring closure. He tied a knot in the fabric at each bottom corner of the pillowcase. He then took the excess from the drawstring and tied each loose end around one of the knotted corners, creating shoulder straps. This allowed the pillowcase to be worn on the back in roughly the manner as a backpack.

"Take this," Gary said. "Put what you need in there from your luggage. Be very selective, because we've got a long way to go and this will not be comfortable with a lot of weight in it."

Randi stared at the pack. "What should I bring?"

"Another pair or two of your thickest socks, comfortable under-wear, an extra pair of pants, an extra shirt, any jacket or raincoat you might have, maybe any extra cigarette lighters. Just the bare minimum pretty much. And wear your most comfortable walking shoes," I instructed.

Randi threw her suitcase on the bed, opened it, and started sorting.

"I'm going to do a quick inventory," Gary said. "I need to get my pack arranged in a more usable manner if I'm going to start living out of it. A lot of the items I have in here are still in store packaging and I'm going to get rid of all that. I also need to make my ammo more accessible."

I went to my own pack, opened it, and removed an LED flashlight that hadn't cost more than a buck. "I'm going to do a quick recon. There may be useful stuff here in the hotel. Normally, I don't approve of stealing and looting but times are desperate. If I find some extra snacks or things that may help us get home, I'm going to take them."

"Understood," Gary said. "I wouldn't mention it to Rebecca and Alice, though. They already think you're some kind of deviant."

"Let them think what they want," I laughed. "I don't give a shit."

"I think they also know that you don't give a shit," Gary replied, grinning.

I slung my pack on my back and headed for the door. "I'll be back in a few."

"Be careful," Randi warned.

I entered the quickly darkening hallway. The reek of human waste in the humid air was getting worse. This hotel would need some serious work when this disaster was over. I made my way down the hall to the stairs. My plan was to start my search for supplemental supplies on the upper floors because they had fewer guests. Since the elevators were not working, the desk clerk was putting everyone on the lower floors.

I found the stairwell to be as dark and fragrant as the hallway. I climbed to the sixth floor and exited there. The floor was bright enough that I could move around without my flashlight but only because there were no obstacles. It was dead still. I guessed from the layout of my floor where the vending room was located so I headed in that direction. I turned on my flashlight and discovered the same machines I'd seen on my floor – two drink machines and a snack machine. With no power, the machines were useless. No lights glowed. No compressors hummed. The drink machines were heavy duty with massive padlocks on them. They were designed to be vandal-resistant and would be impenetrable with the tools I had, but the snack machine was a different story.

I dropped my pack to the floor and removed my Gerber LMF knife. It had a sharpened steel pommel that was designed so a chopper pilot could use it to hack his way out of a helicopter by cracking the plastic shell of his windshield. I gripped the sheathed knife by the handle and rammed the pommel into the Plexiglas window of the snack machine, cracking it instantly. The noise was loud in the tiny room and I hoped there was no one on the floor to hear it. A few more blows and a chunk fell free, creating an opening I could reach through to remove snacks from the corkscrew holders inside. I hesitated and listened for a moment to see if anyone might have heard me but there was only silence.

I avoided the bulky, nutritionally-deficient foods such as chips and pretzels and focused on taking the more calorie-dense snacks. I took all the candy bars, energy bars, the bagged nuts, and the snack crackers topped with cheese or peanut butter. There was a whole row of beef jerky and I cleaned that out. I ended up with about three dozen snacks which I crammed into the various side pockets of my pack so they would be easily accessible tomorrow.

Carrying my pack by the straps, I exited the room and walked across the hall to the housekeeping closet. I turned the handle and it opened. These doors were intended to be locked but rarely were. Inside was the housekeeping cart for this floor, as well as shelves of the various items needed for restocking the guest rooms. On one shelf, I saw a box of the large garbage bags that fit the housekeeping cart. The maids used these bags to hold all the smaller bags they emptied from the rooms. I tore off about a dozen of these, rolled them up, and stuck them inside my pack. They could be used for sitting or laying on wet ground, for constructing a shelter, as a raincoat, or maybe even as a sleeping bag if the situation required.

I took two extra rolls of toilet paper. I had some in my bag but I hadn't planned on travelling this far and with extra people, more might be required. We would likely reach a point where leaves were needed for the task at hand, but I would enjoy the luxury of good ole TP for as long as I could. I also picked up a few bars of soap and stuck them in a side pocket. Staying clean and sanitary on the trail helped prevent stomach bugs. I found a box of the smaller garbage bags that were used in the guest rooms and I took a dozen of those, too. I could use them to wrap items, like the toilet paper, to keep them dry if we got rained on and my pack got soaked.

Finally, I noticed a stack of blankets on a shelf. These were the blankets you usually found in the hotel closet in case you got cold at night. I took three of them, laid them on the floor, and rolled them into a tight roll about the size of a sleeping bag. I took a piece of cord from my pack and wrapped the roll to keep it from coming loose. I took one more of the big garbage bags and shoved the roll of blankets inside. I would attach them to the bottom of my pack later. They would be more comfortable over the coming weeks than using the emergency Mylar blankets I had in my Bug Out Bag. No matter how warm wrapping yourself in Mylar might be, it would never be as cozy as a blanket.

I shouldered my pack and tucked the roll of blankets under my arm. I slipped out of the housekeeping closet, and paused in the hallway. Still quiet. I made my way back to the stairwell, cracked the door and listened. Nothing. I entered the stairwell and descended to the next floor. At the fifth floor, I opened the door and listened. Quiet here, too. I walked from one end of the floor to the next and heard nothing. I slipped into the vending room and checked out the machine. It was untouched. My pack was not big to begin with, not much more than an overnight pack, and it was getting pretty full already. With the TP and snacks, I was having to cram things in.

I knew from backpacking that you burned a lot of calories hiking. With the snacks I'd relieved from the upstairs machine, and with the food I already had in my pack, there might be enough for all of us for a couple of days. Assuming Gary had food also, the additional supplies might add a few more days to our stock, but there was no way to know what resupply opportunities would be available. There might not even *be* any resupply opportunities. It would be best to take food when it was available, like now. I decided I'd better crack open this machine, too. When it was done, I put the contents in one of the small plastic garbage bags to see if Gary could fit it into his pack.

Before exiting the room I listened at the door. Nothing. I put my pack on, tucked the rolled blankets under an arm and carried the garbage bag of snacks in my hand. I walked the carpeted floor to the stairway door and reached to open it. Before my hand touched the pull handle, the door burst open, nearly hitting me. I backed away, startled, my free hand dropping to my weapon.

"Whoa," I said, partially out of surprise, partially to make the person pushing the door aware that I was here.

The guy opening the door was startled too and muttered a curse. I stepped back even farther, wanting to keep some distance until I knew who I was dealing with. Had someone heard the noise? Was it hotel staff? Another guest?

Three men came strolling through the door, close enough that I could smell beer on them. I kept my hand on the grip of my pistol, ready to draw if I needed to. I nodded at the men. They looked at my pack and the load in my hands, then moved on down the hall, trying doors and speaking to each other in Spanish. They obviously had no more business here than I did. One of them turned and looked back at me again. Before they could decide I was a target, I was through the door and headed back to my own floor.

I reached the room without seeing another person, although I heard more voices coming from rooms on this floor. I knocked on our door. "It's Jim," I whispered.

I heard steps and Randi opened the door. When I went in, I could see through the patio door that the sun had dropped below the horizon and it was nearly dark now.

"Are they back?" I asked.

"We're here," Alice said from the dark depths of the room.

"I'm glad," I said. "It looked like it was getting a little sketchy out there."

"More than a little," Rebecca said. "If I have to pee again, I'm going on that patio there. There's no way I'd go back outside."

"We saw an awful fight," Alice said. "I don't know what started it but there were a lot of people standing around watching. One guy was down on the ground, his face all bloody, getting pounded and kicked some big guy. I think he may have killed him."

"You guys didn't try to intervene?" I asked. "I know how you like to mediate other people's conflicts."

"Well, fuck you," Rebecca said. "We didn't. This is not the kind of climate where you try to mediate anything."

"I'm glad you're finally realizing that, Rebecca. That's our new world for a while. Get used to it."

"When we were coming back, two men followed us," Alice said. "They were talking shit and making comments. We got scared and ran. They laughed at us, but didn't follow."

"I'm sorry that happened to you," Gary said. "But remember it and don't put yourselves in a situation again where you're defenseless."

"I won't," Rebecca said.

"I won't either," Alice added. "I'm looking forward to the safety of a government-operated shelter."

"I hope it is safer," I said.

Rebecca moaned. "Let's not revisit that."

"We won't. The time for arguing is over." I walked across the room and gave Gary the plastic bag of snacks. "Got room for this?"

"I do," he said. He tucked it away in his pack without opening it, although I'm sure he could see the contents through the thin garbage bag.

I dropped my own pack and loosened the lashing straps on the bottom. When they were loose, I attached the blanket roll to the bottom of the pack.

"What time are you guys leaving?" Alice asked.

I looked at Gary. He shrugged, which I took to mean he hadn't really thought about it.

"I would like to be out of here about 5 AM," I said. "There's a reason police make raids at that time of day. The lowlifes are usually out cold by that time and you still have a little darkness to conceal your movement. I'd like to leave without anyone knowing we're leaving or wondering what we have in our packs. I don't want any confrontations or questions."

"Sounds reasonable," Gary said.

"The sooner we're out of here, the better," Randi piped up.

"How about we go ahead and sack out," I suggested. "I'll set an alarm for 4:45 and we'll head out then."

"In case you don't wake up when we leave in the morning, I wish you ladies good luck," Gary said, addressing Rebecca and Alice.

"Thanks, Gary," Alice replied. "I hope you guys get home safely, too."

We all settled in for the night – the women in the beds, Gary and I on blankets on the floor. We left the patio door open for fresh air. Outside music still blared, Latin hip-hop trying to drown out AC/DC. A woman was crying in the parking lot below our window. A baby cried somewhere beyond that.

"Could you slide that door closed?" Randi asked in the darkness. "I don't think I can sleep listening to that."

I slid the door closed without a word, sealing out the night.

16

The night was restless and uncomfortable, but somehow everyone was asleep when my alarm went off the next morning. I quickly silenced it and the three of us wordlessly threw off our blankets, slipped on our shoes and gathered our stuff. Gary and I used our headlamps to make sure we didn't miss anything. I gave Randi the backup flashlight from my bag. I had a couple of them in there and a headlamp.

Alice and Rebecca stirred while we packed and we exchanged a few perfunctory good-byes, each of us distracted by the unknowns that lay ahead of us. Once we were all packed and had our gear on, we exited the room, quietly closing the door behind us. We had agreed to maintain strict silence until we were clear of our little interstate community. It was also agreed that I would take the lead until we were clear of town. I removed my headlamp and showed Gary how to carry one with your fingers wrapped around it to diffuse the light. By this method, you could conceal most of the brightness but still see where you needed to go. Randi followed suit and we headed single-file down the hall. We stepped into the stairway, shutting the stairwell door as quietly as possible, then starting down the stairs.

When we exited the stairwell near the lobby, I noticed that the lobby was full of people sleeping on the furniture and stretched out on the floor. This was clearly one of the bottom tier lodging plans that the desk clerk offered us. Despite the unpleasantness of our dark room and the stinking hallway, I was sure it was much quieter and safer than this lobby. I didn't want to walk through that group of people and take a chance on waking someone. I held out my hand to stop Gary and Randi, then motioned for them to follow. I changed direction and headed down the first floor hallway, away from the lobby. At the end of the hall, we exited to the parking lot, pushing the panic bar on the glass door as gently as possible to avoid making unnecessary noise.

Once free of the building, I breathed a sigh of relief. The air was cool, the early morning quiet. The sky had started to lighten at the horizon. I wanted to be out of there before full light. When I went on backpacking trips, I always awoke to a sensation similar to this – a mixture of relaxation, mild adrenaline, and anticipation. This time, however, it was not about the journey, as it was on those backpacking trips. This was entirely about the destination. I was anxious to get this show on the road and get home to my family.

We were on the northwest side of the interstate. I pointed toward the highway, to the south, and started walking through the parking lot toward the back of the hotel. I could tell that Gary and Randi expected me to use the main road leading to the hotel from the highway. That was how we'd gotten to the hotel yesterday. That idea made me nervous now. There were still too many people in their vehicles. I didn't want to rouse any suspicion or have anyone see where we were going. I didn't want to be questioned or followed. Maybe I was just paranoid, but I preferred to think of it as operational security.

In my Bug Out Bag, I carried a Virginia Gazetteer, which is a large booklet containing topographic maps of the entire state. Since most of my work travel was within the boundaries of Virginia I had always believed that if the shit were to hit the fan when I was on the road, odds are it would be on a Virginia road. I also carried a highway map of the United States which was not as detailed but would point me in the right general direction if I were in a different state. I even went to the trouble of plotting return routes and carrying maps like this for family vacations with the kids. My goal was never to be caught unprepared and without a plan to get home.

We've already established that I'm paranoid.

I had a compass but I also went one degree better. Two years ago I had bought a fancy new GPS for my backpacking trips. It was a top of the line Garmin with a color touch screen. When I bought it, I retired my old Garmin Etrex to my Bug Out Bag. It was still a good, functional unit and I'd preloaded it with topo maps for the western half of the state, which was all the older unit's memory would hold. As long as the GPS satellites were still functioning, and I had no reason to think they weren't, this unit would be invaluable. I also had spare lithium batteries for it, which were both lighter than alkaline and longer lasting.

Passing through the back lots of the hotel and adjacent buildings we made it to the interstate without meeting another person. At the edge of the right-of-way, we climbed a chain-link safety fence, crossed the four lanes of I-81, climbed another fence, and took stock of our surroundings. Since the businesses were all located on the north side of the highway, there were only a few stray cars here on this side. I could not see any people or any movement. We walked down the shoulder of the interstate, through tall grass and weeds, at an angle that would eventually intersect the smaller road passing beneath the interstate. The dampness of the grass and weeds soaked our pants legs. My shoes remained dry since they were good quality Salomon hiking boots. I suspected that Gary was wearing hiking boots of a similar quality. I knew, however, that Randi's running shoes had to be getting soaked. When the sun heated up later, it would probably dry out our pants and Randi's shoes. Hopefully it would be before blisters consumed her feet. We stayed in the weeds until we were well away from the exit, then we began walking on the flat road surface.

This secondary road apparently did not lead into any town since there was no roadblock on this side of the interstate. There would be houses and maybe even businesses here, so we would have to remain alert to the possibility of encountering other people. There could also be other travelers, some potentially threatening. It felt strange to be telling myself that I had to consider anyone we encountered as a potential threat, but was that not the world we were now in? How could I make it home thinking any other way? Caution had to be the rule, not the exception.

Randi lit up a cigarette.

I frowned at her. "You need to quit those things."

"You need to kiss my ass."

"Just thinking about your cardio, Randi. Don't want you to be both old *and* slow."

She gave me the finger. "I'll have to quit in a day or so anyway. I've only got one more pack left. Besides, the first one of the day is the most important."

"Wake and bake, huh?"

She laughed. "That's weed, not cigarettes, and without coffee, I need to take what vices I can get."

"Don't get me started on coffee," I said. "I miss it already."

"Now that we can talk," Gary said, "what's the plan? How are we getting home?"

"I've literally thought about this for years. I think safety and security has to be our first concern," I said. "It's too dangerous to take the easy route down the interstate. That's what everyone will be doing. I think we need to take a discreet route with minimal exposure to towns and people. Since we travel to Richmond so often, I made up a plan to get home from there years ago. It involves using the Appalachian Trail."

Gary thought about it, nodding. "I can see the logic in it. It avoids population centers and nearly takes us all the way to Tazewell County. That's only twenty miles from home for me."

"It's about thirty-five miles from my home," I said. "That's still relatively close. I can do that in two days."

"Isn't that trail rough?" Randi asked, a little apprehension in her voice. "Up and down mountains, muddy, sleeping in the woods kind of stuff?"

"Yes," I said. "I've hiked large sections of it and it is challenging but I think it's our safest route."

"How far are we from the AT now?" Gary asked.

"Around six miles."

"That close? I had no idea."

"Yes," I said. "It parallels the Blue Ridge Parkway not far from here. We can be there by lunchtime."

"We can walk six miles *in a day*?" Randi asked doubtfully. "I've never walked six miles in my life."

"Fifteen is a good average day for me," I said. "I've hiked that far and longer with a 45 pound pack many times. Your body adapts. By the time we get home, you'll be able to do a twenty mile day if you want to. Maybe more. Especially if you're not smoking cigarettes."

Randi made a snorting sound like she didn't believe me.

"You can do it, Randi. But if you're having second thoughts we're still close enough to the hotel that you can go back. I'm not trying to run you off. I just want to make sure you know what you're getting into. The options are trust the government or bust your ass to get home. That's the long and the short of it."

She finished her smoke and flipped the butt to the pavement, stepping on it. "First off, I will bitch, moan, whine, and complain but I will fucking well make it. Ain't nothing you guys can do that I can't, short of peeing standing up. Second, if I have to travel with those women I will go off and hurt someone. No doubt about it. They are not my kind of people."

"I think we can all make it, too, but not on the food we've got," Gary said. "We'll have to resupply somewhere along the way. I've got some Clif bars and some dehydrated meals, but it's probably only three days' worth. Then I guess there's whatever was in that bag you gave me last night, the origin of which I shall not ask about."

"I confess," I said. "I busted open the candy machines and we probably have about fifty packs of candy bars, jerky, nuts, and crackers between us."

"You damn delinquent!" Randi teased. "What would Alice say?"

"I know," I admitted. "In my pack, I've got a Gatorade bottle of rice and one of beans. I've also got a Ziploc baggie with a couple of boxed macaroni dinners and a few dehydrated backpacking meals in it. Not enough to get us home."

"Sorry, guys – I got nothing," Randi said.

"Don't worry about it, Randi," Gary said. "Not everyone is as paranoid as we are."

"In light of current circumstances, I would no longer refer to you as paranoid. Let's just call it *prepared*," Randi said.

"So we've maybe got a week's worth of meals?" Gary said.

"I've got a potential resupply point in mind," I said. "My best friend from high school, Lloyd Earhart, lives about an hour's drive from here."

"Or a four-day walk at thirteen miles a day," Randi added sarcastically.

"Yep, about that long," I said. "He runs a barber shop in a small town just off the Appalachian Trail. He's also the mayor."

"The mayor?" Gary asked.

"Yep, think about it. You've got a small town of about two hundred fifty people. Who knows more people than the barber? He's been mayor there for nearly twenty years, usually running unopposed. He listens to people bitch all day long so he's on top of the issues."

"You think we can resupply there?"

"I'm pretty sure," I said. "He kind of lives in the past anyway. I'm sure he's probably holed up in the old building he lives in, sipping moonshine and playing the banjo. He doesn't really care much for the modern electronic age. He also has a friend with a store who might be able to help us out with some supplies."

"What's the name of the town where he lives?" Randi asked.

"Crawfish."

"What about water?" Gary asked. "How are you set for water?"

"I have six bottles left from the original stash in my pack. I picked up another six from the food tent yesterday when we ate. That's way more water than I prefer to carry. I also have purification tablets and my Katadyn Hiker pump filter."

"That's good," Gary said. "I've got four big bottles of spring water and some purification tabs. With your filter we should be in good shape all the way home."

"What's a pump filter?" Randi asked.

"I use it for backpacking. It allows you to pump water out of lakes, streams, and springs. It filters it clean enough to drink. I even used it once on Roan Mountain in Tennessee to suck water out of puddles during a dry summer hike when a lot of the springs were dried up," I said.

"You drank puddle water?" Randi asked, turning up her nose.

"Yes, I did. And I was glad to get it."

"How did it taste?"

"Like rotten leaves," I said. "But in case you ever get the chance to drink water filtered from Whitetop Laurel Creek in Damascus, Virginia, that's the best creek I've ever tasted. The leaf water was probably the worst."

"All this talk of food and water is making me hungry," Gary said. "I'm used to fueling up first thing in the morning. Any objection to stopping to divvy up some candy bars and water?"

"None at all," I said. "Let's do it."

17

We were sitting on the shoulder of the road sucking down water and eating candy bars when I heard the sound of an engine in the distance. I finished my second Snickers bar and wiped my hands on my pants. I threw the wrapper on the ground. After I did, I stared at it for a minute and thought about how I had always adhered to Leave No Trace ethic in the woods. I made my kids carry out every piece of trash they made. I picked it back up and shoved it in my pocket. I could burn it later in a campfire.

Randi shook her head at me.

"Leave your trash if you want to, but I'm burning mine tonight," I said. "I can't make myself do it when I have a choice. I've spent too many years cussing other people when I found their trash in otherwise beautiful spots."

Gary started giggling.

"What's with you?" Randi asked him.

"It's funny, but it's also not funny at all," Gary said.

"What's that?" I asked.

"That you can kill a man and rob a vending machine, but you can't litter," he said, no longer laughing.

"That is pretty funny, now that you put it that way," I said. "I guess a man has to draw the line somewhere. I draw mine at trash. The wrapper stays in my pocket."

The engine noise was getting louder. The road we were walking on was a rural two-lane that passed through fields broken only by the occasional distant farmhouse. Some dogs had barked at us as we walked by but none came close. I was sure that people watched from those houses but no one came out. The engine noise had finally defined itself and was clearly a tractor.

"You hear that?" Gary asked. "Should we hide out?"

"Let's stay put, here on the ground," I said. "We look less threatening sitting here eating."

It was only a moment before an old blue Ford tractor rattled into sight, a hay mowing blade extending from the left side. The tractor carried the blade in the raised position so he could travel down the road without taking out mailboxes. The man noticed us as soon as we saw him, detectable only by a slight swerve in his steering. Other than that swerve, nothing changed until he was directly alongside us. Then he braked, stared at us without expression for a moment, and killed the tractor engine.

He continued to stare, saying nothing in a stoic, farmer kind of way. He wore green pants and a matching green shirt, like a mechanic's uniform, with a white t-shirt underneath. The pants were tucked into dirty rubber boots. The man looked to be in his sixties but it was hard to tell with farmers. They weathered early.

"Morning," I said, nodding in his direction.

He nodded back, then spat tobacco juice onto the road. "You folks lost?"

"Depends on what you mean by lost," I said. "We're a long way from home without a ride, but we do have a plan for getting there."

He thought about this for a moment. "Guess you ain't lost then," he said. "More like you're stuck."

"That's about the size of it. We were on our way back home and got caught up in all this mess going on. We were stuck at the exit back there and things were getting ugly. Today they're making everyone who stays there go to a FEMA shelter so we made a break for it."

The man's eyes got wide. "FEMA? They're putting people in camps?"

"They call them shelters," Gary said. "But we didn't want to find out so we started walking."

"Where's home?" the man asked.

"Tazewell and Russell Counties," I said.

The man whistled. "That's a damn far piece."

"That's a fact," I stated.

"Ain't you going in the wrong direction?" he asked, calculating our route in his head. "You need to be going southwest. You're going due south."

"We're heading for the Appalachian Trail. It'll take us home without having to pass through a lot of towns."

He considered this. "That ain't a bad idea," he said. "Hard walking but safer than staying on the roads."

"Have you heard any news lately?" Gary asked. "What's going on out there?"

The man spat again, then wiped his mouth with the back of his hand. "The White House has gone silent is what I'm hearing on the radio. We ain't got power so I don't know if television news is working or not. They say the president is holed up in a bunker somewhere until they figure out if there's going to be more attacks. All the major cities are declaring martial law. They talked about doing martial law nationwide but a reporter interviewed some retired general and he said they don't have enough troops. Half of what they got ain't showing up for work. Gone AWOL to take care of their families, I guess."

The man twisted around in his seat to face us better. "One of my neighbors has shortwave and he says those terrorists destroyed most of the big oil refineries and they'll take years to repair. They also destroyed so many power stations that there aren't enough transformers to fix them. They can't make more because they don't have any power at the factories that make them. Now ain't that a pickle?

He also said that Nashville was pretty much wiped off the face of the Earth by a busted dam."

We all shook our heads in disbelief. Much of this news matched the bits and pieces we'd heard yesterday but it was still hard to digest. Despite our problems, and they were significant, at least we were still alive and healthy for the moment.

"I'm thinking we're about four miles from the trail," I said. "Do you know if that's right or not? The map shows there's a parking lot down this road that connects with the trail."

"Four miles?" the man said, thinking. "That would be about right."

"Guess we should get going then," Gary said. "We've got a long way to go."

"Then again, it's only about one mile if you cut across my farm," the farmer said.

"I noticed on the map that the trail was up on that ridge," I said. "But without an access trail it looked like it would mean climbing straight up a hillside through rhododendron thickets. They can be damn near impossible to get through without a trail."

"You remember that big forest fire last year?" the farmer asked.

I nodded. It had made the news statewide.

"Forest Service had to cut a fire road right through my property to get to it," he said. "It joins right up with that trail you're talking about."

"That's good news," I said. "You don't mind us crossing your property?"

The man shook his head. "You folks look like you could use a boost. You got enough hard times ahead of you already."

We all agreed to that.

"About a hundred yards up the road is a gate on the right," he said. "Go through that gate and lock it back so the cows don't get out. Follow the gravel road straight up into the woods. It'll lead you right to where you're going. That shortcut will save you about eight miles of walking by the time you walked to that parking lot and back."

I walked over to the tractor and stuck out my hand. "We appreciate this."

The man took my hand and shook. "No problem. You all be careful and remember to close the gate."

I promised him that we would and picked up my pack. He started his tractor and pulled off down the road. Gary and Randi stood and gathered their gear.

Randi stretched. "I'm all for saving miles. This should be easier."

I laughed at her. "We'll see what you think in a couple of hours."

"I'm trying to be positive, Jim."

"Then let's get going," I said, heading down the road for the gate.

When Ellen awoke, she did not initially recall that she was in the middle of a crisis. The children were in the bed with her, which was not completely different than any other summer day where Jim got up early, leaving for work while she and the kids slept late. As a teacher, Ellen enjoyed having her summers off as much as the children did. Their days began slowly and she loved that.

She rose from the bed to go to the bathroom, then remembered that the power was out. It was a dark cloud descending on her, remembering that her husband wasn't at work but trying to walk hundreds of miles home from a business trip gone awry. She could still use the bathroom but couldn't flush right now since the generator wasn't running and there'd be limited water pressure. She knew Jim had some way to hook up the spring water to the house but she wasn't certain he'd finished it. There was always something that needed done.

As she walked by the bedroom window she stopped in her tracks. She backed up, walked to the window, and stood there in shock. About two dozen cows were grazing on her lawn. *Shit*, she thought.

Then remembering her garden, which she could not see from this window, she said it aloud. "Shit!"

She'd slept in one of Jim's t-shirts but their yard was private and there would be no one out there to see her running around dressed as she was. Their house was set back off the road and fairly private. Besides, this was an emergency. She stepped into a pair of flip-flops and went to the kitchen. From the kitchen door she could see more cows strolling through the garden trampling plants and helping themselves to anything that looked tasty.

She was furious and nearly blind with anger. Now, more than ever, they would need that food. She snatched up a broom and flew out the door. From the back porch, she could immediately see the problem. Without power, the two strands of electric fence that usually kept the cows in the pasture next door were of little consequence to the large animals. The cows had pushed the two strands of wire down and walked across them to the greener pastures of Ellen's backyard and garden.

She waded into the cows, trying to urge them out of her garden without doing any more damage. They chewed and paid little attention to her, used to people as they were. That was, until she started swinging the broom. Like a domestic ninja, she wielded it with martial precision, swatting cows and driving them from her garden. They bolted and lunged, taking flight urgently now that they were under attack. Running back and forth, she herded them to the front yard and kept them moving down the driveway.

When she reached the gate, she ran ahead of the cows and opened it. This action startled some of the cows into retreating back toward the house. Ellen cursed loudly, running along the fence line to get back between the cows and the house, turning them in the right direction. Swinging the broom and yelling, she was able to bring them to a stop and get them moving back toward the gate. There, she finally drove them through onto the road in front of the house.

Typically, she and Jim would have driven them back across the fence, back into their own pasture. That would have been pointless now because they'd eventually find their way back into her yard. These weren't Henry's cows but those of another man. She didn't know him very well and had no way to call him to inform him of the escape. He would have to find out on his own. The cows would probably stay in the road in front of her house anyway, eating the tall grass from the shoulder of the road, and their owner could deal with them later.

Driving the last black beast through the gate, she stopped and leaned against it, sweating and catching her breath. It was only then that she realized she had an audience. Two men she didn't recognize stood across the road from her, rifles resting on their shoulders. Their grins revealed that they had apparently enjoyed the show, seeing her running around, driving the cattle in the t-shirt that barely covered her panties. She gripped the broom tightly and a cold fist closed around her heart. She was not only half-dressed, she was unarmed and vulnerable. This could be where it all ended. She immediately thought of her children and how her carelessness could mean the end for all of them.

One man was bearded and wore the reflective work clothes of someone who from the coal mines or natural gas business. She didn't know the man, nor did she recall seeing him in the vehicles that came and went from the trailer park up the road. She knew nearly everyone in the valley, with the exception of the more transient population that moved in and out of the trailer park. The other man was also bearded and wore hunting camouflage with a John Deere hat. Ellen did not recall him either. He had a single rabbit hanging dead from his belt.

They're just hunting, she told herself. Be cool and get back to the house. Act with authority, or at least as much authority as a woman with her ass hanging out can act with.

"Them your cows?" the man with the rabbit asked.

"No," she said, trying to keep her voice steady. "They came through the fence."

The men continued to look her over, leaving her feeling very uncomfortable. One averted his eyes and looked toward her house.

"Where's your husband? Why's he got you out here playing cowgirl?"

Ellen stared at the man, understanding that it must have dawned on him that there must not be any man at her house. If there was, she wouldn't be out chasing cows dressed as she was. Cut it off now, she told herself. Get back to the house.

"If you'll excuse me, I have work to do," she announced. She swung the gate shut and latched it. She would have to remember to put a padlock on it today. She turned and walked back toward the house, feeling the men's eyes on her backside.

The men said nothing at her departure. She worried that their awareness of Jim's absence may be the beginning of a problem, though she wasn't sure what she could do about it. They would just have to be careful, vigilant, and stay armed at all times. Not having her gun with her could have cost her dearly. She could have been raped, robbed, or killed. Her children could have been killed. She would have to focus on not reacting so quickly. When anything happened from this point on, she would have to examine it from all angles before taking any action. She would have to make safety the first priority.

In her fear and rush of paranoia it hit her that this would have been a perfect ruse to draw her out of the safety of her house. Someone could have let those cows loose to make her come outside. She didn't feel like that was what had taken place this time, but it could be next time. She decided never to leave the house unarmed again. She would need to return to Jim's binder. There was useful information in there about securing the house. Information she might need today.

She was not able to relax enough to draw a full breath until she reached the steps of her house. Up until that point, she had listened carefully for the clank of the gate latch or the sound of footsteps coming up on her from behind. She didn't know what she would do if they came after her. She supposed she would have run, maybe even fought for her life. Would she have screamed for the children to help her? To bring a gun? What would she do? Maybe they needed a plan for that.

When she climbed the steps and reached the front door, safety just feet away, she found it locked. It was then that she remembered she'd come out the back door. Another painful mistake, another reminder of how she needed to be doing a better job of this. She turned and went back down the steps. When she took a glance at the road, she found the men were still there, still watching her. When she got to the corner of the house, she lost all composure and ran to the back door as fast as she could, climbing the steps two at a time and hurtling herself through the door.

Once inside, she threw the latches and locked the door. Only then did the tears come. She shook and sobbed, sliding down onto the floor and curling herself into a ball. She would have to think differently to survive. She could not fail so miserably again. Her life – and the lives of her children – depended on it.

By the time Pete and Ariel woke up, Ellen had regained her composure. She'd changed clothes and made coffee on the camp stove out back. She had also dug a thick belt from her closet and now wore the S&W Shield in a kydex holster. On the opposite side of her belt was a nylon pouch that held two spare mags. The faithful Ruger LCP was in her back pocket. She would not be caught unarmed again.

While she drank her coffee, Ellen made breakfast. She cooked refrigerated food that needed to be eaten soon. There were eggs, bacon, and biscuits. With them, she served slightly soft butter and homemade peach preserves. The softening butter reminded her that it was time to run the generator. She was able to start it with less trouble this time. The noise of the engine was better than an alarm clock and had both children roused in no time. They found their way to the kitchen and ate groggily while she sat with them.

"You guys okay this morning?" she asked, sipping her coffee.

They nodded but said nothing, nibbling sleepily at their food.

"What would you think about your grandparents coming out and staying with us for a while?"

"That would be fine," Ariel said.

They were silent for a while then Pete furrowed his brow. "Why do you want them to come out here and stay with us?"

"Two reasons," Ellen said. "I'm worried about them being out there alone. I'm not sure they have as much camping and survival stuff as we do."

"They don't," Ariel said. "They think Daddy is silly for buying all this stuff."

Ellen wondered if they still thought he was silly under present circumstances.

"Why else?" Pete asked.

Ellen carefully considered her words. "Because I think we need some extra help," she said. "I think it would be safer to have everyone together. We would have more people to keep an eye on things."

What Ellen left unsaid was that Jim's dad could handle a gun if needed. Jim's mom could keep Ariel entertained and help around the house. She'd already tried to send them a text this morning, having been unable to reach them with a call. They only used their cell phones sporadically so it was hard to know if they even had them turned on or not. She would probably have to go out there and speak to them in person.

Had it not been for the incident at the gate this morning, she would have been fine with leaving Pete home, locked in the house and keeping an eye on things. He was at the age where he could stay home for short periods of time by himself, albeit under less concerning circumstances. Now that she was aware they'd drawn some unwanted attention, she couldn't take a chance on Pete being home if something happened. She would have take the kids and they would make a quick trip to Jim's parents' house, hoping that their home was safe when they returned.

19

J im's dad, known to everyone as Pops, was in the yard, walking their dog when Ellen and the kids pulled up. Ellen had been concerned about making the trip but it had been relatively uneventful. She'd avoided using the main road out of the valley because she was concerned about people seeing her leave. She didn't want them to know the house was vulnerable. She'd cut through a neighbor's field and used a farm road to cross his property, exiting at a gate that was closer to town and outside of their valley. Ellen had never driven the road before but had heard about it from Jim who often cut firewood on the neighbor's property.

The kids jumped out of the car immediately and ran to Pops – Pete to hug Pops, Ariel to hug the dog. Ellen climbed out, then reached back inside and removed the Remington 870. She hung it over her shoulder and joined the kids.

"What's with the firepower?" Pops asked, smiling.

"Things must be calm here," Ellen said. "I'm not certain they're going to stay that way, though."

"You could always come join us here," Pops said, coming over and giving Ellen a squeeze.

Ellen hugged him back. "That's not why we're here. Besides

checking up on you guys, I was interested in seeing if you wanted to come stay with us."

Pops scratched his chin. He handed the leash to Ariel, who wanted to lead the dog around the yard. "I don't know," he said. "Things have been really quiet here."

"That's because you're close to the Emergency Operations Center and the State Police substation. The bad guys are probably avoiding this neighborhood. I think we're better prepared at our place, though."

"We have some emergency preparations," Pops said.

"You know this could last a year, right?" Ellen asked, her voice low to keep Pete from hearing. He was wandering off to see his grandmother.

"Why that long?"

"Jim read a lot about this," Ellen said. "There's no manufacturing capacity to repair all the electrical components that have been damaged. There's no refinery capacity to provide enough fuel to keep commerce moving. Food will start running out soon. Fuel is already restricted. Without power, people will start dying off."

Pops' expression had gone from the joy of seeing them to one of grave concern. "I'll have to talk to Nana and see what she thinks."

"That's fine," Ellen said, starting to walk toward the house with Pops.

"You guys think you can hold out for a year?" he asked.

"I'm certain of it," Ellen said. "We have a lot more preparations than you might think. We have some solar, we have food, we have a spring and a way to purify the water. We also have enough weapons to defend ourselves if need be."

Pops laughed. "Surely you don't think things will get *that* bad. Has Jim planted those seeds in your head?"

"It's not just Jim," Ellen said. They entered the garage and started through the laundry room. "Things will disintegrate rapidly as people start to run out of food and water. One of the neighbors stopped by and said things were already starting to get a little sketchy in the trailer park up the road from the house. Those are the least prepared people in our valley. When they get desperate, they'll start to look at what they can take from their neighbors."

Pops considered this.

"This morning I had a little encounter with two men at the gate. It left me feeling a little uncomfortable," she added.

Pops stopped and turned to her. "Did they hurt you? What happened?"

Ellen stared at the ground, not comfortable with admitting her own carelessness. "Cattle got loose in the yard. They were in the garden so I went outside to drive them off. I ran them all the way to the front gate and didn't notice there two men were down there."

"Doing what?"

"Hunting," she said. "They had guns and a dead rabbit."

"Did they say anything to you?"

"They asked if my husband was home," Ellen said. "And they watched me all the way back to the house. It made me feel uncomfortable because I didn't have my gun. That was my mistake and it won't happen again."

Pops reached over and hugged her again. Ellen fought back tears, not wanting to appear weak in front of anyone.

"It'll be fine when Jim gets home," she said. "We just don't know when that will be."

"Let me talk to Nana," he said. "We'll pack up some stuff and come out until Jim gets home. I really think this whole mess will be over soon. Give me some time to convince her and to get our stuff packed."

Ellen experienced a wave of relief. Even though they were older and of a different mindset where preparedness was concerned, just having adults to share the load would be helpful.

"Thanks, Pops," she said.

20

E llen and Ariel were back home less than ninety minutes from when they first left. Although it went against every instinct Ellen had, she left Pete with Nana and Pops. She'd been afraid of them separating for any reason, but Pete convinced her that he needed to help them load Pops' truck. Pops agreed that it would indeed be helpful to have a strong young man there doing some of the legwork. Ellen kept telling herself that Pete staying behind would get Nana and Pops to the house that much sooner.

Returning home, Ellen approached their property through the same secluded farm road she'd used when leaving. When she could finally see her home she noticed nothing amiss. They crept toward the front of the house, sitting there for a moment with the engine running. Ellen watched for movement, for anything out of place. She saw nothing suspicious. She killed the engine and exited the vehicle.

"Wait here," she told Ariel. "I'm locking my door behind me."

Ariel, who was unaware of the incident that morning, appeared to sense the tension in the air and didn't question her instructions. Ellen drew the shotgun into a low ready position and clicked the safety off. She circled the house carefully, checking the locks on the outbuildings and on the house. There were no indications of any visitors. She put the shotgun back on safe and slung it over her shoulder, returning to the car.

"We're good, little girl," she said. "Let's get inside the house."

Ellen expected she'd have a couple of hours to burn before Pops made it there. She knew she'd probably need to have a meal fixed for everyone, too. With the morning's events fresh in her head, though, she wanted to review the binder Jim left her and see what he had in the section on "Securing the House". She'd not had a chance to read it yet but it was looming over her as something that she needed to focus on. Perhaps with the extra hands arriving, they'd have time to implement some of the measures Jim's manual suggested.

She retrieved the manual from the nightstand in their bedroom and took it to the front porch swing. She had the manual tucked under her arm, a glass of water in her hand, and her shotgun hung over her shoulder. She placed the water glass on the porch rail, propped the shotgun within reach, and sat down. She thumbed through the tabs and came to the section she was looking for.

This section is a work in progress and not as detailed as I'd like it to be. If you're reading this without me, I apologize in advance.

Those words stung her heart.

The idea behind this section is to let you know how to secure our home in the event of a crisis. I don't have space for all my ideas so some of them will require a little creativity to put into effect. All I can do at this point is list what we have on hand and some ideas for what I planned on doing with it.

1. Wood – We have scraps of plywood of various sizes in the shop building. These can be installed over windows using a cordless drill and three inch screws. In theory, I would also cut gun ports into these. Nails can be driven through scraps of wood and those boards left with the nails pointed up so that intruders will step on the nails. Those can act as simple booby traps.
2. Wire Fencing – Behind the shop are several rolls of old fencing of different sizes and patterns. This can be put over windows if need be, although they provide no protection against breakage.

3. *Barbwire* – There are two old rolls of barbwire behind the shop building that can be used to create barriers on the property.

4. *Steel* – there are various pieces of steel, from plates to beams, that could be used for different things. The steel plate could create a bullet resistant barrier. The steel beams, placed with the excavator, could block the road and would be too heavy to move out of the way by hand.

5. *Lighting* – There is a six-pack of solar, motion-activated security lights in the Daddy Shack that I never got around to installing. Since they don't need power, they can be installed anywhere: on a tree, on a post, or on the side of a building.

6. *Nails* – there are lots of nails in the buildings. Driven through an old scrap of plywood, they could be used to create spike strips that might prevent someone from driving a car or an ATV up to the house.

7. *Party Poppers* – there is a gross (144) of Party Poppers in the building. These are the little fireworks where you pull a string and the thing pops and shoots confetti out the end. Used in conjunction with a tripwire, these can create a primitive perimeter alarm.

8. *Tripwires* – There are several rolls of masonry string for creating trip-wires with the party poppers. There are also several big rolls of fishing line for creating tripwires, but they can't be tied easily to the party poppers. You can take the fishing line and tie a little bell to it, or a can full or rocks, or some wind chimes --- anything that makes noise.

9. *Battery Operated Perimeter Alarms* – when Lowes was closing out a line of cheap home security products, I bought a couple of driveway alarms. These are battery-operated devices that you can stick outside. They shine a beam onto a reflector that bounces it back to the device. If this beam is broken by a car or person, an alarm sounds in the house. The thing runs on batteries but has a limited signal range so test it before trusting it.

10. *NVD* – The most valuable piece of equipment may be the Night Vision Device that is in the bottom of the gun safe. I keep one in my bug out bag when I travel, but there is a spare in the gun safe. They use AA batteries. It's the same one that I've shown you how to operate before. It's not the greatest device in the world – the image is cheesy, the optics not so great, and there's no magnification, but you can clearly see if someone is walking around the

house at night. They will not be expecting this so you will have surprise on your side.

11. There are many more things you can do. Be creative. Get Pete to apply his creativity to it, also. If you have lots of time, the excavator can be used to dig strategic ditches that you could use as shooting trenches.

ELLEN CLOSED the book and stared out at the vacant land surrounding her house. She had never looked at it before as a place that might have to be defended. Seeing the vast open spaces around it, she questioned whether it could even be defended at all. She quickly brushed that aside. She could not have that attitude. It was her job to keep things safe until Jim returned.

She got up and went inside. She needed to get started on clearing a room for Nana and Pops, then start a meal. After dinner, she would walk the yard with Pete and Pops. They would come up with a plan together.

The shortcut across the farmer's land was deceptively easy going for the first half mile and had us in good spirits. We were pleased at making progress and taking our fate back into our own hands. We felt confident in our decision to set out on foot. Beyond that first half-mile, the road quickly became steep. Before long all conversation ground to a halt as we huffed and puffed our way uphill. This was the point on the topographic map where the contour lines got closer and closer together. No matter how fit you were, climbing a steep hill with a load got the heart pumping. I frequently checked on Randi, who was red-faced and breathless but keeping at it.

"Need another smoke break?" I yelled back to her, smiling.

She gave me the middle finger and kept plodding along. You had to respect someone who could be a smartass while so clearly suffering.

Though hiking and backpacking could be very strenuous, it felt good to be doing it. Ten years ago I'd suffered from bad allergies and had developed what my doctor called "allergic asthma". My breathing sucked and I would sometimes get short of breath while walking between buildings at work. I saw several doctors, including specialists, and nothing helped. I took four medications a day and only got worse. In a last ditch effort to find something that would work, I read a promising study on acupuncture. That led to one of the greatest health care discoveries in my life – Dr. Wu.

Dr. Wu was a diminutive Chinese lady who had a practice about an hour from my home. She was from San Francisco originally, had received a degree in Traditional Chinese Medicine, and was a licensed acupuncturist. She probably saved my life. Within six weeks I was improving. My pulmonologist, who saw me monthly, monitored me throughout those early weeks and was astounded at my progress. Within a year, I felt well enough to buy a bike.

On my inaugural ride, I coasted the bike fifty feet down my driveway and then turned to pedal back. About halfway up, I was gasping for air, and my hamstrings spasming. I wondered if I could get my money back. I kept it up, though, and my conditioning steadily improved. That was eight years ago and I had few allergy symptoms at all anymore. I could run a 5K and I could road bike a full one hundred miles. I wasn't setting any records but in my late 40s I felt stronger than I ever had before. I knew that I could walk home. I would suffer but I would get there.

At the top of a ridge, the fire road crossed a well worn path. I removed my pack and sank to the ground, a sweaty mess. I retrieved the GPS from my pack and checked the coordinates. It appeared that this was indeed the Appalachian Trail. We were here.

I was draining a water bottle when Randi and Gary topped the ridge and joined me. Gary lowered his pack to the ground, took a water bottle from it and stood there, sweat rolling down his face. Randi sat down abruptly, then flopped over backward, pack and all. She was breathing hard but not hyperventilating. She'd live and I knew that she'd make it home, too. She was tough.

"Shit," she muttered when she was able to speak.

"She's alive, Gary," I said. "I wasn't sure there for a second."

I dug in my open pack, took out another candy bar, and began devouring it. I leaned my pack toward Gary, an offer to take one if he wanted.

"I think I'll eat one of my own," he said. "It will lighten my load by a tiny bit."

I asked Randi if she wanted one but she was still unable to string together enough words to make a sentence. I picked a candy bar from the mix and pitched it toward her collapsed form. "Eat it between breaths. You'll need the energy."

An electronic ding startled me and I realized that it was my cellphone. Gary and Randi's phones were not far behind, beginning to chime their own alerts. Soon, we were all receiving text messages that had been unable to reach us before.

"This ridge must put us in range of a functional network," Gary said, digging for his phone.

All my texts were from my wife. I started at the beginning and went through them in order.

RECEIVED YOUR MESSAGES BUT NOT SURE IF YOU'RE GETTING MINE. FOUND YOUR INSTRUCTION BINDER AND HAVE CARRIED OUT ALL INSTRUCTIONS. BE CAREFUL.

Her next text was two hours later.

BOUGHT LAST OF SUPPLIES ON LIST AT STORE. WAITING IN LINE FOR MORE FUEL NOW. KIDS WITH ME. USING CAUTION.

That phrase about using caution was straight out of my instruction manual. I'd told them to go to the store and pick up last minute supplies with cash if there was the opportunity, even though we were well-stocked. I also advised them to go armed and I took that statement of hers to mean that she'd heeded my warning. There was another text from 8:55 PM last night.

EVERYONE HOME AND SAFE. KIDS HELPING. FOLLOWING MANUAL.

Then one from this morning.

WORRIED ABOUT YOU. LOVE YOU AND HOPE YOU ARE SAFE. WE'RE FINE HERE SO TAKE CARE OF YOURSELF AND GET HOME SOON.

I was suddenly aware of their absence in a very immediate and painful way. We were a close family and did a lot together. I fought back tears but I knew that it was as much a result of stress and fatigue as missing them. I reined it in and composed a quick text back.

HAVE SIGNAL FOR A MINUTE AND GOT ALL YOUR TEXTS. I'M FINE AND STARTING HOME ON THE ROUTE I PLANNED. MAY TAKE WEEKS. BE CAREFUL. LOVE YOU AND THE KIDS VERY MUCH.

After sending it, I tried to call her but got a message that all circuits were busy. I looked up to see Randi and Gary doing the same thing, composing texts through-tear filled eyes. "Well, ain't this just a shit sandwich?" I said.

"You could sat that," Randi said, her voice quavering.

I pulled out my trail map while they continued reading and texting. My GPS gave me an accurate picture of where we were on the map so I went right to it. It appeared to be about six miles to the next shelter. Since it was our first day on the trail, the shelter might be a good place to stop and spend the night. We could cook dinner, rest up, and start fresh the next morning. With this being the peak hiking season, there might be other hikers there, perhaps even a full house. If that was the case, they were just going to have to make room. I had a small tarp and the garbage bags for improvising a shelter, but I would prefer not to if there was a structure we could use.

"We could go about six more miles and stay at the next shelter, if that's fine with you guys," I said.

"Shelters?" Randi asked. "What kind of shelters?"

"There are overnight shelters scattered along most of the trail at intervals so through-hikers can spend the night in them, if they're so inclined. They allow you to get out of the weather or avoid setting up a tent if you want to save some time. Most of them are just three-sided stalls with a roof, but some of them are two-stories with a loft. Some of the most popular shelters even have outhouses."

"There will probably be other hikers there," Gary added. "This is prime time for hiking the AT."

"We'll know when we get close," I said. "You'll smell the hikers before you see them."

Randi wrinkled her nose, but she wasn't complaining about not having to sleep on the ground. I decided not to tell her that most of the shelters had mice, too.

"Is the rest of the day going to be as steep as what we've done already?" she asked, a note of concern in her voice.

I got up and sat beside her. I laid the map out and pointed to the contour lines between us and the next shelter. "See how the lines are mostly loops and the spaces between the lines are consistent?"

She nodded.

"That means for the most part this will be an afternoon of ridge-running, with some brief rolling climbs, primarily staying at the same elevation."

She looked at me blankly. "What the hell does that even mean? Put it in language a grandmother can understand."

"Not flat," I said, "but no more major climbs today either."

"Thank God."

When I folded the map and turned away to tuck it in my pack, I heard the flick of a lighter. I turned back to find her relishing a cigarette.

"I can't believe you're doing that," Gary said.

"I might as well enjoy it while I can," she said.

After a few more minutes I rose to my feet, stiff from the first climb of the morning, and stretched my muscles. It wasn't a bad stiffness, though. It felt good to be using my muscles and following a trail.

"I guess that means you're ready to walk?" Randi asked.

I continued stretching the sore spots. "We have six miles to cover. We can probably do about two miles an hour, all things considered. That would put us at the next shelter by early afternoon."

"There will still be hours of daylight left," Gary said. "Are you sure we shouldn't just push until the daylight runs out?"

"It's up to you guys," I said. "I'm fine with pushing. I just thought we might benefit from a shorter day and a good night's rest in a shelter. If we push on there's no guarantee we'll make it to another shelter when we stop. We may have to sleep on the ground in the woods."

"But we could be miles closer to home if we walked until dark,"

Randi said, dropping her cigarette and grinding the butt beneath her shoe.

I hated seeing her litter but didn't feel like I could ask her to carry a pocketful of cigarette butts under the current circumstances. It was a different world now. I had to remember that.

"We would be," I conceded. "If you all want to try it, I'm fine with it."

"Let's do it," Gary said. "Those texts we received gave me a second wind."

I bent over and picked up my pack, closing any open pockets and zippers. With everything tucked back in its proper place, I swung the pack onto my shoulders and buckled the waist belt. Randi and Gary weren't far behind, showing a new determination and less doubt about following this trail home.

Once we hit the trail, we made good time. Everyone was walking strong and keeping a steady pace. We stayed on our feet while taking a few standing breaks to suck down water and eat candy bars. I was already beginning to tire of the candy bars and was anxious for a change of menu. We didn't see another soul on the trail until we approached the Bear Den Shelter a little after 4 PM.

"Shelter dead ahead," I announced.

22

E llen was relieved to discover that the truck she heard approaching the house belonged to Pops. She'd been expecting him through the front gate, but Pete had obviously guided him onto the same farm road they'd used that morning. The truck was creeping as if it was loaded down and Pops was pulling his enclosed dual-axle cargo trailer behind him.

Ellen thought for a moment about having him park the rig around back, but decided it was probably better to have it parked around front. It made it look like more people were staying there. Maybe that would make them less of a tempting target for anyone looking to steal.

Pops pulled up beside her vehicle and killed the engine. The doors opened and Pops, Pete, Nana, and their dog Rosie all came spilling out. Ariel went running down the porch steps and hugged Nana, then took the dog's leash and began showing him around the yard.

"Thanks for coming," Ellen said as Nana came and hugged her.

"It's okay," Nana told her. "We couldn't really do much at our house anyway. We have the generator but we didn't want to burn up all our gas in case we needed it for the vehicles."

"We've got a few tricks up our sleeves out here," Ellen replied. "Jim has prepared for something like this."

Nana looked around and shook her head. "I always thought he was a little paranoid, but I'm not so sure now. He always said that a few hiccups in the wrong place at the wrong time could bring the whole house of cards toppling down."

"His paranoia came from being better informed than most of us," Ellen said. "He was aware of the risks and vulnerabilities."

"I'm kind of glad I didn't know all that," Nana said. "I'm not sure I would have been able to sleep at night."

What Ellen didn't say was that feeling as if her family was prepared helped her to sleep better at night.

"Come help us unload some of this stuff," Pops called.

Ellen and the kids helped Pops and Nana unload for the next hour. They had brought suitcases with their clothes and toiletries. Not knowing what the weather would bring, or how long they would be staying, they also brought a wide variety of outerwear and shoes. They had filled two coolers with the remaining food from their refrigerator and freezer, as well as boxes with canned foods and other staples. Ellen and Pete carried those to the kitchen to deal with later. Pops brought a few cans of Coleman fuel, two cases of one pound propane cylinders for the camp stove and lanterns, and over a dozen five-gallon fuel cans of gas and diesel fuel. He'd even brought all the toilet paper they had in the house.

He'd cleaned out his gun safe and the contents were piled in the trailer too. There were milk crates full of ammunition. Ellen had not realized that Pops was such an ammo hoarder. She'd never heard it discussed, but she was certain she was looking at ten thousand rounds of assorted calibers. Maybe Jim wasn't the only paranoid one in the family.

There was an old college footlocker in the trailer and Pops raised the lid to show her that it was full of pistols and magazines. There were nearly two dozen rifles, some in gun cases, some wrapped in blankets stacked in the trailer. It was the lifetime firearm collection of a man who enjoyed occasional hunting and target shooting.

"Let's stash those in the basement," Ellen said.

"Fine with me," Pops said.

"I think you need to start wearing a gun all the time," Ellen said. "I'd also pick a rifle and shotgun to keep handy, something you've got plenty of ammo for."

Pops dug into the trunk and pulled out a Ruger SR9 in a holster and clipped it onto his belt. A little more digging produced three spare mags. He took three boxes of 9mm hollow points and stacked those with the magazines.

"I don't have anything fancy," Pops said, eyeing his rifles.

"What's accurate and easy to load?"

"The Remington 700 is a tack driver if there ever was one," Pops said. "It's not a fast reloader but not too slow, either. It's a .270 and I have a couple of hundred rounds for it."

"Is it scoped?"

"Yes."

"Good. Use that one. You never know when we may have to reach out and touch someone."

Pops smiled but it was a rigid, tense smile. He was clearly hoping that it didn't come to that. He was a man who loved to shoot, but preferred the ring of a steel target over the scream of a human one.

They ferried weapons, ammo, and assorted items until everything was unloaded and stashed away. By that time, everyone was starving. Ellen already had dinner heating on the grill prior to their arrival so throwing it together only took a few minutes. Nana and Ariel helped. Pete walked Pops around, showing him some of the things they'd done with Jim gone. Twenty minutes later, they were seated outside eating pork roast, noodles, fresh broccoli, and biscuits.

"The disaster sure hasn't impaired your ability to put together a meal," Pops said enthusiastically.

Ellen smiled. Pops loved food. "We camp so much that cooking outdoors is second nature," Ellen said. "We're also eating a little higher on the hog right now because we have so much in the refrigerator that needs to be eaten. We have some beef roasts, too, that I might slice into jerky and dehydrate if we can't eat them fast enough."

"There's a roast or two in our coolers, also," Nana said.

"If we can slice and marinate some of that tonight I'll start drying it tomorrow," Ellen said. "It will keep longer that way."

"What else needs done around here?" Pops asked. "Anything Pete and I could be doing?"

"Jim left us a manual," Ellen said.

Pops chuckled. "That boy was always more organized than anyone else I ever knew," he said with admiration.

"The manual gives us a few ideas and tells us what materials we can use to increase security around the property."

Pops started to say something else but paused when they all became aware of a distant clanging sound. It was a steady, metallic banging that came from around front. Ellen rose first, followed by Pops. She went in the house and opened the front door. Looking through the storm door, she could see a cluster of people at the front gate, beating on it with a stick. There were two ATVs and what looked like four people standing there.

Nana looked puzzled. "I wonder what they want."

"Only one way to find out," Ellen said.

"You're going down there?" Pops asked.

"What else am I supposed to do? If I ignore them, they'll probably cross the gate and come up here. I don't want them up here seeing what we have."

"How do you propose we do this?" Pops asked.

Ellen was glad that he used the word "we".

"I'm going to drive down there in my car," Ellen replied. "I'll wear this sidearm and make sure it's visible. I'm also going to carry Jim's tactical shotgun because it's about the scariest gun in the house. I'd like you to ride with me, keeping a gun visible so you can cover me. I want them to see that we're ready for trouble."

Pops took a deep breath and sighed. "Okay. Let's do this."

"I want to go," Pete said.

Ellen put her arm around him. "You need to stay up here to take care of Nana and your sister. You can get your gun and keep it with you, but I want the chamber empty. You have to be safe with it, okay?"

Pete looked pleased with that. Guard duty was a big responsibility.

Ellen and Pops retrieved their weapons and went to her SUV. Pops seemed nervous. Ellen was slightly nervous, too, but even more pissed about the manner in which these people were calling her to the gate. She drove quickly, leaving a cloud of dust behind the Suburban. When she reached them, she hit the brakes and slid to a stop by the gate. She sat for a moment, sizing up the group. There were two men and two women, the entire group appearing to be older adults, maybe in their forties.

Ellen opted for the assertive approach. "What the hell are you all doing beating on my gate?"

The group stared at her for a moment, then one of the women stepped forward. She was overweight and rough looking. Her hair was unkempt and her teeth looked rough. Ellen figured anyone who had let herself go that badly did not work, which irritated her since there were jobs to be had.

"We wanted to talk to you a second," the woman called out.

Ellen flung her door open and climbed out. She reached back in, grabbed the shotgun, and held it across the front of her body. Leaving the Suburban running, she stepped around the open door, stopping at the front bumper.

The group was taken aback by her weapons, staring at them.

"Then talk," Ellen said. "I've got stuff to do."

The woman cleared her throat. "We was wondering if you had any food to spare," the woman said. "We're about out. The whole trailer park is about out. There's probably forty or fifty people up there ain't got nothing."

"There's nothing I can do for you," Ellen said. "We've got just enough for my family."

"Surely there's something you can give us," the woman said with a hint of anger. "We figured if we collected a little from every family in the valley we might have enough to get us through the day."

"Like I said, I've only got enough for my family," Ellen said. "We're not rich people sitting on a pile of food. We were taken by surprise just like you all were. Now you're expecting us to feed your whole neighborhood?"

Ellen wondered if the woman was used to getting handouts, used to government checks, rental vouchers, all the benefits awarded to those too sorry to work. Of course she knew that there were people who legitimately couldn't work for health reasons, but there was also a whole culture dependent on being coddled and taken care of. They were not her problem. Her concern was with her children, her in-laws, and the husband that she missed terribly. She fought to control her anger.

"So you ain't gonna give us nothing?" the woman asked. "What are we supposed to do?"

"I just told you that I have nothing to give," Ellen said. "We have a little food for ourselves but I don't know how far it will get us. I can't give anything away. As far as what you're supposed to do, I suggest you get out and start looking. See if there's someone needing work done. Do some hunting. Walk into town and see if any of the churches are giving out food. There's still time to set out a garden."

None of those were the answer she wanted to hear. "Well that ain't good enough!" the woman yelled. "Neighbors are supposed to help neighbors."

"And you are not my damn problem!" Ellen yelled back, bristling.

"Fucking rich bitch," one of the men said under his breath, loud enough for Ellen to hear. "We can *be* your problem if that's the way you want to play it."

Ellen leveled the shotgun at the man, racking a round into the chamber. "Let me make this crystal clear. I have nothing for you. I am not responsible for taking care of you. The best thing you can do is get the hell out of here and never darken my doorstep again."

One of the men spoke and she realized it was one of the men from earlier that morning, one of the rabbit hunters. "This here's a public road. Ain't no law against us being on the public road."

Ellen met his eye. "No there isn't," she said. "But my suggestion is that you stay on it and stay on that side of this gate."

"Or what?" the man asked belligerently, jutting his jaw out defiantly.

"Let's just say that my husband has an excavator that digs a hole eleven feet deep and I have access to hundreds of acres for digging holes. Anyone crosses that gate, they'll never be seen again."

"You got the balls to kill a man?" the guy asked.

"I don't recommend you find out," Ellen said. "You might not like the answer."

With that, Ellen backed up, got in her vehicle and slammed the door. She laid the shotgun across the center console and accelerated backward, executing a perfect bootlegger turn in the gravel driveway. In her rearview mirror, she could see the people still standing in the road, awash in the cloud of dust she left behind.

"That went well," Pops said sarcastically.

"If you hadn't been with me, and if we hadn't have been armed, I think they might have tried to make their way up to the house."

"You really think so?"

"I do," Ellen said. "If they only wanted sympathy, they would have just sent the women, hoping that we could talk it out woman-to-woman. With the men coming, too, I think the idea was to try force if diplomacy failed."

They pulled back in front of the house and Ellen killed the engine.

"What now?" Pops asked.

"I think we need to set out some tripwires and barricades before dark. We may even have to pull some guard duty tonight just to keep an eye on things."

23

The Bear Den Shelter was a three-sided structure made of the type of milled logs used in log home construction. It had an overhang on the front that covered a porch. The porch, as well as the picnic table out front, was piled with packs, boots, and assorted pieces of well-used gear. In between the piles of gear there were tired, dirty hikers lounging around eating, drinking, and tending to blistered feet. Our approach drew little attention initially, other than hikers looking up to see if they recognized us, hoping we were a trail friend they'd encountered along the way. When they saw we weren't, they went back to what they were doing. As we got closer, though, some began to give us a second look. Our gear was obviously not standard backpacking gear and we were cleaner than the rest of them.

"Let's take a break here," I said as we neared the shelter.

Randi and Gary hung back a little, but as a veteran of many AT section hikes I was comfortable with shelters and hikers. I mean, really, they were backpackers, not a street gang. They may stink but they aren't scary. I approached the picnic table and dropped my pack on the ground.

"How's it going?" I asked the man and woman already seated at the table.

The guy appeared to be in his twenties, with a thick beard, long hair, and a bandana wrapped around his head. The girl appeared to be about the same age. She was wearing a tie dye shirt and had brown hair worn in dreadlocks. A ring glistened from one nostril.

"Good, man," the guy said in a friendly tone.

The girl looked at me and smiled. The guy checked me out and glanced at my companions. "You guys day hikers?" It was a typical starting point in a trail conversation, determining whether the person you were talking to was a day hiker or through-hiker.

"You could say that," I said. "We don't look like through-hikers?"

He shook his head and laughed. "Not hardly."

"Too clean," the girl added.

"That'll change," I said.

"You spend any time out here it certainly will," the guy said.

Randi and Gary approached about this time and dropped their gear. Gary took a seat at the picnic table while Randi wandered off to relish another of her precious cigarettes.

The guy nodded to Randi's pack. "Is that a pillowcase?"

Gary laughed. "Yep. She's into ultralight homemade gear."

The couple at the table began to eye us a little cautiously. The girl leaned forward conspiratorially. "Are you guys like fugitives or something? I mean, if you are that's cool and all. Just don't kill us."

I laughed this time. "Not hardly. More like refugees than fugitives. We're just making our way home."

"Dude, there are a lot better ways to get home than the AT," the guy said. "Like about any other way possible in the world is faster than this."

Gary and I exchanged a glance. Could they not know what had happened?

"How long has it been since you guys have resupplied?" I asked.

The girl looked at her friend as if trying to recall. It was easy to lose track of time out here when every day revolved around walking, eating, and sleeping. "Maybe three days," she said. "We've got a package waiting for us tomorrow up ahead. That's our next supply point."

"Have you not seen anyone else in the last day or so?" Gary asked.

"Nobody new," the guy said. "We hiked most of the last couple of days with this group here. This is a pretty remote section of the AT so we just stuck together. We crossed paths with a few SOBOs but that's been it."

"SOBOs?" Gary asked.

"Southbounders," the girl piped in. "Hiking the trail from north to south. We're NOBOs – northbounders."

"You guys haven't heard any news from outside?" I asked.

They shook their heads in unison. I looked over at Gary again, not quite sure how to say it delicately.

"Guys, things are getting crazy out there right now," I said. "There have been major terrorist attacks and things are pretty much fucked. That's why we're not on the road."

I could see Gary out of the corner of my eye and he was grimacing. I looked over at him. "What?"

"That was delicate," he said. "You certainly didn't sugar coat it."

I shrugged. "What can I say? I'm plainspoken."

"Hey guys!" the girl yelled, turning back toward the shelter and calling to the people inside.

"What's up?" came a voice from the shelter.

"Get out here," she said. "You all have to hear this."

Randi had finished her cigarette and pitched the butt in the fire pit in front of the shelter. She wandered over to us. "What's going on?"

"They don't know," Gary said to her.

"Don't know what?" she asked, confused.

"Don't know about any of it," Gary told her. "They haven't seen people or heard any news in days."

"Oh shit."

There was the sound of boots on wood and a handful of other hikers streamed from the shelter. I counted five of them, roughly around the same age as these guys. The girl turned back to me and waited expectantly.

"I was just telling your friends here that things are pretty bad out there in the world," I announced to the group. "There were over a dozen major terrorist attacks yesterday. They've knocked the power out to most of the country, blown up roads and dams. You can't get any gas."

The group stared at us, stunned.

"Were a lot of people killed?" the guy at the table asked.

"We don't really know," I said. "I did hear a report that they blew up a dam in Kentucky that caused Nashville to flood. They blew up the Chesapeake Bay Bridge Tunnel and several oil refineries. It's hard to get information so we don't know a lot. With the power outages a lot of stations are not broadcasting anymore. Now they've frozen the gas supply and left stranded travelers all over the country with no way to get home. That's how we ended up here."

"Isn't the government doing anything to help?" one of the group from the shelter asked.

"The only thing we know for sure that the government is doing," Gary said, "is sending some buses down the interstate to gather stranded folks up and put them in emergency camps. Some of our folks went with them, but we didn't want to."

"Shit," someone in the group muttered. "That's messed up."

"Why aren't you walking the roads?" one of the group asked. "What the hell are you doing all the way up here? The road is easy walking compared to this. Maybe you could even hitch a ride."

"It's not safe," Randi said. "The cops are all busy with emergencies so people are pretty much doing whatever they want. There have been attacks on people walking the interstate. We've seen shootings and had to defend ourselves, too. The trouble is unavoidable if you stay down there. It's extremely dangerous."

There were other questions about specific regions of the country, presumably where these hikers had family, but they were areas we hadn't heard anything about.

"We haven't had cell reception all day," the guy at the table said. "I was hoping we'd get some today to call home. Now I'm worried about my parents."

"There's reception further up the trail," Gary said. "We've didn't have any all day until about six miles back. There's a fire road that crosses the AT and there's a pocket of reception there. "

The guy got up from the table and started gathering his gear. "Let's pack up," he told the girl. "I won't be able to sleep tonight until I've at least tried to get a hold of my family."

She got up also and began gathering her gear.

"Try a text if you can't make a call," I told the guy. "We could text but we never could get any calls through."

"Thanks," he said.

"Sorry to dump all that bad news on you guys," I said. "I know it's a lot to take in."

The guy started shoving items in his packet. "Are the rest of you going?" he asked the group that had come out of the shelter.

They looked around at each other, nodded, and went back to start gathering their own gear. One guy stuck around. He was similar to the others in appearance – scruffy, sweat-stained, and tanned.

"Where exactly are you guys headed?" he asked.

"Why?" I replied, my paranoia kicking in instantly.

"Tazewell County," Gary replied. "At least that's where I'm headed. The others live in that general area."

"My girlfriend and I are students from Emory and Henry College," he said. "She's back in the shelter packing her gear."

"We're familiar with Emory and Henry," I said. "Gary has a daughter who attended there."

"We were hiking up from Damascus," he said. "We were going to go to Shenandoah National Park and have some relatives pick us up there. Our families live in the Bristol area."

"I would head home," I said. "No telling if anyone will be able to get there to pick you up with the fuel restrictions. You may not even be able to get a call out to your relatives to pick you up. You could end up isolated and on your own. Not a good place to be."

"Can we hike with you?" he asked.

I expected this and had no problem with it. As a parent, I would hope that someone would help my kids in a similar situation. "Sure. We're fresh on the trail and won't be able to keep your pace, though."

"That's no problem. We can slow it down for you old folks," he said with a grin.

I looked at Gary. "I'm having second thoughts already."

The guy extended his hand to me. "I'm Walt. My girlfriend is Katie."

I shook his hand. Then he shook with Gary, waving to Randi who was a little further back.

"Pack your stuff," I told him. "And we need to eat a bite, so give us a few minutes."

He nodded and wandered off to tell his girlfriend of their new plans.

Gary, Randi, and I shared a quick meal of jerky, crackers, and water. We bid goodbye to the departing hikers as they moved out, taking large strides to gain more ground with each step. Walt and Katie said their goodbyes to their trail friends and exchanged contact info so they could get in touch at a later point.

"So that's what I'm going to smell like when I get home?" Randi asked.

I nodded. "Maybe even worse," I said.

She shook her head at the repugnant thought.

"It keeps the bugs away," Walt assured her.

"And everyone else," Gary added.

By my GPS, we averaged 2.5 miles per hour over the next three hours of walking, which did indeed gain us a few additional miles before stopping for the night. As the sun fell over the horizon and our weariness grew, the sound of insects and night birds began to emerge. Walt and Katie dropped their packs when we selected a frequently used group campsite for the night.

"Do you guys even have any gear?" Katie asked. She was an athletic, smallish waif of a girl with short hair. We'd learned over the course of the past few miles that she was a triathlete who'd competed throughout the world. She carried her fifty pound pack like it was nothing.

"Some," I replied.

"We have a tent," she said. "I feel kind of bad about sleeping in a tent with warm sleeping bags while you guys are roughing it."

"No worries," Gary said. "We'll be okay. Use the gear you have and be glad you have it."

Walt and Katie found a good tent site and set up their camp quickly and efficiently. You could tell they'd done this many times. One rolled out a protective ground cloth while another found the tent. One rolled out the tent while the other put the pole together. Before you knew it, they'd assembled their camp, said goodnight, and climbed inside.

"I know you told me we'd have to rough it if we passed up the shelter," Randi said. "But how the hell are we going to sleep out here? I mean, I've camped before, but not like this. I had actual camping stuff. What do I need to do? I don't even know where to start."

I dropped my pack and looked at Gary. "What do you have in the way of shelter?"

"I've got a tarp and a piece of painter's plastic," he said.

"I've got a tarp and a piece of Tyvek house wrap. Between us I think we can put together a quick shelter."

"What do you need me to do?" Randi asked.

I was impressed that she was eager to help. I knew she was not used to this level of activity, spending most of her time at a desk, and not really having any physical hobbies. She had to be exhausted. We were all tired, though, and the job would go faster with more hands.

"Gather some leaves," Gary said. "Find a forked stick and use it to rake leaves into a square pile about eight feet by eight feet. Make it about a foot thick and pull out any big sticks. If Jim doesn't mind, we can put his Tyvek over that and it will give us a soft bed. We'll string one of our tarps over top of it to ward off any dew or overnight rain."

With a plan in place, we all went to work with the same weary efficiency that Walt and Katie had demonstrated earlier. In about twenty minutes, we had a functional shelter. I had planned to eat a little more and drink another bottle of water. That went out the window when we completed the shelter and all sat under it for a test drive. Within seconds, we were fumbling with the purloined hotel blankets and covering ourselves. I put my pack at my head and used one soft corner of it for a pillow. I could feel my pistol poking me in the side. I started to remove the holster and slide it under the pack, but I was asleep before I could complete the action.

At some point in the night, I thought I heard the sound of an ATV nearby but I couldn't be sure if it was real or if I dreamed it. Either way, I rolled over and went back to sleep.

24

Working until darkness closed around them, Ellen, Pops, and Pete strung a series of tripwires around the house. There were three layers of tripwires that any trespasser would have to get through to make it to the house. Those farthest from the house used the fishing line because they had more of it than anything else. Attached to the fishing line were clip-on bells from the fishing aisle at Wal-Mart, strings of cans that would clatter together, and even a set of wind chimes from the back porch. Anything that would notify the person on watch that someone was coming. The next two layers utilized mason's twine and party poppers. Someone activating one of those tripwires would set off a small firework. Hopefully it would startle the visitor and perhaps send them running the other way.

Ellen was going to do the first watch that night, Pete the second, and Pops would take over in the early morning. They planned to try that arrangement for the night and see how it worked. They could always tweak things if it didn't.

Ellen's shift went without any hitches. She moved from the front porch to the back and walked around the house several times. The night was warm and quiet. At one point, coyotes began yipping and howling in the distance. Rather than being scared by the sound, she was always thrilled by it. That wildness was part of why she loved living in the country. When her shift ended, she gave the yard one last scan with the night vision and went to wake Pete up.

When she was sure Pete was fully awake and not going to nod off in the porch swing, she went over the basics with him. She hung the night vision monocular around his neck and made sure he knew how to use it.

"I've used it before, Mom," he reminded her. "Several times."

"Just checking," she said. "This is important work. We're all depending on you. You're such a big boy now."

She leaned over and kissed him on the head, then gave him the shotgun. She showed him that there was a round in the chamber and that it was ready to fire when the safety was switched off. She went over this in great detail, even though she knew Pete had a lot of gun experience for someone his age. She knew that repetition was how things became committed to memory, even if it was irritating.

"Remember how loud this will be if you shoot it," she reminded him. "Don't be startled. Just make sure you have a firm grip on it so that it doesn't kick the fire out of you."

Pete nodded.

"If you have things under control, I'm going to bed," Ellen said. "Wake me if you need anything."

"I'll be fine."

He was fine. For most of his shift, anyway.

It was around 2:30 AM when the tinkle of a bell, followed by a hissed curse, told him that someone had found the outer ring of trip-wires. From his dark observation post on the front porch, Pete quietly raised the night vision monocular to his eye and looked out in the direction of the noise. He could clearly make out two men walking toward the house through a field to his left. They were not men he recognized. He could see well enough to know that neither man was his father. One man was carrying something in his hand that may have been a pistol but it was hard to tell. Neither man had any sort of long gun.

Pete started to go wake Ellen and Pops. He stood and the porch creaked beneath his feet. He took another step and there was another creak. His heart rate accelerated. He could feel the fringes of panic clawing at him. He knew that his own sound was broadcasting through the silence of the night as clearly as the bell had. He turned back toward the field without moving his feet and took another glance through the monocular. The men were closer now, crouched low and moving quickly across the damp grass. They would be on him soon.

Pete dropped the monocular back to his chest and took another step toward the front door. There was another creak of boards beneath his feet. How had he never noticed that the porch was so loud?

Another step and he could hear the men talking, whispering back and forth. One more and he groped through the darkness for the door handle. He knew he was close, knew the handle was within reach. He felt tears burning down his cheeks and his breathing increased. He wanted to run but had a job to do. Everyone was depending on him.

A bang behind him scared him nearly to death. In his panic, he could not tell if it was one of the party poppers or if one of the men had opened fire on him. He spun and clicked the safety to the Fire position. He pointed the muzzle of the shotgun toward the last sound he'd heard in the darkness and he pulled the trigger. The fire erupting from the shotgun barrel temporarily blinded him as the noise from the blast set his ears ringing. When he recovered, he could hear a man screaming.

"Shit! Mike, you okay?" the voice said. "Mike, get up!"

Pete snapped to attention and racked the slide on the shotgun, ejecting the spent round and chambering a fresh one.

"Mike!" the voice in the darkness demanded.

The shotgun erupted again, Pete still in a state of blind panic, adrenaline pouring through his body. He racked the slide again.

BOOM!

He pumped the slide again.

BOOM!

Pump.

BOOM!

He continued until there were no more rounds. Behind him the porch door opened and he spun his head in that direction. He was nearly blinded by panic and adrenaline but caught himself before he turned the gun in that direction. Ellen rushed out the door, a pistol in her hand. Pops was behind her with another shotgun at the ready.

"What's happening?" Ellen demanded, shining a flashlight onto Pete's chest, illuminating his face. In the chaos, she didn't realize this could have made Pete an easy target for any shooter still out there in the darkness.

From his wide-eyed expression and the streaming tears, she could see that this was no false alarm. Then she heard the groan of a wounded man in the dark. She started to shine her light toward the sound but Pete snapped into action. He grabbed the light and turned it off.

"No!" he hissed. He handed her the night vision monocular from around his neck, all the while pointing his shotgun in the direction where he thought the intruders were.

In the green glow of the night vision, Ellen could see two men lying in the yard about thirty feet away. One was still. The other was moaning and moving around. She dropped the monocular to her chest. The awareness of what had taken place here staggered her. "Oh, Pete," she whispered.

Pops took the shotgun from Pete. Pete collapsed into his mother's arms, sobbing loudly and holding her tight. She held him for a moment, but then pulled herself away, still worried about any danger presented by the wounded man.

"Go to Pops, baby. Mommy has to make sure it's safe." She turned on her flashlight and trained it on the two men. Her weapon was raised in the other hand. Occasionally, she would sweep both the light and weapon across the yard, making sure there were no other people with them. In a dozen or so steps, she reached the men. She kicked the still one and there was no response. The other was conscious, blood pouring from a wound in his stomach. He pressed his hands to it, trying to stem the flow of blood but it poured around his fingers. It was the rabbit hunter who'd been at the gate earlier.

"You shouldn't have come here," Ellen said.

"You'll go to jail for this, bitch," the man hissed. "If you live long enough. My family will come for you."

Ellen could hear crying behind her and knew it was Pete. The emerging man inside Pete had known what he had to do tonight and had risen to it. The little boy inside of him was having a hard time seeing what he had done.

Noticing the shotgun in Pete's hand, the man taunted him. "Look what you done to me, boy! They'll put you all in jail for this. And if the cops don't get you, my brother will. He'll kill your whole family right in front of you!"

Ellen dropped her pistol and fired a single shot into the man's head, ending his rant. She'd heard all she was listening to. Pete was having a hard enough time dealing with this. The last thing he needed was to be threatened. Ellen knew there would probably be no consequences to a shooting like this, under these circumstances, but Pete didn't know that. He would worry. She mourned for her poor, soft-hearted child.

"Stay with them," Ellen told Pops. "I've got to get the excavator."

Jim had taught her how to use the machine but she wasn't very efficient at it. Once she had it in place, the digging went quickly. Pete and Pops watched in silence. They were in a hollow behind the house, out of sight from everyone but the waning moon. An owl broke the night with its mournful sound. The hole was beneath a feedlot where the neighbor's cattle came to eat. The ground was in a constant state of trampled, muddy carnage. No one would ever know.

As she returned the machine to the barn, Ellen wondered how many more bodies they'd bury before things were back to normal.

25

It was 5:24 AM when my internal clock woke me up. Either that or my bladder, which was ready to explode. I rolled out of the crinkly bed and took shelter behind a nearby tree to take a leak. I wasn't particularly shy but it seemed the polite thing to do. What I could see of the sky looked clear, giving me hope of a dry day for walking, even if it might be hot and humid. With pressing business attended to, I walked back to our shelter. My legs were stiff from the previous day's walking and I could tell that I was slightly dehydrated.

I lifted my pack from beneath the tarp and sat down against a tree. We'd been munching candy bars and sucking down water bottles all day yesterday and I needed to take inventory of my supplies. I was glad that we were drinking up some of the water bottles because I was tired of carrying all that water weight. The bottled water was too precious to toss out, though, because we needed it to keep going. This was a constant dilemma for the trekker and backpacker – how much water to carry. Too much weighed you down; too little and you found yourself fighting dehydration.

I still had eight full bottles remaining and a few empty bottles I'd saved for refilling when we found a good water source. I knew Randi had a few and Gary had an unopened eight-pack in addition to whatever bottles he might have accumulated on the way. We could get by on what we had in the bottles today, but may need to start filtering some stream or spring water tomorrow. The Katadyn filter in my pack was more than adequate for keeping us supplied until we got home. It was a veteran of many backcountry trips and had never let me down. Clean water was essential. Nothing could ruin a backpacking trip faster than spewing from both ends.

As far as food went, I had not yet tapped into the emergency food that I kept in my Get Home Bag, relying instead on what I'd pilfered from the vending machines. In the bottom of my pack was a Chinese knock-off of the MSR Pocket Rocket that I backpacked with. The knock-off had been less than $10, including shipping from China, and functioned much the same as my MSR stove except it had a pushbutton ignitor that the MSR didn't have. I had one unused canister of gas for the stove. It wouldn't be enough for the whole trip so I only planned on using it when I couldn't build a fire due to rain or security concerns.

I was also carrying a one quart pot from an old Coleman backpacking set. I had since replaced it in my primary backpacking gear with a titanium pot that had been a Father's Day present from my wife and kids. This pot was the right size to boil water for drinking or cooking. It was also the perfect size that the can of stove fuel and the stove itself would fit down inside it and still allow me to get the lid on. That protected the whole setup and kept it together in one place. I had some used Gatorade bottles that held the food rations. One held a two pound bag of white rice, the other a two pound bag of red beans. I had marked the clear bottles in one cup increments to make measuring portions easier.

There was a large baggie that held a couple of expired Mountain House freeze-dried backpacker meals, two MREs that I'd bought at a gun show, and a mixture of various energy and protein bars. There were also a few drink mixes that could boost electrolytes, provide carbs, or just help cover the taste of bad water. I'd once backpacked a section of the Appalachian Trail around Roan Mountain in Tennessee during a particularly dry summer. Many of the normal watering holes and springs where backpackers traditionally refilled their water had dried up. At one point I'd become thirsty enough to filter water directly from a leaf-filled mud puddle. I knew the Katadyn would filter out anything unhealthy from the water but it did nothing to erase the taste of old leaves. I had since started carrying a few drink mixes for that very reason. Even nasty-tasting water can save your life if you can make yourself drink it.

The stack of candy bars, granola bars, and jerky from the vending machine at the hotel had dwindled. I had divvied up the haul in a tentative fashion soon after the Great Vending Machine Heist, giving Gary some to stash in his pack. During a rest break yesterday I'd given Randi some to stash in her improvised pack so that she would have access to fuel when she needed it without having to ask for it. You can burn several thousand calories a day hiking trails with a pack and if you don't constantly refuel you will "bonk" and reach such a deficit state that you crash and can't continue. We couldn't risk a bonk.

I had nine snacks of different types left from the vending machine. I knew those would be gone by the end of the day. I figured Randi had fewer and I wasn't sure what Gary had. Since no one else was moving yet, I decided to boil up some water and dig into one of the freeze-dried backpacking meals. I needed something besides junk food to get my engine started.

After sorting through the stack, I arrived at Spinach Fettuccini for Two. Not usual breakfast fare but my only concern at the point was packing calories into my body for the day's trek. Carbs would be great. I set up the stove, poured some water in the cooking pot, and balanced it atop the stove. While that water heated, I took another bottle of water and began to rehydrate myself.

Rather than the soft whisper produced by a gas range, a canister stove sounds like a small jet engine, producing a roar that eventually had Randi and Gary stirring. Murmurs inside Walt and Katie's tent indicated that were waking up too.

"Is that garlic I smell?" Randi asked.

"It is," I said. "Guess your sense of smell hasn't been damaged by all that smoking."

"What in the hell are you eating for breakfast that has garlic in it?"

"Spinach fettucine," I replied. "It's about done. Want some?"

"I don't know," she said hesitantly.

"You'd prefer more candy bars?"

"Fettucine it is," she replied, sitting up and throwing back her blanket.

Gary got up and raided his own pack for an MRE, although I offered him a portion of the pasta. Fortunately, I had two plastic sporks in my pack so Randi and I didn't have to share a utensil. The meals were cooked by pouring boiling water into the bag that the meal comes in, then closing the bag up while the meal rehydrates and cooks. When the correct amount of time has passed, you simply stir the meal and eat it from the bag. Since I didn't have any plates in my pack and didn't want to dirty up the pot, Randi and I passed the bag back and forth until we decimated our spinach fettuccini breakfast.

"Best breakfast pasta I've ever had," Randi said, digging for a cigarette.

"I think I'd have to agree," I said. "What did you end up with, Gary?"

"Huevos rancheros," he replied. "Real breakfast food."

"I'm eating with him tomorrow," Randi said, winking at me.

Walt and Katie had been packing up their gear while we ate. When they finished they joined us, each of them nibbling on a Clif bar.

"How are you guys set for food?" I asked.

"Getting low," Walt said. "We'd just come through a five day section with no resupply, which is a long haul for us. We usually don't carry more than three days' food. We were planning to resupply today before plans changed."

"How many meals do you have left?" I asked.

Walt looked at Katie. She held up a lone finger.

"Lunch," she replied.

I wasn't to the point of singing Kumbaya with these folks yet. Not was I going to tell them that what was mine was theirs. I had a lot of reservations about sharing supplies with everyone I met, potentially depleting them. As co-workers, Gary and I had already assumed responsibility for helping Randi get home, which would put a dent in our supplies. We had accepted that, though. If we assumed responsibility for everyone we met along the way, we may eventually run out of resources and fail in our mission of getting home to our families. I couldn't accept that.

Feeling a need to address this since it was hanging out there, I thought of the plan I'd been turning over in my head during our walk yesterday. "I don't have a lot. I can get you through dinner tonight. We're also facing a resupply issue, though. We don't have nearly enough to get us home."

"Getting on this trail is the first time I've felt safe since leaving Richmond," Randi said. "Don't tell me we're going to have to get off it and go back into the world again? Where all the crazy people are?"

"Yes, we are," I said. "There's no alternative. You can't travel fast and live off the land. We don't have time to hunt and fish. If you're going to travel fast, you need to carry your food with you."

"Are we still shooting for Crawfish?" Gary asked.

"Crawfish?" Katie asked. "Your plan is to live off crawfish?"

"No," I said. "Crawfish is a town. My best friend from high school, Lloyd, runs a barbershop in a town on the outskirts of Buena Vista. He's also the mayor. I think he can help us if we can get to his place."

"How far is that?" Katie asked.

"Maybe thirty-five miles," I responded. "If we can make good time, we could be there tomorrow night."

"You think he'd take us in?" Gary asked. "All of us?"

"I think he'd at least be willing to put us up for the night. I can't make any promises beyond that," I said. "There's probably a party going on at his place right now. He's an old time musician and he kind of lives in the past. I doubt any of this has fazed him at all."

26

The day's walk began fairly well considering the circumstances. I'd always found long walks to be meditative and it was easy to lose track of time plodding along a mountain trail. I was a little sore that morning, which was a combination of age and pushing it yesterday. Though I was in fairly good shape and did a variety of activities, backpacking can be more extreme than people think. My shoulders were sore from the weight of the pack pulling on them. My knees were sore from stabilizing the combined weight of my body and my pack on uneven, hilly terrain. My calves and quads were sore from climbing. My back was stiff from everything it had been through, including a night of sleeping on the ground. The bottom of my forefoot was hot from a day's walking, which was a sign that a blister might be forming. I'd taped it with duct tape this morning and hoped it would wear better today. I knew if I was experiencing all this, the rest had to be in as much pain or worse.

I'd tried to text my family again and found my iPhone dead. I pulled it from my shirt pocket and checked it again, hoping it had miraculously charged in my sleep but it had not. While I was staring at it, Gary pulled his from his pocket and checked it also.

"Dead," he muttered.

"Mine, too," I said.

He stuck his back in his pocket. "Even unreliable communication was better than nothing."

"Let's take a short break," I announced to the group.

Everyone gladly stopped and dropped their loads for a moment. Usually on backpacking trips, people string out a little based on their individual pace and they catch up at with each other at the rest breaks. It's no big deal for people to be thirty minutes apart when the path is clearly marked and there are no hazards or navigational challenges. Due to the unusual circumstances of this particular disaster, and the way strangers were not always well-behaved, I warned people this morning that it was best to stay within sight of each other as much as possible. I'd also told them that if they were pulling off trail to take a bathroom break they needed to let someone know so we didn't leave them behind. Everyone agreed with the plan. I didn't necessarily consider myself the leader of this bunch but there were things that needed to be discussed. If no one else brought them up, I would.

I dug around in my pack and found a padded nylon case about the size of a hardcover book, maybe around an inch thick. I unfolded the case to expose the solar cells lining the inside. It was an Anker portable solar charger with a USB port that could charge a phone or tablet. I carried a spare iPhone cable inside the case and plugged my phone into the charger. Using two carabiners, I hung the charger from the back of my pack so my phone would charge as I walked. The charger worked best in direct sunlight, but a day of walking should leave the phone usable by the time we stopped. That was no guarantee you'd have signal, though.

"That's a trick," Gary said. "I've been wanting one of those."

"Start backpacking," I said. "It gives you the excuse to buy a lot of prepper gadgets. My wife would have rolled her eyes at me purchasing this for 'the apocalypse' but she was fine with me buying it so I could call her and tell her how much I love her from the trail."

"I might enjoy backpacking under different circumstances," he said.

"Not this girl," Randi said from where she rested against a tree. "I think this will be my one and only backpacking trip. Hell, once I'm home, I may never leave town again."

"Can't say as I blame you," I remarked.

After another candy bar, we hit the trail again. I stared at the empty wrapper before I stuffed it into my pocket, recalling a day when I had looked at a Snickers bar as a treat. I expected it would be a long time before I ever craved another one. What I really wanted was a club sandwich with tater tots. That would have been perfect.

We stopped for an early lunch at the empty Blackwood shelter, another of the sparse overnight huts scattered along the trail. Every shelter had a trail register where hikers could sign in with their trail name and even include a short message if they wanted. There were no entries dated for the previous night. Perhaps word was reaching the trail that things had gone to shit and people were peeling off to try to get home. Come to think of it, we hadn't passed any hikers all day, and that was unusual on the AT. This time of year, it was practically a freeway for the great unwashed and overburdened.

Walt and Katie finished the last of their food, sharing sandwiches of tortillas, sliced cheese, and summer sausage. Gary, Randi, and I had jerky, peanuts, and – you guessed it – candy bars. We'd come thirteen miles already but everyone was feeling good. Over the past day, we'd reacted promptly to any hot spots in our shoes, putting duct tape over any areas that rubbed to prevent blisters. If anyone was suffering, they were hiding it well. I'm okay with a little suffering on the trail. I'm something of a Mountain Masochist – I love to suffer with a pack on. If it hadn't been for worrying about my family, I'd have actually been enjoying this.

Thinking about them prompted me to dig out my phone and check it. It had about twenty percent charge. This was not surprising since I'd only had it on charge about two hours and we were in and out of wooded cover all morning. I appreciated that the device worked at all. Even though I'd not received any texts since last checking it, I composed one to my family, updating them on the turn of events. It balked when I sent it, the progress bar refusing to move all the way across to indicate a successfully sent message. I left the phone on, hoping it might go through if we found a pocket of signal along the way.

I noticed that Gary had field-stripped his Glock and was wiping sweat from the components with a bandana. I wasn't as Glock-obsessed as Gary but you had to admire the ease with which you could tear the damn things apart for cleaning.

"I'll be adding a gun cleaning kit to this pack when I get home," he said. "I hadn't thought about the effects of daily carry in these conditions."

"They do get nasty," I said.

I was gathering my trash to burn in the shelter's fire ring when I saw Walt and Katie staring at Gary. More specifically, staring at Gary's Glock.

Walt noticed that I was watching him and raised his eyes to meet mine. "We're not big fans of guns. Guns kill people."

I looked at the ground and shook my head. Where did these people come from? "When treated with respect, guns can be very useful. It's just a tool and, in this case, it's an important survival tool. Our guns saved our lives several times over the past few days. I expect it won't be the last time, either."

"You have one, too?" Katie asked, concern in her eyes and her voice.

"I do. When I hiked the southwest Virginia section of the AT – the same section you two were just hiking – I carried a gun then, too. People have been murdered along this section of the trail. Not all by guns, either."

"They make me uncomfortable," Walt said.

A switch inside me flipped and frustration took hold. "Would someone raping your girlfriend make you uncomfortable?"

Both Walt and Katie recoiled. They hadn't seen this side of me – the unemotional, coldly practical side. The side I'd inherited from my grandfather. This time, however, rather than trying to soften my words and deescalate the situation, Gary followed my lead.

"You guys haven't seen what it's like out there," Gary said. "It's like Lord of the Flies or some kind of depressing futuristic movie. Bad people are figuring out that the cops are all occupied with bigger emergencies and they're doing whatever they want. They're robbing, murdering, and raping. They're getting away with it. We've seen a lot of violence in the last two days. Several times, our guns have been all that stopped us from becoming victims, too."

"You seem like normal people," Katie said. "I'll try not to judge you."

She appeared to be sincere in what she said, but I didn't know her well enough to give a damn if she judged me or not. As much as I wanted Walt and Katie to get home, I wasn't taking on new pains-in-the-asses. I decided I needed to make that clear.

"We're glad to help you as long as helping you does not stand in the way of our objective," I said. "Our goal is to get home to our families safely. The minute I feel like you're judging me for protecting the interests of our group, we'll have to part ways. This group is not a democracy. You are welcome to travel with us as long as our interests coincide. When they don't, we part ways with no hard feelings. Is that clear?"

Walt and Katie exchanged glances, then met my eyes and nodded.

"I'm sorry if I pissed you off," Katie said, tears in her eyes.

"You didn't piss me off. I'm just a very determined, very blunt man who misses his family. I don't have time for debating my actions with sheltered and misguided children."

"He's the bluntest," Randi agreed. "No sugar coating with this guy. He doesn't mind peeing in your cornflakes."

"Definitely not," Gary chimed in. He reinserted the mag in his Glock, racked the slide to chamber a round, and placed the weapon on his pack beside him.

I stood and picked up my pack. "As long as we've cleared up who America's biggest asshole is, let's get this show on the road. We're burning daylight."

As I shouldered my pack and began buckling the straps, I heard the sound of an engine. I froze and listened. Randi started to say something, but I waved her silent, cupping my ear. In a moment it was clear something motorized was coming up the trail.

Gary removed his Glock from the top of his pack and placed it beneath his thighs. It was concealed but within easy reach.

"It's a four-wheeler," Randi said quietly.

A green Suzuki ATV came pounding through the brush, over-hanging the narrow trail by a foot on each side and leaving a wake of crumpled foliage behind it. It looked incredibly strange and out of perspective. This National Scenic Trail was off-limits to motorized vehicles and the last thing I expected was one to come crashing out of the woods. It was just another indication of how quickly the world was changing in the wake of this disaster.

There were two riders. In the front was a scrawny man-boy some-where between fifteen and twenty-five wearing a wife-beater, jeans, a gold chain, and hunting boots. He had a faint mustache and a dark mullet. Behind him was a harder-looking man of indeterminate age who bulged with muscles. He wore a sleeveless camouflage t-shirt, with full sleeves of homemade tattoos that were either a remnant of jail or a misspent youth. I guessed jail. He had the look of a man who had done hard time.

Both carried weapons. The boy in front had a single-shot shotgun hanging over his shoulder from a homemade rope sling. The one in back balanced a lever-action carbine across his lap. When they came with fifteen feet of us, they killed their engine. In the silence of the woods, the only sound was the pinging and ticking of their cooling machine. When they stopped in front of me, my eyes were immedi-ately drawn to the front and rear cargo racks of the ATV. Strapped to the racks with bungee cords were two bulging backpacks.

We stared at each other, and I broke the ice, nodding at the two. "How's it going?"

The driver nodded back, spat, and met my eye. "Alright, I reckon. You folks camping?"

"Nah," I said. "Not hardly. Just trying to get home. What are y'all up to?"

The two men were no longer meeting my eye, nor were they simply ogling the women as I might have expected. Their eyes moved over us in a calculating manner, seeing what we carried, how many packs we had, and if we had weapons visible. They were assessing us, both as foes and for the potential value of what we might be carrying.

"We're doing some hunting," the rider in the back said. "Y'all seen any deer?" His speech was slow, heavily accented, and he wore an inappropriate smile. It was the expression of someone impaired by drugs, suffering a mental disability, or perhaps even that of a sociopath. I noticed a scar under his eye and several missing teeth.

I shook my head. "No, haven't seen any deer."

"Got a smoke?" he asked. "We're out."

I looked around to confirm that Randi wasn't smoking, then replied. "No," I said. "No smokers here."

He nodded at me, not saying anything. He continued to study me, smiling that odd smile, sizing me up. I could feel tension rising. The driver of the ATV wrung his hands on the handlebars, not sure where this was going, not sure if he should stay or drive off. It showed me that the dangerous man, the decision-maker, was the one in back. If this turned violent, my first shot would be aimed in his direction.

It was at this point that the offended liberals in our newly-formed group could contain themselves no longer. "You shouldn't have that four-wheeler on this trail," Walt spat. Apparently the idea of people both hunting on and defacing the trail was too much for him. "Look at what you're doing to the trail. It will take years for that damage to repair itself."

The two riders glanced at each other and grinned, each revealing teeth coated in flecks of smokeless tobacco. They were truly amused by the comment.

"What you gonna do?" the rider in back asked. "Tell on us? Who the fuck you gonna tell, college boy?"

"I w-will if I have t-to," Walt stammered. "When I get out of here."

Walt raised his cell phone, snapping a quick picture of the men on the ATV, and making a big show of collecting "evidence".

I intervened then, waving an arm toward Walt to hush him up. "He ain't telling on anybody. You all know as well as I do that there isn't anyone right now who gives a shit if you hunt up here or not. No one cares if you ride on the trail now. None of that matters."

"Damn straight," said the man driving the ATV. "Nobody can't do shit about it. You thinking you can do something about it, college boy? You going to stop us?"

It was about this point that Walt realized his mouth had written a check his ass couldn't cash. He'd stuck his foot in it and he started to backpedal. "I'm sorry. I didn't mean it.'

I rolled my eyes. First Walt had provoked them and then he revealed his weakness by folding like a wet noodle. This wasn't going to end well. "Forget him," I told the men. "He's all talk. We're out of here. Good luck with the hunting."

"Where y'all headed?" the passenger asked, his attempt at friendliness chilling my blood. He was definitely a killer and there was nothing friendly about his question.

"West," I said.

The driver gave us all another once over, then started his engine. He thumbed the throttle and accelerated away, his passenger giving us a parting nod and a grin that could have meant just about anything.

"We haven't seen the last of those two," I said as the sound of their engine faded down the trail.

"What do you mean by that?" Walt asked.

I looked at him and shook my head. "It means you stirred a hornet's nest. Let's get out of here."

27

W ith our group divided by the tension around our earlier discussion about firearms, we cliqued up for the afternoon's hiking. Walt and Katie hiked together, while my group stayed to themselves. We made good time, chugging away like machines and cresting a four thousand foot peak known as The Priest. By early evening, we gradually lost elevation and were within an hour's walk of the Blue Ridge Parkway. My plan was to overnight a good distance from the road, where we would hopefully be safer. Tomorrow, we would get on the Blue Ridge Parkway and follow it until we came to another road that would descend even further. If all went well, by nightfall we would be at my friend Lloyd's place.

We had yo-yoed with Walt and Katie all afternoon, taking turns between our group leading and them taking the lead. I was in the lead when we reached a point where my GPS told me I was as close to the Blue Ridge Parkway as I wanted to get. I didn't know for sure that the road was being used by travelers, but my gut told me to avoid it for as long as possible.

"Before you set up your gear, I have a plan," I told them when we all made it to the clearing. "I don't think we should set up right here beside the trail."

They stared at me blankly. Everyone was tired and ready to settle in.

"We can pitch camp here in this clearing, but I think we need to sleep a little further back in the concealment of the woods," I continued. "My gut tells me we might have company tonight."

"Those men?" Katie asked. "Aren't you being a little paranoid? They're long gone."

I shook my head. "No, I'm not. Gary, did you notice the firearms?"

Gary's face was slick with sweat and he appeared exhausted. "Single shot shotgun," he stated. "Looked like a twelve-gauge Harrington & Richardson or something similar. The lever gun was probably a Rossi .30-30. I know it wasn't a Winchester because I'm familiar with those."

"Were the men's guns expensive guns?" I asked.

"No," he said, shaking his head. "The shotgun is probably something you could pick up for under a hundred bucks. The Rossi is a little more but still on the low-end of the price scale."

"Do you think those guys were locals or backpackers?" I asked Walt.

"Locals for sure," he said. "They probably just wandered up here to look for game, like they said."

"Did you see their packs?"

"I saw they had packs," Walt replied. "Didn't see what brand."

"Gregory Baltoros," I said. "You ever price one?"

"We did," Katie said with surprise. "They were close to $350 each."

"What about the sleeping pads tied to those packs? Did you get a look at them?"

No one said anything.

"I did," I said, answering my own question. "They were Thermarest Neoair. One on each pack. Anyone ever price one of those?"

Katie replied again. "Around $100 each."

"So, we're at nearly a thousand bucks and we're not even to the contents of the packs yet," I said. "Who carries that kind of gear in the woods? Local hunters or through hikers?"

The group responded with a dawning recognition of where I was going with this. Their faces wrinkled and their expressions grew dark.

"You think they may have killed hikers and taken their gear?" Walt asked.

"They got it somehow and I doubt anyone would give up that kind of gear willingly."

Randi and Gary said nothing, aware enough at this point in our journey that they should not be surprised with this possible scenario. They knew what people were capable of. We'd seen it with our own eyes.

"What do you propose?" Gary asked.

I took off my pack and set it in the cleared center of what was obviously an established and well-used campsite. It was right beside the trail and large enough for group camping. A ring of blackened rocks formed a fire pit in the center.

"I think Walt and Katie should set their tent up here, just as they would if they were camping. We pitch a tarp here in an A-shape that restricts anyone's ability to see inside it. We can leave a fire smoldering here and give the camp the appearance that we sacked out here for the night," I said.

"But we don't?" Randi asked.

"No. We make a rough camp about a hundred feet over in that direction. It's not likely to rain tonight so we don't really need a cover over us. We can lay out a tarp and sleep on it with our blankets. I want to be close enough to know if anything crazy happens."

The group pondered this.

"If they do come, and they find empty tents, won't they just keep looking for us?" Walt asked. "Won't we still be in danger?"

"We post a watch," Gary said.

"Exactly," I said. "With a group this size, a ninety minute shift should be sufficient. We rotate in and out until morning."

"I won't carry a gun," Walt announced defiantly.

I couldn't stifle a laugh, but it was not a friendly laugh. "I wouldn't give you a gun. I'd rather deal with an armed intruder than deal with someone who is scared of guns, doesn't know shit about guns, and is wandering around my own camp with one. Both are dangerous."

Walt's virtue deflated. With nothing else to say, he dropped his pack and removed his tent, clearly too beat to argue. His action broke our inertia and we began setting up our own decoy shelter.

Since we weren't actually intending to sleep in them, it went pretty fast. As usual, Walt and Katie had their tent up in a matter of minutes. For our own shelter, Gary strung paracord between two trees, draped a tarp over it, and weighted the ends down with rocks. Randi packed both ends with leaves to make it appear that we had created a leafy sleeping pad. When everything looked right, we moved to an area a little deeper in the woods. We found a sufficient spot and spent a few minutes dragging branches and debris out of the way. The area was covered in a thick moss that made any further padding unnecessary. We simply spread our Tyvek tarp over the moss and had a surprisingly comfortable bed.

We offered to share with Walt and Katie but they found their own spot about a dozen feet away, rolling their sleeping bags out directly onto the moss. Walt and Katie were out of provisions, so I planned on digging into my stash of rice and beans for dinner. After some discussion, we agreed that we could probably build a fire in the fire ring of the established camp, where our decoy shelters were set up. Leaving some burning embers in there would only help create the picture of it being a real camp if we did end up having visitors that night.

Using a butane lighter and twigs, we had a blaze going in no time. Gary ended up digging into his stash for the beans and I provided the rice. He also had a pot about the size of mine in his pack. Both pots had wire bails on the top for lifting them, so we rigged a system for hanging the pots over the fire. It was easier to control the temperature if you had the ability to raise and lower the pot. Both the rice and beans took some time to cook so we spent that time going over the details of the watch and determining where the sentry would be positioned.

By the time dinner was cooked, darkness was beginning to fall. We built up the fire in the decoy camp, scraped our pots clean and rinsed them with some of our water. That done, we all headed back to our bivy further in the woods. The plan was that Katie would take the first watch, then Walt, followed by me, Gary, and finally Randi. As we settled down for the night, I checked the chamber on my Beretta and made sure that there was one in the pipe. I considered the option of sleeping with it tucked under my side, but decided instead to leave it in the holster. If I awoke and took off running in a half-dazed state I didn't want to forget the pistol and have to come back for it. In my exhaustion, I rested my head on my pack and was out in just a couple of minutes.

28

A gunshot in the night jolted me from my sleep. More came in rapid succession, deafening in the stillness. I bolted upright, flinging my blanket to the side. My first reaction was to reach for my headlight, but I hesitated, not wanting to have a blazing target on my forehead. I knew at least one shot was from a shotgun. The last sounded like a pistol. My left hand shot out, patting along the ground cloth for Randi, who should have been beside me. Her spot was empty, only a crumpled blanket left.

A scream split the night. It was a man, screaming in pain.

"Gary!" I hissed.

"I'm here. There's a fire. Something's burning."

We each stood, rising unsteadily on the uneven and unfamiliar terrain, our muscles stiff, uncooperative. I could see Walt and Katie's empty tent was on fire. I stumbled toward it. In the dim glow, I could see Walt seated in the spot that we'd designated for a sentry. He was frozen in terror – the terror of a man jolted from his sleep.

"Where the fuck is Randi?" I whispered.

Walt shook his head rapidly but no words came out. I would have to deal with him later.

"Randi?" I called, trying to keep my voice low.

The scream came again, from the woods past the burning tent. The same scream. A man.

My Beretta was in my hand. I'd drawn it from the holster at some point. I couldn't see Randi in the light from the fading fire and I didn't want to go charging out into the open without knowing what was going on. I dropped into a crouch and crawled forward, staying concealed as best I could.

Another shot rang out, this one definitely from a high-powered rifle. It was followed by another that struck a tree high over my head, whistling as the round punched through the leaves. The shooter didn't appear to have anyone in his sights. He was firing randomly. He was scared.

"Randi!" I said in a louder voice.

"Jim!"

"Where the hell are you, Randi?"

The screaming started again. "You fucking bitch!" the man yelled. "You shot me!"

Ahead and to my left someone lit a flashlight and held it in the air. It was Randi. She waved it around, trying to get my attention.

"Turn that off and stay down," I ordered. "I'm coming to you."

I scrambled toward her position, branches raking me across the face and neck. When I got to her side, I could barely see her but I could tell she was rolling around on her back, her hands groping at her waist. I dropped to her side.

"Are you hit?" I asked urgently.

"No dammit," she hissed. "I'm trying to get my freaking pants back on."

I didn't get it. "What happened?" I asked. "Who is that screaming?"

She cursed and wallowed around some more, finally managing to get her pants fastened. She rolled into a sitting position. "There was someone out there. I heard a lighter and I thought someone was smoking."

"Guys?" Gary called from behind us. "You okay up there? What's going on?"

"Keep low," I said. "There's someone still out there."

"I'm coming," Gary said. "Don't shoot me."

There was the sound of movement in the underbrush behind us, then Gary emerged and knelt beside us. He had a headlamp in his hand, the lens wrapped in a bandana to dim the light. "What happened?"

"I was working on that," I said. "Randi hasn't told me yet."

Gary looked at Randi. She was scared, her eyes wild in the diffused light of the covered headlamp.

"I was up and I heard the sound of a cigarette lighter being flicked," she said. "In the quiet, I could hear it clear as day."

"Why were you up?" I asked. "I haven't done my watch yet so it couldn't have been your turn."

"Dammit, I had to go to the bathroom," she said in a hostile whisper. "I haven't been in days. I wanted some privacy so I got up to go. Walt was asleep on his watch. I was going to wake you up and tell you when I was done but then all this happened."

"Okay," I said. "Sorry I asked. Keep going."

"So, I hear this lighter and think that someone is smoking. I'm about out of cigarettes so I was excited to think that Walt and Katie might have some. I raise up from where I'm squatting, take a look, and see someone is flicking a lighter over next to that tent. Then the tent starts glowing."

"They set it on fire?" Gary asked.

"Yes! Then while the fire was spreading, one of those guys from earlier steps out from behind it with a shotgun and fires right into the side of it."

"That must have been the shot that woke me."

"I was so scared that I must have made a noise," she continued. "He looked right at me, his shotgun pointed at me."

"You had the pistol I gave you earlier?" I asked.

She nodded. "I had it in my hand because I was scared a bear would sneak up on me."

"Did you fire at him?" Gary asked.

"Hell yeah," she said. "I was afraid he was going to shoot me. I pointed the gun at him and started pulling the trigger as fast as I could. He kind of fell or moved or something. I couldn't see him anymore. Then I saw the other guy was behind him so I kept shooting at him until the gun stopped."

"Where is the gun now?" I asked.

She reached behind her and pulled it from her back pocket. "I needed both hands to get my pants back on."

The urgency of the screaming was diminishing, the cries more sporadic. There were attempts at words, wet and garbled, the sound of a man drowning in his own blood.

"We need to take a look," I said to Gary.

He nodded.

"Without getting killed," I added.

He nodded again.

"You stay here," I told him. "I'm going back to my pack to get something."

Without waiting for a response, I felt my way back in the direction I'd come from, trying to avoid taking any branches to the eye. I finally saw the white glow of my Tyvek sheet and reached down for my pack. In one of the outside pockets, I felt for a black zipper pouch with a lanyard string attached to it. When I found the string, I tugged the pouch free, unzipped it, and removed a Bushnell night vision monocular from it. I hung the lanyard around my neck and headed back toward Gary and Randi.

"Night vision," I stated, reaching for the power button.

"Night vision?" Randi asked sarcastically. "*Really?* Why wouldn't you have night vision, right?"

"It's nothing fancy. Nothing like the military has."

Once the monocular screen came to life, I scanned the woods in the direction of the burned tent. I could see a few glowing embers around, but not much star light penetrated the thick canopy of trees. A second button on the monocular activated an infrared spotlight. The spotlight greatly increased the effectiveness of the scope and was invisible to anyone not wearing night vision.

With the assistance of the IR illuminator, I could see a pair of legs extending from the brush past the tent. The legs slowly drew up at the knees and then relaxed again. The screaming was nearly gone now, replaced by crying. I scanned the rest of the bushes and couldn't see anyone else. I passed the monocular to Gary.

"Take a look," I said. "I only see the one guy."

Gary put the scope to his eye. "This thing is cool. How much was it?"

"Under $150. It's only first generation so it's kind of cheesy."

"It does the job," he said. "We know what's out there now."

"Not exactly," I said. "We're missing one guy."

There was another choked cry from the man lying in the weeds near the burned tent. He was down, but not out. I kept the monocular to my eye, holding it with my left hand, the Beretta in my right. I stood and advanced slowly. The poor optical quality of the monocular would be difficult to use if I was running, but it was more than capable of dealing with the slow speed I was moving at now. The man was less than thirty feet away and as I turned around a cluster of Rhododendron I found him sprawled on the trail, his legs still moving without purpose, his hands curling and uncurling. His eyes were open, his chest saturated with blood that appeared black through my scope. The sodden mass bubbled when he breathed. Blood flowed from his mouth and ran down his ears, cheeks, and neck. There were multiple wounds but one was clearly a lung shot, fatal in these conditions.

I scanned the bushes around me for as far as the IR illuminator would go. I saw no one.

"I can't see anyone," I called out. "Gary, you come up. You can use your light but keep it low."

Gary closed the distance quickly, his Glock held at the ready. When he reached me, he ran his light over the wounded man. "Jesus Christ."

I put the night vision in Gary's hand. "Take a position over there near the trail and keep an eye out with this thing. We're going to start packing gear. I think it's time to get moving."

Gary moved toward another clump of bushes to set up a watch. I removed my headlight and turned it on, aiming it toward the ground to cut down on stray light. I turned around to head back to my gear and ran straight into Randi. She'd been standing immediately behind me, her flashlight glued to the face and chest of the man she'd shot. She stumbled backward and I reached for her, gripping her arm and steadying her. She yanked away, twisting, and spraying vomit into the weeds.

I stepped back and gave her a moment. While she retched and gagged, Walt and Katie approached with another light.

"Get her some water," I said to them. "There's a bottle beside my pack."

Walt hurried off.

"He's not dead," Randi said, wiping her mouth with her sleeve.

"No," I said. "He's not."

"I did that," she said in a low voice.

"You *had* to do that," I corrected. "He *made* you do that."

"He's my daughter's age," she said, her tone mournful.

"He's likely a murderer and got what he deserved."

Katie approached with the water bottle Walt had retrieved. Walt was apparently too scared to come near us. That was insightful on his part. This was partially his fault for falling asleep on his watch and I felt like I could hurt him for endangering all our lives. Punching him in the face would make me feel better, but it wouldn't help anything. I took the water bottle and passed it to Randi. She rinsed out her mouth and spat in the bushes. I could see tears in her eyes when she turned back to me.

"What are we going to do with him?" she asked.

"We're going to leave him," I said.

"But—"

"But what?" I interrupted. "There's no 9-1-1, no ambulances up here, and I'm not carrying a man that tried to kill us. I'm also not particularly interested in putting a bullet in his head to put him out of his misery, either. Nature will take care of this."

"You seem like you could do it," she said.

"Do what?"

"Put a bullet in his head. You seem like you're good at this," she said. "Like you were ready for it. Almost like you enjoy it."

I shook my head. "I don't enjoy this. Things in the world weren't perfect but they were better than this. I may be a little bit better prepared than the next guy but that's because I worked at it. I read a lot of books, I watched a lot of videos. I chose to spend money on preparing for something like this rather than wasting it on a boat, a Harley, or renting a house at the beach."

"You weren't in the military?"

I laughed at that. To anyone who had been in the military, the answer would be obvious, but Randi was sincere in her question.

"No, I was never in the military," I told her. "I'm not a soldier. I'm a paranoid hillbilly wanting to get home to my family. Under the right circumstances, a determined father is every bit as dangerous as the most highly-trained soldier."

She took a deep breath and braced herself. "Then maybe a determined grandmother can survive, too."

"A determined grandmother may have saved some lives tonight," I told her. "Now harden the fuck up, Granny, and let's get out of here."

I patted her on the shoulder. When I did, she dropped the beam of her light from the gasping man on the ground, turned, and went to pack up.

Within fifteen minutes, our gear was all packed and we departed camp by flashlight. Each of us strolled by the wounded man, his eyes blinking as he watched us go, his mouth moving wordlessly. When he passed the wounded man, Gary leaned over and picked up the single shot shotgun from where it lay in the weeds. He opened the breech and ejected the spent round. He leaned over and patted the wounded man's pockets, finding a half-dozen or so shells. I waited on a comment from Walt and Katie, but there was none.

The last surprise of the night came about a mile down the trail. We came to an area where the trail was torn up and the bushes were disturbed. It was clear that the ATV had been parked here, probably while our attackers stalked the trail looking for us. Whoever had been parked there left in a hurry, swinging wide and accelerating too fast, causing the rear end of the four-wheeler to slew around on the muddy trail. They had grazed a thick cluster of rhododendron in their haste, losing one of the packs we'd noticed on their ATV earlier. It lay in the dense brush, a single shoulder strap caught on a broken branch.

I looked at Gary and shrugged. "In different times I wouldn't take another man's gear but I think the original owner of this pack is probably dead or long gone. The last owner had no right to it. I'm not going to pass over supplies that may help us on our journey."

"I can't carry that," Randi said, staring at the large and overstuffed pack. "I can barely carry what I got."

"You're not ready for it yet," I said. "For now, we'll dump your gear into my pack and you can carry it while I carry the Gregory pack. We'll sort through the stuff later and adjust the loads."

"Works for me," she said.

She wasn't so enthusiastic about the arrangement once she actually slung my pack onto her back. Even though it was only a low-volume weekend pack, it was still pretty heavy. Her eyes widened for moment and she staggered, adjusting to the weight. Once I adjusted the straps and hip belt for her she decided it was definitely more comfortable than the pillowcase pack she'd been carrying.

Now that it was empty, I started to toss the pillowcase pack off into the weeds, but ended up stuffing it into a side pocket on the Gregory pack. I shouldered the heavy pack and it was clear that this was indeed a through-hiker's setup. It must have weighed fifty pounds, though the pack's excellent suspension did a good job of handling the weight. I quickly adjusted the straps, belt, and load lifters, and tuned it to my liking.

When everyone was ready we started walking again, heading for the Blue Ridge Parkway and my friend Lloyd's house.

29

W e reached the Blue Ridge Parkway while it was still dark and followed it west. After the isolation of the deep forest, the open road made me feel exposed and vulnerable. In the circle illuminated by our flashlights this could have been any road. By the time the sky lightened and the world became visible around us, we found that our path was little more than a paved ledge looking out over dozens of rounded peaks and fog-filled valleys. Under other circumstances, it would have been a breathtaking sight.

By 6:30 AM, we'd been walking about four hours and we took a break at a scenic overlook. There was a picnic shelter and, more importantly, pit toilets. Even though they were simple cinderblock outhouses painted in Park Service Brown, they were a luxury after what we'd become used to. Under the shelter, we sat at log tables watching the sun rise.

After a short break and a trip to the facilities, Walt and Katie gathered their gear. "We appreciate the help," Katie said. "We're going to take off and find our own way home from here."

They'd apparently been talking among themselves as we walked and come to the conclusion that they wanted to venture out on their own. I shrugged by way of a response. Gary had no comment, either.

"We appreciate your help," Walt said. "Really, we do. We're just going to hit the highway and see if we might be able to catch a ride from there. It'll be faster."

It was obvious they were just being polite. There were philosophical differences between our groups and they didn't agree with our tactics. With their lack of information, they had no idea what they were walking into. The world had changed since they left it. They thought things would be better on the road, that they could hitchhike or walk and everything would be okay. We tried to tell them differently but you couldn't make people's decisions for them. They would have to find out on their own.

"Be very careful," Randi warned. "And don't trust anyone. It's really bad out there."

Katie smiled at Randi. "We appreciate it. We'll be careful. We'll look out for each other."

"Good luck," I told them. "You'll need it."

They pulled on their packs, took up their trekking poles, and strode away. I'm sure they were relieved to be free of us. I hoped things went well for them. If they couldn't handle what they'd seen with us over the last day or two, they would most certainly have a hard time finding their way in the world that awaited them.

"I'm hungry," Gary said.

We divvied up some of the remaining vending machine loot and tore into it less than enthusiastically. Holding a granola bar in his teeth, Gary dug in his pack and came up with a flattened cardboard sleeve wrapped in electrical tape. From the open end, he shook out half a hacksaw blade and began sawing the barrel off the shotgun he'd taken from the wounded man. He obviously wanted to reduce the weapon to a more concealable size. While he worked on that, I took time to get my own gear reorganized.

Starting with the outside pockets of the Gregory pack, I began sorting through the gear I'd been carrying for the last couple of hours. I unzipped the pocket in the pack lid and came up with a blue nylon wallet. I opened it and found a drivers license, a little cash, and a credit card, all wrapped together with a rubber band. The license

had been issued in Vermont to a Larry Baxter, a fifty-six year old man
with a graying buzz cut and blue eyes. From the picture I could see
that neither of the men on the ATV was Larry Baxter. I considered
whether I should hold onto the wallet and attempt to get it back to
Larry Baxter when I made it home – if he was even still alive. This
was outweighed by my concern at being caught with another man's
identification and possibly being accused of theft, or even worse. I
gathered the wallet with all its contents and tossed the stack into a
nearby trash can.

The rest of the pockets contained bits of gear that a hiker might
need during the day: spare batteries, a headlamp, ibuprofen, mole-
skin for blisters, a water pump, and a bandana. There was a cellphone and charger in one of the pockets. The phone was dead and I
threw it in the trash. There was a copy of Paul Bowles' *The Sheltering
Sky,* which was bookmarked about halfway through and showing
significant trail wear. Inside the main compartment of the pack, I
found a nice down-filled Marmot sleeping bag, which I kept.

There was a one-man MSR tent, which I did not keep. It was a
good tent and one I'd specifically looked at before when shopping for
tents. I knew it was less versatile, though, than the shelter materials I
already carried and my pack was heavier than I wanted it to be.
Throwing away good gear gave me a pang of guilt, but I still had a
long way to go. Both speed and agility were affected by carrying too
much gear. It also increased the risk of injury. I'd once strained my IT
band – likely from carrying a too heavy pack – and had been forced
to walk twenty-seven more miles on the injured leg. It made for a very
difficult hike and I spent three months limping when I got home.

There was some clothing and I checked the tag for a size. None of
it fit me. I set aside the shirts and rain gear for Randi. The pants were
too small for any of us so I tossed them onto the pile I'd started with
the tent. I would leave that gear here under the shelter, hoping that
someone down the road may find it and benefit from it. I kept two
pairs of hiking socks, a pair of light gloves, and a toboggan. There was
a folding twig stove, which cooked food by means of a tiny fire built
from twigs. With the stove was a cook set, which I put in the pile to

discard. I did keep the utensil set, though. There was no food, no water bottles, and no other personal gear.

I set about repacking the pack, taking the majority of my items from my Get Home Bag and finding room for them in the Gregory. I helped Randi repack my original pack with her gear and made certain that the strap adjustments were working for her. By that time, Gary had finished removing the barrel from the shotgun. I knew he was done from the heavy clang of the barrel dropping to the concrete. It bounced a few times, then rolled across the shelter and off the edge into the grass.

Gary pulled a Leatherman multi-tool from his pack, selected a file, and removed any burrs from the barrel tip. When he was done with that step, he closed the file blade and unfolded a wood saw blade from the tool, sawing the shotgun's stock into a crude pistol grip. Despite the short blade length of the saw, it was extremely sharp and Gary had his weapon done in short order. It was crudely done, but would pack a devastating punch at close range. He loaded a live round into the chamber and drew the hammer slightly back to the safe "half-cock" position.

"You gonna carry that thing?" I asked.

"Not in the open," he said. "In my pack. It was too good a weapon to leave behind."

"I agree," I said. "I wasn't thinking clearly last night. I should have thought of it. We need every asset that can help us get home. It would have been dumb to leave it."

"We were all a little rattled," Gary said. "Even soldiers have to get used to war. Our war is just starting."

I thought about what Gary said. Since shooting that man who tried to wrap a crowbar around Gary's head in the gas station parking lot, I'd been going through a lot of self-talk about focusing on our mission and not getting hung up on the violence. We were all still in shock from the past few days. I'd studied how people react in times of stress and chaos, and had tried to prepare for it. It's a hard thing to train yourself for. I thought of my grandfather again, who'd carried a gun and knife every day of his adult life, dropping them in his pockets when he headed out the door like I did with car keys and a cell phone.

I recalled a story my uncle told me at a family reunion, one of the few he attended. He was not very social, either. He told me he'd been riding my grandfather's truck route with him one evening when he was about twelve. This would have been in the early 1950s. It was fall and my grandfather picked my uncle up from school so he could ride his route with him. He drove a truck for a living, delivering meats and produce to small country stores.

When they finished their route, it was around 7 p.m. The sun had already gone down and the night had cooled. They stopped to eat at a little beer joint on the side of the road called Buster's. It was a classic Appalachian roadhouse with a low ceiling and stained hardwood floors covered in sawdust. My grandfather ate there whenever he made this run and assured my uncle that their cheeseburgers were hard to beat. He was right. They both had large cheeseburgers with fried potatoes and my uncle said it was one of the best burgers he'd ever had.

On their way out, my grandfather lit a cigarette and smoked as they walked across the dark parking lot to his refrigerated truck. Their path took them by a shed that housed the refrigeration equipment for the restaurant. When they passed that shed, a man stepped out of the shadows. My uncle said he could see the glint of a knife in the man's hand and he froze.

"I need some money," the man demanded. "Y'all gonna gimme your fucking money."

My uncle said he peed in his pants right there, but my grandfather dipped his hand into his pocket and came out with a Schrade pocket knife, opening the blade. In those days, they didn't have all those fancy lock blade knives, tactical knives, and knives with pocket clips like they do now. It was just a plain old pocket knife with a long blade that my grandfather kept razor sharp.

There was no discussion, no threats, and no warning. My grandfather lashed out at the man, slashing him across the face, then stabbing him in the chest. The man staggered backward and dropped his knife. He grabbed his chest, trying to contain the dark ooze that seeped around his fingers. My grandfather stepped toward him and lashed out again, his knife flashing across the man's throat before he finally fell.

My uncle said that my grandfather stood there over the fallen man, his shoulders heaving as he sucked in air around the cigarette he hadn't even dropped in the scuffle. He'd acted so quickly and with such finality that he seemed like a warrior of some distant culture brought forward to modern times.

Immediately behind the restaurant was a steep bank that dropped to the lead-colored Tug Fork River. It was here where the restaurant threw their trash. It was also where the sinks and toilets of all the local homes emptied. It was into this river that everyone in the county threw their old tires and appliances. On that night, it was where my grandfather threw the drunken, bleeding, and dying man who'd dared pull a knife on him and his son. He rolled the body and listened to the splash, watching the reflection in the water to see that it was moving downstream as it should and was not hung up on a root or rusting car frame.

"Get in the truck," my grandfather said.

Once they were inside, he pulled a greasy rag from under his truck seat and cleaned his knife, then his hands. The rag was thrown out the window on the way home. They drove on and not a word was said about it. Not then. Not ever.

That was the kind of man I was going to have to be to make it home to my family. The kind of man who acted without hesitation during life and death situations. I was going to have to harden the fuck up. Sixty years ago this might have been the kind of country where a man could travel home and get help along the way from decent, trusting people. It was not that same America. For every good man in America, there was a drug addict wanting to steal from you. For every good woman, there was a deadbeat too lazy to work and waiting for a handout. For every child, there was a gang member, a sex offender, or a carjacker. This was not a group of coworkers coming home from a business trip anymore. This was war and getting home was our mission.

Gary's pack had a long pocket between the main load compartment and the padded back plate. It was for carrying a hydration bladder, which Gary did not bring on this trip. He doubled a piece of paracord and tied a single point sling around the grip of the sawed-off shotgun. He then shoved the weapon into the hydration bladder pocket like it was a scabbard. It was completely concealed from view. He fastened the other end of the paracord to a D-ring on the shoulder strap of his pack. His intent was to use the sling to draw the weapon from his pack. The success of that plan would depend on how stuffed his pack was and how much pressure the contents of his pack placed on that sleeve.

He must have read my mind, or my look, which I have never been very good at masking.

"We'll see how it works," he said. "Hopefully I can yank it out of there without shooting myself or someone else."

I hoped so too. I powered up my GPS. While I waited for it to sync with the satellite network, I double checked my weapon and made sure the magazine was full. It was then that it occurred to me I had not replenished Randi's magazine from when she emptied it last night. "Randi, pass me that LCP."

She removed it from her back pocket and offered it to me. I pressed the magazine release and dropped the magazine into my palm. Empty.

Good thing I thought of it before she needed the weapon. The hollow point ammunition came in boxes of twenty-five and I refilled the magazine from the partial box of Critical Defense rounds in my pack. When I ran out of those, I still had a full box of fifty rounds of .380 ball ammo. It would still punch holes, just considerably less damaging ones than the hollow points.

When I returned the full LCP to her, I reminded her that the weapon was ready to go and to be careful with it. She rolled her eyes at me.

"Grew up with guns," she reminded me in a sarcastic, lilting voice. "Remember?"

My GPS was fully synced at this point and indicated that it was accurate to within fifteen feet of my position. I zoomed out and used the GPS's waypoint tools to do a quick measurement from our current location to where I approximated Lloyd's house to be. This type of route measurement was not completely accurate because the handheld unit made it difficult to trace all the twists and turns of the road. Still, I came up with a distance of around 8.3 miles. I repeated the distance out loud for the benefit of the others.

"How does that translate into hours?" Randi asked. "How much longer am I going to have to be walking?"

"If we're going mostly downhill on this paved surface we might do three miles an hour or better," I said. "With breaks, let's say three hours or so."

"I can do three hours, I think," she said. Then she added, as an afterthought, "I'm out of cigarettes now."

"Good," I said.

"Bastard," she snarled. "You're the one who's going to have to listen to the complaining."

I smiled. "No, I won't. You'll be too winded to complain. If you have breath for complaining, we're not walking fast enough. If you complain, I'll just step up the pace until you can't complain anymore. Keep that in mind."

She mulled this over. "You're not just a bastard, you're a *cruel* bastard."

"Let's go. We've got miles to burn."

30

When I hike, I'm always excited to return to walking after a break. I enjoy the breaks, slumped against my backpack, taking in a view, but there was something about the resumption of the trip that carries great potential. It's when the world opens up to you. Walking the trail is where you see things – the views, the wildlife, the indescribable play of light that photographs always fail to capture.

The pleasure of resuming our walk on this beautiful day, in this beautiful place, was short-lived. We were walking in a straight line on the shoulder of the road, taking long strides and eating up ground. I was on point, Gary at the rear. We stayed close to the shoulder so we could duck over the edge of the road if we saw or heard someone coming. For the first mile or so there was nothing to be concerned about. Then a scream cut through the near silence.

We all flinched, hands moving toward weapons, muscles tensing.

"What the fuck?" Randi said.

"That was close," Gary said. "Just ahead."

The road followed the contour of the mountaintop, snaking around every shoulder, ridge, abutment, outcropping, or draw in the mountain, making it nearly impossible to see for any distance at all.

"What are we going to do?" Randi asked.

Another scream came, dropping to an anguished wail. The sound tore at us like nails on a blackboard.

"Oh God, that sounds like Katie," I said.

"Oh no," Gary muttered.

"I'm going to take a look," I said. "You guys staying here or coming with me?"

Gary and Randi exchanged a quick glance before replying that they were coming with me. I dropped over the weedy shoulder of the road and kept moving, walking along an angled bank that offered some concealment from the road. The grass was dew-soaked and we were constantly losing traction, our feet sliding out from under us. After several minutes of fighting with the wet bank, we closed in on the screaming.

I held a hand up, stopping Randi and Gary behind me. We flattened ourselves against the bank, creeping higher on the shoulder. Through the weeds, we saw three ATVs, one of them with a trailer hooked to it. Four men and two women were standing among the ATVs. I recognized one of the men and one of the machines from the day before. It was the passenger with the jail tattoos. He was probably with the man we killed last night. He'd made his way back to his family or some other group of lowlifes that gave a shit about them. Now he was back with reinforcements.

Katie was at the center of this group. She was on her knees, her hands resting on Walt's still body, a puddle of blood running from beneath him. I could not immediately see how he'd been injured or killed but there was a lot of blood. The older of the two women stepped forward and grabbed a handful of Katie's hair, wrenching her away from Walt's body. She dragged her a short distance then began kicking and stomping her, still holding her by the hair. Katie screamed and sobbed, trying to protect herself but it was futile. All she could do was cover her head from the blows and kicks raining down on her.

"What did you do to my son, you fucking bitch?" the woman kept screaming at Katie, her voice hoarse and rasping. "Did you kill my son? Was it you that killed him?"

Katie sobbed, unable to form words. She looked like she was going into shock. The other woman, much younger, likely a sister or someone's wife, stepped forward and kicked Katie in the back, right over her kidney. She drew back her fist and landed a series of punches on the side of Katie's face, one after another. After the last blow, the mother slung Katie by the hair and she collapsed onto the pavement. The younger woman bent and spit into Katie's face.

The men surrounding the fight did nothing to stop it. In fact, they looked vaguely amused by the whole thing, smiling and joking. One even lit up a cigarette.

"I like a good cat fight," the man from last night said.

"What I wouldn't give for a scoped rifle," Gary whispered beside me. "Even a .22 caliber would be an improvement. We've got nothing accurate at this range."

It was probably around seventy yards to where all of this was taking place and our handguns with open sights were insufficient for the job. We might hit them but we might not.

"What do we do then?" I asked. "Do we wait for them to leave and let things play out?"

"That girl hasn't done anything," Randi said. "I killed that old bitch's son. I can't let Katie to die for something I did."

"What do you propose we do?" I asked her.

She looked at me like I was an idiot. "Why don't we just rush them?" she said. "They're all looking the other way. By the time they notice us, we'll be close enough to shoot."

Gary and I looked at each other.

"Might work," Gary said. "We'd have to be quiet and move quickly."

The younger woman who'd punched Katie and spit on her now stood over Katie's body, staring down at her with disgust, her breath heaving. "Fucking bitch," she screamed. "By God, let's just kill her now. She ain't gonna tell us shit."

The woman reached into her back pocket and withdrew what

looked like a .22 caliber mini-revolver, probably a North American Arms model. She put a thumb on the hammer and pointed the gun at Katie's head. "Let me kill her, Mom," she said coldly. "Please, just let me kill her."

The older woman looked down at Katie's trembling, blood-spattered form and shook her head. "No one's killing her until I know what happened to my baby." She walked to the ATV cart and returned with an old-fashioned butcher knife.

"Last chance, girl," she told Katie. "You start talking or I start cutting your pretty little face up. I've butchered livestock my whole life and I ain't scared of a little blood."

"She'll do it," the man with the tattoos said. "She'll cut you, bitch. You better start talking."

"We have to do this now. Randi, you take the two on the farthest left," I said. "I'll take the two on the farthest right. Gary, you take the center two."

"Why do I get the center two?" Gary said. "That's where Katie is. I don't want to hit her."

"I don't either and you're a better shot."

Gary didn't have anything to say to that.

"Let's hit it," I said. "Walk quickly toward them with weapons up. Don't run. Don't draw any attention. Take firm, quiet steps. As soon as the first one turns, we start shooting. Remember your shooting lanes."

"What the hell is a shooting lane?" Randi asked.

"Just shoot the ones I told you to shoot."

"Why didn't you just say that instead of trying to be all tactical?"

I frowned at her. "Let's do this."

We shrugged out of our packs and checked our weapons. I confirmed everyone was ready and stood, climbing the guard rail. No one on the road noticed. Everyone ahead of us had their eyes glued to the old woman waving a butcher knife in Katie's face. I started to walk toward the group, checking to see that Gary and Randi were with me. I checked my speed so that we were aligned as closely as possible. No one should be out ahead and in the line of fire when the chaos started.

Ironically, it was Katie who saw us first. We'd closed half the distance when Katie peeled her hands from her face. She was clearly in shock, accepting that she was going to be tortured and then die on this lonely road with her boyfriend. The woman stood over her, talking to her in a low voice that kept us from hearing the words.

We closed ten more yards. Katie raised her head and looked straight at us, blood smeared on her face. Ten more yards and the old woman noticed Katie's eyes, noticed her distraction. Hell, maybe she even saw our reflection in her pupils.

We were fifteen yards and closing when the first head turned to us. It was the old woman with the knife. Her hate-filled eyes widened and she opened her mouth to yell. The words never escaped her foul mouth. Gary's .40 caliber Hydra-Shok round caught her in the face and sheared everything from frontal lobe to brain stem. She instantly dropped the knife and fell onto Katie.

The man I'd seen the previous day, the partner to the one we'd killed last night, was in my sights. I planned on him being my first target. I was set to double-tap him center mass when he dropped behind an ATV. I started to pursue him but saw my secondary target turn toward me.

It was exactly like a shooting drill I practiced at home, shooting at spaced targets. The man was a little older than me with a shaggy gray beard and long, unkempt hair. He wore a greasy t-shirt and blue mechanics pants. He raised a shirttail to reach for a revolver, but I caught him before it came free of his waistband. I double-tapped him, one slicing a chunk from his neck, the other punching through his sternum. He twisted and fell with a grunt.

I returned my attention to my first target in time to see him roll into the ditch, partially obscured by another ATV. I fired at what I could see, but didn't connect. He scrambled up a short bank, dodging my shots, and disappeared into the treeline.

Randi was blasting away, not having much luck at hitting her targets. The LCP had nearly non-existent sights and her first shot, targeting center-mass as we'd told her, went a little wide. It caught a skinny guy that looked like a meth dealer in the arm. He grabbed at his arm and she emptied the pistol at him. She caught him in the shoulder and once in the abdomen before he went down. The remaining man, fortyish with greasy black hair, took cover behind the ATV trailer. Gary and I both plowed rounds into it, punching holes in the plastic sides of the trailer. The man caught several rounds and collapsed behind it.

I turned my attention to the remaining woman in time to catch her raising that tiny revolver on Randi. Before my sights found her, she thumbed and dropped the hammer, firing a .22 round in our direction. I flinched. Randi screamed. The woman's thumb began to draw the hammer back for a second shot. I aimed but before I could fire there was a blur of movement in front of her. The sudden movement caused me to hesitate for a fraction of a second because I knew Katie was downrange.

She had found the old woman's butcher knife and raised it in her bloodstained hand. There was a flash as the light caught it, a brief reflection from the blade, before it plunged into the vile woman's abdomen. She doubled over in pain, dropping the revolver. Katie withdrew the knife and attacked. She pulled the woman down to the pavement, plunging the knife into her chest and neck repeatedly. Katie's violence was the only sound in the great silence of the Parkway.

Gary and I watched stunned until her movements slowed and she dropped the knife. She fell over sobbing, curled into the fetal position.

"Cover me!" I yelled.

I scrambled up the bank and looked for the man who'd escaped me. I saw the trail he'd taken – the broken branches, displaced rocks, missing chunks of moss – but I would not pursue him. He was probably in there somewhere waiting for me to do just that. I knew, though, that leaving him alive was also a risky move. He might catch up with us again.

Aside from the one that got away, everyone in that group had been hit at least once. They'd all dropped but that didn't mean they were out of the fight. Gary and I made a quick pass to confirm they were all dead or close to it, then I went to check on Randi. She was sitting down in the road, holding her face, blood seeping between her fingers. She was cursing in a low voice, repeating the same words over and over. I took that as a good sign. She still had some fight left in her.

"Randi, where are you hit?"

She continued her mumbling curses. I took her by the wrists and gently pried her hands from her face. It was immediately obvious that a round had simply grazed her cheek.

"I'm a nurse," she hissed. "Give it to me straight. How bad is it?"

"It's okay," I said. "The bullet just grazed you. You'll be okay. You may not be able to smile for a few days, though."

"Good thing there's nothing to fucking smile about then, isn't it?" she said. "It burns like hell."

I yanked a bandana from my pocket and pressed it to the side of her head. "Hold this on the wound."

"Great, a snot compress," she mumbled. "I'm sure it's sterile."

She did as I asked, though, and I went to assist Gary. He was doing a more thorough check of the bodies. He was bent and digging in the pocket of one of the men.

"What you got?" I asked.

He held up a pack of Marlboro Lights with a grin on his face. I held out my hand and he tossed them to me. I shook one loose and pulled it from the pack, sticking it between my lips. I took the lighter from my pocket, flicked it, and sucked the flame to the tip. At the sound, Randi's eyes opened and widened. I removed the cigarette from my mouth and handed it to her.

"Good for what ails you."

"Bless you, my child," she said.

"Don't thank me, thank Gary." I turned to him. "They all dead?"

"No, but the ones who aren't will be that way before long. Nothing we can do." Gary holstered his weapon and went to check Katie, who'd crawled over to Walt's body. Gary checked Walt first, then slowly drew his hand back. He was dead.

I looked around, found a ratty old blanket in the ATV trailer, and draped it over Walt's body. Katie was no longer crying, but emitted a tired, wailing moan. Gary helped her stand and led her to one of the ATVs, helping her take a seat on the rack. It looked like exhaustion, hysteria, and shock had taken control.

I jogged over to the shoulder of the road, where we'd left our packs, and returned with a first aid kit. I removed an antiseptic wipe, a butterfly closure, and set to work on Randi's cheek. She was in a much better state with a cigarette in her hand, but still winced when I applied the antiseptic to her cheek. She called me a variety of colorful names but I took it as a sign she was in good spirits. I wiped her cheek, my hands shaking as my body tried to burn off the excess adrenaline. It was a bad feeling, one that I had become more familiar with lately than I cared to be.

From the corner of my eye, I could see that Gary really didn't know where to start with Katie. He was working on wiping the blood off her, first using a handkerchief and water, then using alcohol wipes from the first aid kit. From the noise she was making, it was clear that she needed more than just bandaging.

When I finished with Randi's cheek, she flipped her cigarette butt away and stood up. "I can take care of her. She needs a woman's help."

"I'm sure Gary won't argue with you."

With Katie in Randi's hands, Gary and I regarded the scene around us.

"Did we really have to kill all these people?" Gary asked. "This is a slaughter."

"I don't know," I said. "Did you see an option I missed?"

"Not one that would have saved Katie's life, but this is a lot of dead people."

"I agree. I'd be a lot happier if there was one more among them. That one that escaped worries me."

"Is this what we turn into when things start going to hell?" Gary asked.

I thought about his question for a moment. "Them or us?"

"All of us," he said. "Them *or* us. Do we all just turn into animals and start killing each other?"

"I don't know about that," I said. "I don't feel like I've turned into anything. I want to get home and I'll rise to whatever level of violence is required to get me there. I don't think we've killed anyone except people who left us no choice. If that's the kind of people that lay between us and home, I'll pave the road with their bodies." I was dead fucking serious.

I could tell there was a lot going on in Gary's head. Among all those things bouncing around in there, I was sure he was asking himself if he had that level of resolve, if he was hard enough.

"That guy may come back," I said. "We need to get our shit together and get out of here."

We set to work, piling the scant useful possessions of this group into the ATV trailer. There was a .270 caliber bolt-action rifle, an old Smith & Wesson .38 revolver, and the .22 mini-revolver that Randi had been shot with. There was no boxed ammo, but we found several spare rounds for each weapon in the pockets of the people we'd killed. There were several knives of various sizes. We kept a single hunting knife but the rest were of such low quality that we left them on the bodies. We also collected some packs of cigarettes and lighters. If Randi didn't smoke them all, maybe we could trade them for ammo or something useful. There was a feed sack in the trailer that held some canned food and utensils, as well as a couple of flashlights.

"We need to get rid of these bodies, Gary. I don't want people seeing this and thinking we murdered innocent people."

"I agree," he said. "But I want someone keeping watch. I don't want that straggler shooting us in the back if he returns."

"Can we use the ATVs?" Randi asked.

"I guess so," I shrugged. "On those machines we could be at Lloyd's in less than an hour, I bet."

Randi maintained watch while I fetched our remaining gear from over the hill. Gary and I carried all the bodies and rolled them over the embankment. He got the feet, I got the shoulders, and it was tiring work. It was completely clear to me now where the term "dead weight" came from. When we were done, Gary stepped over to a rhododendron and sprayed it with the meager contents of his stomach. I turned my back. Funny that killing didn't have any adverse effect on me, but seeing people throw up always turned my stomach. Didn't make a lot of sense but that's how I was made. What the hell could I do about it?

While Gary lost his lunch, I took all the gear we didn't need and tossed it over the shoulder onto the bodies. As I stood staring over the bank at the results of our conflict, Gary walked up to my side.

"I think we should conceal them a little better," I said.

Gary nodded. We each pulled out our belt knives and hacked off branches, throwing them over the bodies. We spread out and collected branches from a wider area to avoid making any one area look too cut back. When we were done, the bodies were at least camouflaged. We had one more body to deal with, still lying on the road beneath the blanket I'd placed over him. We looked at Randi for help.

She shrugged and took the direct approach. "Katie, what do you want to do with Walt's body?"

Katie looked at Randi, unsure. "I don't know. What should we do?"

Randi looked back at us for ideas.

"We don't have any tools for burying him, Katie," I said. "We can leave him here or we can take him with us. That's all I know."

She sighed heavily, her eyes tearing again. "Let's take him. Can we do that? I don't want to leave him here with the people that took his life."

The arrangement for transporting Walt's body was less dignified than I would have preferred. The ATV trailer was on the small side, about four feet wide and six feet long. In order to make everything fit and to avoid soaking all the gear in Walt's blood, we had to place his blanket-wrapped body on the bottom. We put the guns beside him, along with the sack of gear we'd recovered from Katie's attackers. We covered the guns and Walt's body with our individual packs. We would keep our personal weapons handy, but it seemed prudent not to ride into a strange town on stolen ATVs with weapons and a body on display.

As we prepared to head out, I looked at Randi. "You ever drive one of these?"

She gave me that look again. "I'm a country girl. I was practically born on one of these."

"Gary?" I asked. "What about you?"

"I've ridden motorcycles all my life but ATVs only a couple of times. I know the basics, though."

"Then how about I drive the ATV with the trailer," I suggested. "Gary you take one for yourself. Randi, you take the other and Katie can ride with you. We have a little more than seven miles to go. Surely to God we can get there without getting killed or having to kill someone else."

31

It was a somber day for Ellen and her family. Pete had been very upset last night after shooting the two intruders. Pops had taken guard duty for the rest of the night so Ellen could lay with Pete and help him get to sleep. He'd asked a lot of questions and she didn't have answers for all of them. She grieved for what circumstance had forced their son to do. It made her worry more for Jim and long for his return. It was only after Pete fell asleep that she could think about her own actions. How had she reached the point where she could so resolutely and easily end a man's life?

Pete slept late that morning and felt somewhat better after breakfast. He helped Pops use the excavator to block the gate with a series of steel beams. The beams were scrap from an old bridge and weighed more than five hundred pounds each. They had several and placed them at random intervals all the way up the driveway. It would make it very difficult for anyone to drive up to the house. There was a hill on one side of the road and a steep embankment on the other so they'd be difficult to drive around. With the driveway blocked, the farm road at the back of the property would have to be their primary way in and out.

Pete and Pops also took the box of driveway alarms Jim had purchased and began installing them around the house. They had a limited range, but would set off an alarm in the house when the devices sensed movement. Pops explained that the sensitivity of the device may require some fine tuning to avoid false alarms. In the meantime, they could expect dogs, cats, possums, or even cows to trigger an alarm. Every signal would have to be visually verified. Everyone understood they wouldn't replace guard duty, either. There would still need to be a live sentry at night.

By afternoon, everyone was focusing on their chores. Ellen was cycling the generator to keep the freezers and refrigerators cold. Nana and Ariel were running a canning operation. They'd hot-packed many of the meats from the freezers and there were jars cooling on every flat surface of the kitchen. They had the pressure canner on the back porch, heating on the side burner of the gas grill. They still had a lot of frozen foods left but were trying to save as much as possible. They'd already put up thin sliced beef for sandwiches, beef cubes for stews, and several varieties of chicken and pork. One of the nice things about this canned meat was that it would be much easier to prepare than the original roasts.

Pete and Pops decided to barricade the front windows too. They found some scraps of 1/8" plate steel and bolted it over the windows using three-inch lag screws. Some windows were covered with a single piece while others were pieced together from two smaller scraps. This method left a shooting port that could be accessed by raising the window sash from inside the house and sticking a gun barrel through the horizontal gap between the plates. When they ran out of steel plate, they found some pieces of ¾" plywood that they doubled up over the remaining front windows, creating a 1 ½" thick barrier. Neither the steel nor the wood was likely to stop a rifle bullet but it would slow one down.

While Pops and Pete were putting up their tools, they heard a call from the gate. Pops spun around and put his hand on the butt of his pistol. Pete ran for the rifle he'd leaned against the house.

"That's Henry, isn't it?" Pops asked, squinting toward the road.

Pete returned with his rifle and looked. "I think so."

The man at the gate waved at them, then started climbing over it.

"Go tell your mother that Henry's here," Pops said before heading down the road toward him.

Pete ran for the house.

Henry and Pops met up about halfway down the driveway.

"Well, hey there," Henry said. "Didn't know you were staying here."

Pops shook Henry's hand. They'd known each other for years, although Henry was about ten years younger than Pops.

"We came down yesterday," Pops said. "Ellen was a little worried about being here by herself. We decided to come help her out with the kids and all."

Henry nodded. "Probably a good thing," he said. "There some people in this valley that worry me a little."

"Ellen said the same thing," Pops said, not wanting to bring up last night.

"The folks in that trailer park are living like some crazy tribe," Henry said. "I drove by there last night on my four-wheeler and I swear they were roasting big chunks of beef over an open fire they'd built out of someone's porch. I stopped by because I knew it was somebody's steer and I wanted to make sure it wasn't mine."

"How'd that go?" Pops asked.

"I had a rifle with me and I asked where they got the meat. They didn't want to say. I kept asking and one of them finally told me he hit a cow with his truck and they butchered it."

"You believe it?" Pops asked.

"Could be true," Henry said. "Could be a lie. There are a lot of cows running loose right now. People are too damn busy living like pioneers to check their fences like they used to."

Pops nodded.

"They showed me the cowhide and it wasn't my cow," he continued. "I told them that I better not have any cows turn up missing or I would be up there to pay them a visit."

"How'd they take that?"

"There are some rough characters in that trailer park. If it does come to it, I'll take some backup and be prepared to shoot. I halfway expected someone to start something yesterday but they let it go."

"I don't know what this world is coming to," Pops said.

Henry looked around, feeling no pressure to speak. Farmers were like that – content just to stare at the land and not say much, sometimes. Henry threw up his hand and waved. Pops turned to find Ellen and Pete approaching.

"What brings you down here, Henry?" Ellen asked.

"Just wanted to check on you guys," Henry said. "The Kisers that live between me and the trailer park said they thought someone tried to break in on them last night. Their dog got a hold of them, though, and they ran off. You all see any trouble?"

Pops turned to Ellen, gauging her reaction.

"No," Ellen said. "Not really. A bunch from the trailer park came down here yesterday wanting me to give them food and I had nothing for them. We did hear some shots last night."

"Really?" Henry asked.

Ellen nodded. "There were several shots. I got up and looked out the window but didn't see anything. I couldn't really tell where they were coming from."

"That right?" Henry said. "Couldn't hear anything from my place, but that ain't surprising the way sounds bounce around in these hills."

"Yeah," Ellen said. "I reckon it could have been anywhere up or down the road, I couldn't tell."

Henry mulled this over. "Well, I got to get back to work," he said. "Keep your eyes open. I think things will get worse before they get better."

Pops nodded. "I think you're right about that, Henry."

"Call me on the radio if you need to," Henry reminded them. "We may have to team up on these people if they continue being pushy. They seem to feel like we're obligated to take care of them. I've got news for them, though."

"I agree," Ellen said. "Everything we have, we worked for. I'm not handing it out to people because they show up and demand it."

"Well, I need to get back. Just wanted to check in with you folks." With that, Henry turned and walked off.

32

It was my eternal predisposition toward sightseeing that saved my life. I was in the lead and we were puttering along cautiously on the ATVs, winding our way down the mountain. Coming around one bend I could see Lloyd's town in the distance, easily recognizable by the tower of the town hall. I turned sideways, raising my arm to point toward it. "There's the town," I called to the others.

I had barely closed my mouth when everything went to shit. A strand of barbed wire that had been lying across the road, hidden by leaves, was suddenly jerked tight to the level of my neck. Because of the way I was turned sideways, with my arm upraised, the wire caught the inside of my bicep. It dislocated my shoulder rather than catching the inside of my neck and dislocating my head. In an instant, I was lifted from the seat of my ATV and thrown backward. In another fluke of timing, I landed on my back in the trailer I was pulling, then continued rolling backward into the road. The trailer broke my fall sufficiently that I was not severely injured, but I hit my head on the pavement and lay there stunned. Randi, riding behind me, reacted quickly and swerved to the left, only missing me by a hair.

A little further back, Gary eased off the throttle and slammed on his brakes. Even with my eyes closed, I could identify the hollow sound of ATV tires skidding on pavement. With their focus on me, my companions didn't notice the man with the gun climbing down the high bank of the road until it was too late.

"Don't you fucking move," he warned, leveling a pistol at them.

I recognized the voice, but continued to lay still, my eyes closed, my head spinning. I could feel warmth spreading under my arm, blood running from a deep burning gash. This asshole had sliced me open with that wire. A barb had gone under my arm pit and cut me at the same time that the wire wrenched my shoulder from the socket. The pain from the dislocated joint was excruciating and my only defense right now was to feign unconsciousness. My shoulder screamed. It was all I could do not to writhe from the pain and cry like a baby. It felt like a red hot knife was being twisted around inside the joint.

"Turn them machines off!" he yelled, gesturing at the four-wheelers. One ATV turned off, then the next. I had no idea where mine ended up. I could only hear the ticking of cooling engines and the scuff of footsteps walking across the pavement toward us.

"You're the bitch that killed my little brother," the man said. "And now the rest of my family is dead too. Any good reason I shouldn't shoot all of you right now?"

No one replied.

"Well, I got my own good reason to not shoot you," he told them. "It's because I want to slice you open and let you bleed to death slowly. I want you to have time to think about the mistake you made when you crossed my family. That sound like a party?"

I cracked my eyes open as faintly as I could and saw the man standing in front of Randi, an old revolver pointed right at her. Katie sat behind her, eyes wide in fear, still traumatized by her earlier encounter with these people.

"Looks like you got a little cut there on your cheek," he said to Randi. "We do that?"

"I didn't do it to my damn self," Randi answered defiantly.

"We gonna do more than that in a minute," the man said.

From my cracked eyelids, I saw the man insert his index finger in his mouth and suck on it. Then he pulled it from his mouth and extended it toward Randi's mouth. He rubbed his wet finger across her lips before forcing it between them. She did not cooperate, but she never closed her eyes, never wavered from his direct gaze.

"Open your mouth, bitch," he hissed, putting the gun to her forehead.

She let her jaw go slack and his nasty finger probed her mouth, moving in and out. He smiled the disturbed smile of someone a few sockets short of a set. His delight turned to shock, then pain, as Randi bit down on his finger as hard as she could. She ground it between her molars, attempting to pulverize it flat.

When the man's brain was finally able to process the incoming flood of pain signals, he responded quickly and backhanded the revolver across Randi's face. She released him and crumpled to the ground. The man grimaced, shook his injured finger, and then examined it. It was bleeding heavily. Randi clearly had bigger balls than most of the men I knew.

"You're gonna hurt for this, bitch," the man hissed, raising his foot in the air, intent on stomping Randi's face into the ground. In seconds her head was going to end up like his finger.

"No!" Gary yelled.

The man spun toward Gary and fired a single shot. So much for killing everyone slowly. He was ready for this to be done. Katie screamed when Gary dropped. The man turned back toward Katie, steadied his pistol, and shot her in the face without a word. The man was a sociopath, a cold-blooded, remorseless killer.

Knowing that I was next, that the man would put a bullet in my head to make sure I never rose again, I took the opportunity to grab for my handgun. Because my right arm was injured, I had to reach across my body with my left hand. The gun was not positioned for a left hand draw since I was right-handed. It left me grabbing the weapon awkwardly, then laying it down on my belly to adjust to a proper left-handed grip. It was a difficult move that I wished I'd drilled on, but I'd never imagined this scenario. Fortunately the safety was ambidextrous and I was able to release it after a slight bobble. I raised the gun as the man began to turn in my direction.

The front sight wavered over his body and the 9mm barked once, catching him in the lower left quadrant of his back. He twisted in pain and I hit him again in the chest. He dropped his gun, clutched his chest but remained standing, his eyes glued on me. I fired again, steadier this time, and hit him in the throat, clawing out a chunk. A geyser of blood erupted as he toppled over backward.

I dropped my gun, unable to move my injured body and hold the weapon at the same time. I crawled toward the closest ATV and used my good hand to pull myself up. I could do nothing until I reset my shoulder. Trying to recall how to reduce the dislocation by myself, I could think of nothing to use except the ATV. Every movement was excruciating.

I leaned over and clamped my hand as tightly as I could around one of the steel tubes of the cargo rack. I straightened my back. In an explosion of movement, I used my legs to push straight up while holding to the ATV as tightly as I could. There was a blinding burst of pain, then a sickening pop as the shoulder joint reseated itself.

I let go of the rack and staggered around in a daze, eyes watering, clutching my arm. I was suddenly aware that my head ached from the impact with the pavement and I felt dizzy. My head started spinning and I fought to stay conscious. I remembered the shot, Gary, and my gun on the pavement. I'd killed another man. Randi had been knocked out. Or had she been killed? I couldn't remember.

I scanned the pavement for my Beretta and leaned over to pick it up. I probably would have passed out from bending over had I not experienced a fiery wave of pain from using my recently dislocated shoulder. My mouth filled with vomit from pain and dizziness. I spit it out, getting some on my clothes.

I passed the Beretta to my left hand and checked the guy I shot. He was dead for certain. I kicked his pistol to the side in case he experienced some kind of spontaneous resurrection. I wasn't taking any chances. I scanned my surroundings and saw no other threats.

I moved to Randi. There was a whopper of a bruise forming on her left cheek and around her eye. I touched it to see if the cheekbone was broken but it didn't seem to be. The pain from touching the bruise made her stir. She'd be okay.

At the rear of the ATV, Katie lay on the ground in a pool of her own blood. Her face was a misshapen and damaged pulp that I wish I'd never seen. It was the kind of memory that never left you. There was no doubt she was dead.

I delayed checking Gary. I didn't want to see my friend dead. We'd been through too much together. He'd taken a round that had dropped and silenced him. I had nothing to treat a chest wound. If he was still alive, maybe I could get him to town, to a doctor, but there was nothing. No sound, no cries of pain, and no pleas for help. I had to assume the worst. He was dead.

What would I tell his family?

I stepped around Gary's ATV and studied his fallen body. There was a light smear of blood beneath his head, probably from hitting the pavement. I watched him for a moment and was shocked when I saw his chest rise. I immediately began looking for the wound, ready to plug it despite the inevitable futility of my actions. I finally found an entrance wound but there was no blood around it. I set my pistol down, put my left hand over his chest and probed the wound with my finger, but it felt odd. I found hot metal.

The slug?

I drew my finger back and ripped open the loose button-up shirt he was wearing. Beneath it was soft armor. *Body armor.*

Gary was wearing fucking body armor.

"What happened?" asked a voice behind me.

I spun, making myself dizzy in the process. I winced. My head throbbed and I felt a wave of nausea. Randi stood there, probing her face gently, checking her wound as I'd just done with her a moment ago.

"He took a bullet coming to your aid," I said. "I thought he was dead, but he's wearing some kind of body armor."

I finished unfastening his shirt, spread it open, and it was clear that his vest had caught the round, stopping it. Of course, I also knew that blunt trauma over the heart could present its own problems. I removed the Velcro straps under his armpits and lifted the vest up. There was no evidence the bullet had penetrated the vest. No blood underneath it.

"Bring me some water," I said.

Randi went to her ATV. I heard a loud intake of breath.

"Katie," Randi said. "Oh sweetie! Oh shit!"

I realized that Randi had already been knocked out when Katie was shot. She hadn't known.

"Water," I reminded her, trying to draw her attention from the grim scene in front of her.

In a second, Randi was behind me, passing me a bottle of water. I unscrewed the cap and splashed some across Gary's face. He stirred, then bolted upright immediately, his eyes wide in fear. He gasped, hyperventilating, trying to take in the scene. He was trying to figure out if he was dead or alive. He frantically patted his chest, searching for a wound. He found no bullet hole, but did grimace in pain when his fingers probed his chest.

"Oh, Jesus," he croaked. "I've got a broken rib."

I put a hand behind him and eased him back down onto the pavement.

"I'm sure you do," I said. "But you're still alive. A broken rib we can deal with."

"The vest," he said. "Police surplus. Kept it in my bugout bag."

"Why didn't you say anything about it?" I said. "I didn't even realize you had it."

He reached for the water bottle and took a long drink. "I never said anything because I felt bad that I didn't have one for you guys. I felt guilty."

I laughed. "No need to feel guilty, man. The damn thing saved your bacon."

"Katie's dead," Randi said.

Gary's smile left his face and he looked around at the scene surrounding us. He shook his head.

"On the practical side, there's no need to haul Walt any further," Randi said. "We can lay them to rest off the road somewhere. Together."

I looked at Randi and nodded, not sure I really had any words left in me for this experience. I knew losing Katie really hurt her and she was just trying to distance herself from it. She was trying to stay tough. To stay hard.

Things kept getting crazier every day. How long would it take us to get home? How many bodies would we leave behind? Would we all make it or would one of us end up buried on the side of the road, too?

33

Throughout the day, Ellen and her family focused on the variety of jobs that needed to be performed to keep things functioning. They continued to run the generator at intervals. They processed frozen meats into longer lasting products for the day the generator fuel ran out. They tended the garden, charged batteries, and scanned radio stations for news. Even all the basic tasks, such as cooking and washing dishes, now took much longer. Above all, they maintained vigilance, keeping an eye on the road and the perimeter of their property.

There had been more traffic today on the road through their valley. Several different groups had gone by, both on foot and on ATVs. There was even a pickup that coasted slowly by earlier, the bed full of people. Whoever was on watch kept a set of binoculars handy and dutifully reported what they observed. From what they were seeing, it appeared folks were looking for the missing men. The ones Pete had shot and Ellen had buried in the pasture.

Later in the evening, they had a dinner of rice topped with canned soup. It was a simple, filling meal that was easy for a group. They ate from paper plates, with plastic utensils, which limited cleanup to the pots used for making the rice and the big spoon used for serving it. At the children's prompting, they concluded dinner with coffee, hot chocolate, and some cookies. While they sat around enjoying dinner on the back porch, the clanging at the gate came again.

Though she'd been expecting this, the sound filled Ellen with dread. Conversation came to an end and her anxiety turned to anger. She grabbed the AR-15 that lay nearby, stood and slung it over her shoulder.

"Pops, I'll need you to cover me from the truck. You can use the 870 shotgun. Let's go," Ellen said.

Pops nodded, obviously distressed by how ugly things were turning. He was a social being and not prone to violence.

Ellen drove toward the gate. She could see the pickup from earlier stopped in front of it. A man and a woman stood at the gate, beating on it with a stick. Ellen drove to within twenty feet of the gate, stopped, and threw open her door. She exited the vehicle, but remained behind the door, speaking to the group through the open window.

"What the hell do you people want?" she asked. "I thought I told you I had nothing for you."

The woman at the gate was the same woman Ellen had spoken with yesterday. "We're looking for my husband. He didn't come home last night."

"What was he out doing last night?"

"Hunting," the woman said.

Ellen mulled that over. The men had been hunting, alright – hunting for things they could steal. "We haven't seen him."

"We heard shots last night," said the man standing beside her.

Ellen assumed it was the woman's son. He looked to be around seventeen or eighteen years old. "We heard them, too," she said. "They didn't come from here."

"You mind if we come on through and look for him?" the woman asked.

"I fucking well do mind," Ellen replied. "He shouldn't have had any reason to be on my property, so I don't see that you have any reason to go tearing through my property looking for him."

"I ain't asking," the boy said, tightening his grip on the top rail of the gate. "I'm fixing to come across this gate and I better not find out that you done anything to him."

Ellen raised her AR and leveled it at him. "I'll kill the first person that steps onto my property."

The group didn't move, sensing Ellen's seriousness.

"You kill my husband?" the woman asked. She was on the verge of tears.

"I didn't kill anybody," Ellen replied flatly. "But if your husband was out stealing from people last night and got himself killed, he brought that on himself, didn't he?"

The woman glared at Ellen. "If we have to steal to feed our families, we'll do it."

"Then I'll just lay it out here plain and simple for you," Ellen said. "We're done talking. I ain't coming to this gate anymore to powwow with you folks. My suggestion is that you head out of here and see if there are shelters set up to help people. I strongly suggest you don't start stealing off your neighbors or a lot of people will end up dying."

No more words were exchanged. Ellen climbed back in the truck, reversed up the driveway, and parked the vehicle behind the house. "That went well. Wouldn't you say?"

Pops was shaking his head. "I think we should just get out of here and go back to our house in town."

"No," Ellen said. "You all can leave if you want, but the kids and I are staying here. It will get worse than this in town soon. There are fewer people with the resources to grow their own food. We can survive here on this farm for a long time if we can manage to keep it."

Pops patted Ellen on the arm. "I just don't want to see anyone get hurt. I couldn't live with it."

She looked at him and there were tears in his eyes. "I don't want to see anyone hurt, either," she said. "And we have a backup plan that would be safer than the house. Maybe it's time to use it."

"A backup plan more secure than what Jim already set up for you?"

"You have no idea," Ellen said. "We have a cave. A fortified cave. Jim's been working on it for years."

34

The rest of the ride down the mountain was surreal, following the smooth pavement of the Parkway down into the town of Crawfish. The road was empty, although there were a few abandoned vehicles sitting on the shoulder or pushed off into the ditch. We passed no other people until the road flattened out into farmland and then we saw a few folks. A farmer splitting wood with heavy maul stopped to watch us go by. I started to raise my hand into a wave, but the pain from the dislocation curbed my gesture. It wasn't likely anyone would have waved back anyway. Such was the consequence of being a stranger in a strange land.

As the country became more populated, dogs barked at us and children watched us from behind fenced-in yards. Adults eyed us through screen doors and windows, deep within the shadowy interiors of powerless homes. We drove on, slow enough to stop if we came upon a hazard, but fast enough to discourage anyone from stopping us to chat.

In front of a ramshackle sharecropper's house we drove by an old man in a t-shirt and a diaper standing by the road, bearing silent witness to our passage. His mouth hung open, his eyes empty, and his hand wrapped around the neck of an old open-back banjo he'd been dragging behind him. The diaper appeared close to collapsing under its own weight.

The pain of my dislocated shoulder continued to wrack my body, made worse by the effort of steering the machine. Several times a sharp pain in my arm made me hug it to my mid-section, trying to make it go away. It didn't work. When we stopped for the night I intended to take the strongest pain medication I could find and pray that Lloyd had some kind of liquor put back for company.

Twenty-five minutes after our journey began, we passed a crooked green sign that welcomed us to Crawfish. It was a railroad town that in its day had been the crossroads of this community. It was where people arrived and departed. It was where the community's cabbage, beet, and tobacco crops had once left for markets around the country. It was where the local payroll for long-closed industries had shown up on the train for disbursement.

At its peak, it held sprawling wooden hotels and spas with siding of local poplar clapboards. There were mineral springs where the sick came to consume the limestone-rich spring water and to purchase bottles to take home with them. Now it was the sleepy bedroom community for larger nearby towns. It was where college professors moved to restore Victorian homes and open bookstores that few ever visited.

I'd never entered the town from this direction, always approaching from the interstate. When we reached the railroad tracks, the dead center of the town, I killed my engine and tried to orient myself. Randi and Gary pulled alongside me, killing their engines also.

"Is this it?" Randi asked.

I nodded. "Just trying to get my bearings."

From the corner of my eye I saw Gary cock his head.

"You hear something?" I asked.

"Sounds like music," he said.

I smiled. "That would be it. Follow that banjo."

"You're asking us to go *toward* the banjo music?" Randi asked.

"Didn't you see *Deliverance*?"

I cranked up my ATV, pulling away from Gary and Randi as they exchanged glances. I turned off Main Street and passed a restored railroad caboose donated by the railroad. It sat on a short section of rusty track that led nowhere in either direction. I swung a right turn up a back street and in the distance saw a series of storefronts that were all part of a single, immense brick building.

That was it.

With Gary and Randi bringing up the rear, I headed in that direction. The building was one of the oldest in town, dating to just after the Civil War. A wide wooden porch connected all the storefronts, just as it had over a hundred and fifty years ago. There was an electric barber pole mounted to the wall, stilled by the lack of power. One of the wide plate glass windows had a painted sign that read Lloyd's Barber Shop. Beneath that a script read: Haircuts, Shaves, Lies, Music. Indeed, as I came to a stop and killed my engine, I could tell that the entire front of the building was practically vibrating from the sound of banjos, guitars, fiddles, and an upright bass playing traditional old-time music.

The music trickled to a stop and an odd assortment of faces appeared in the dirty window. Some wore old-fashioned hats, others had unwashed hair that pointed from their head in violent shocks. Finally, I recognized Lloyd's face among his musical brethren and he broke out in a grin. A moment later, the door swung open and a man in the vintage clothing of a 1930s hillbilly musician burst onto the porch, a silver revolver protruding from a vest pocket.

"Brother Jim!" Lloyd said. "You look like hell."

I smiled a weary smile back at him. "You have no idea. What's going on in there?"

"I had folks over playing when all this shit went down," Lloyd said. "They stayed. I don't even know how long we've been playing and drinking. Days, I guess."

"Got room for more?" I asked. "We need a place to stay for a day or so while we regroup and try to get some supplies. We got stuck in Richmond and we're trying to get home."

Lloyd, always host to an inappropriate sense of humor, locked eyes on Randi. "That's no problem. We've got plenty of room and I see you brought a woman to trade."

Lloyd winked at Randi about the time her hand was creeping toward her pistol.

"Careful, Lloyd," I warned. "Our humor is a little low at the moment. It's been a hard trip. The world has pretty much gone to shit."

Lloyd gave a little laugh. "The world went to shit a long time ago. You're just now noticing. I noticed a long time ago. Why do you think I live in the past?"

"Got a place we can hide these machines?"

"Garage is open," he said. "You'll have to make a place for them. When you're done, come on in. You'll know a few of these boys."

35

I stood on the sidewalk outside of Lloyd's Barber Shop, watching the sun settle over the horizon. It threw a warm orange glow over the pastures surrounding Crawfish and onto the white clapboard walls of the old Victorians that filled the town. I sipped moonshine from a plastic cup and listened to the thump of Old Time music. I couldn't remember the name of the song. As we'd hiked these last few days, my grandfather had been on my mind a lot, providing a well of strength that hardened my resolve. He helped me get this far, both on this journey and in my life as a whole. As day faded on the town, I was remembering the end of his life.

He had a massive stroke and had spent several days in the ICU. When they'd finally moved him to a room of his own, my dad and I made the four-hour drive to visit him. My mom and uncle had been with him since they'd first received the news of his stroke, but they'd been the only visitors allowed. It looked like my grandfather might survive, barring any further strokes, but he wouldn't be the same man. He was paralyzed on one side of his body. His speech had been affected. All of those things were relayed to me by my dad on the trip to West Virginia. He didn't want me to be shocked by what I found.

Shock was inevitable, though, when we reached the hospital in

Williamson, West Virginia. The vital, powerful man I'd known my whole life – the man who'd been indestructible in my eyes – had been decimated by the stroke. I saw it as soon as I walked into the room. My mom sat at his bedside holding his tanned, rough hand. He did not turn to face me. I wasn't even sure if he was awake.

My dad prodded me in the back and I moved closer. As I approached his bed, my mom turned and smiled painfully, reaching out to me with her other hand and squeezing my arm. I was seventeen at the time but I instantly felt like a child again. From where I was standing, I could see that my grandfather's eyes were open but he did not turn to face me.

I walked around the bed until I was directly in front of him. It took everything in me to do that. His face was slack and saliva ran from the corner of his mouth. I'd never been so close to this kind of personal devastation. I felt paralyzed, too, completely without control of my body and mind. I raised my hand slowly and put it down on my grandfather's shoulder. He was not a person who touched a lot and it was an unfamiliar gesture in our relationship. However, it was all I knew to do.

He twisted his head violently into his pillow, startling me. I jumped. I could see tears in his eyes. I knew that he felt ashamed – in pain that I was seeing him that way. We stood that way for what felt like hours, all of us locked into this painful moment from which there seemed no escape.

It was only broken when my grandfather twisted his head back in my mother's direction, catching my eyes briefly as his glance passed over me. He raised his left hand, the one my mother had been holding, pointing at her and my father, and then pointing at the door. He made a sound, a soft grunt, that sounded like *row*.

"You want us to go?" my mom asked.

My grandfather pointed again at her and my dad, then the door.

"You want to be alone with Jim?" she asked.

My grandfather bobbed his head in an awkward jerking nod.

My mom looked at my dad and rose stiffly, the two of them leaving the room. I had no idea what was going on. My grandfather turned his head slowly back to me and caught my eye. I was frozen, shaken to my core by the depth of pain and anguish that I saw there. The memory of that look would not leave me for a long time. I felt as if he were conveying a steady stream of regrets, goodbyes, and things left unsaid. I heard it all, watching until his eyes drowned in the tears that poured from them.

He pointed to a notepad and pen sitting on the tray table by the bed. He gestured that he wanted to write something. I lay the pad in his lap and placed the pen in his good hand. With great concentration, he scrawled in large shaky letters: BRING GUN.

My eyes widened and I looked at him, shaking my head. "No," I whispered, my voice a mixture of fear and anger. I was completely appalled that he would ask that of me. That he would consider doing such a thing to himself.

When he looked up at me again and what I saw was not anger at my refusal but desperation. Those eyes told me that I was the *only* person in the world he could ask. I felt a crushing mantle of responsibility drop onto my shoulders. I felt sickened at his request, but imagined myself in that bed, unable to carry out my final wish and unable to convince anyone to help me. Would it be love to condemn him to rot in this bed, never walking the woods, never seeing the river flow behind his house again? Is that how I would repay the man who helped shape me?

I had to do it. I had to be the man he was asking me to be, knowing that I could never, ever speak of it to anyone. I would help kill my grandfather if that's what he wanted me to do. "Where can I get one?"

He placed the pen to paper again, scratching slowly, writing: RED TOOLBOX BASEMENT LOADED.

"In the red toolbox in your basement," I repeated. "And it's already loaded?"

He nodded at me.

"When?" I asked. "I don't want anyone to know I brought it to you."

TOMORROW, he wrote.

I frowned. "We're leaving tomorrow. We're going back home for a couple of days."

He stared at me, desperate, his thinking not clear enough to help me solve this problem, but his will was clear. I knew in my heart that what he was asking me was truly what he wanted. This was not the delusion of a sick man. It was not shock from the suddenness of his plight. He would never get better. He would never be the same. He would never be happy again. In everything I knew about the man, I knew all of that to be true.

I thought about the situation. "We're staying at your house tonight. I'll get the gun and take it back home with me. I'll come back in a few days. Instead of driving to school, I'll drive here. No one will ever know I was here."

This was in the days before video surveillance was common. There were no access cards or security. There would be no record of my visit. I could walk in, slip him the gun, and leave unseen.

"Can you hold a gun?" I asked.

He awkwardly raised his hand, turned it to his head, and curled his index finger as if he were pulling a trigger. His eyes met mine. He could do it but my heart broke at the thought of it. We had made a bargain.

The following Friday, I left for school as if it were any other day. My parents had plans to return to West Virginia that night after they got off work. I had eight hours to get to his bedside and back without raising any concerns. It would be tight. Under my seat, wrapped in a red bandana, was a Colt .38 revolver. I wondered why he stored that particular gun in the basement in a toolbox instead of upstairs with his other guns. The question was partially answered when I removed the gun from the oily rag in his basement and found the serial numbers were ground off. Perhaps this gun had killed a man before.

Back in Williamson, West Virginia, I parked in a half-full lot outside of the hospital. The gun was tucked in my jacket pocket, still wrapped in the bandana. I pushed through a glass door and took the elevator to the third floor. I raised the hood on my gray sweatshirt. I knew where I was going and exited the elevator confidently.

I looked up and down the hall. It was empty. I walked to my grandfather's room. The door was closed halfway and I pushed it open. He appeared to be asleep, the light from the window illuminating him in a way that made him appear very peaceful. His features were relaxed in a way they'd not been a few days earlier. I shut the door behind me and walked to his bedside.

I considered turning around and leaving. He would never know I'd even been there. I couldn't live with the guilt, though. The knowledge that his final feelings toward me were not love, but disappointment and betrayal. I leaned over him and whispered in his ear. His eyes opened slowly, taking a moment to focus on me, to understand who I was and why I was here. I was the grim reaper. I was death come to take him.

He smiled with half his mouth and his eyes teared up again. He mumbled and I knew he was thanking me.

"Do you still want to do this?" I asked.

He looked me in the eye and nodded.

"You can't do it while I'm here," I said. "No one can know I was here."

He nodded again.

"If I slide it up under your hip and cover it with the blanket, can you get to it after I leave?"

He nodded.

"I will miss you so much," I said, my eyes beginning to pour. A sob wracked my body.

"No," he hissed at me, clearer than anything he'd said since his stroke.

I knew what he was saying. He was telling me to harden up. Sometimes men had to do unimaginable things for the people they loved. They pulled their dead fathers from the house and took them to town for burial, as he had. They went to work as children to make sure their brothers and sisters had shoes, as he had. They killed men who threatened them, as he had. I dried up the tears and controlled my breathing.

"I love you," I whispered. "I've got to go."

His eyes stayed glued to mine. "Love you, too," he said, his speech slightly garbled but understandable.

I knew he meant it. Hard as he was, he loved me and he was proud of me. I pulled the hood of my gray sweatshirt back up and left the room without looking back. Passing no one in the hall, I opted for the stairs to avoid standing around waiting for the elevator. I left the building, drove back to Virginia, and as far as I know my visit there is a secret that only I hold.

I got home around the normal time, but my parents were already home. When I walked in the house, I heard my mother's sobbing and knew he'd done it already. I was surprised to feel relief along with my grief. I was happy that he was released. Happy that he had left on his own terms. We'd pulled it off.

No one ever figured out how he got the gun. My mother was certain one of his old buddies had slipped it to him. There was a constant stream of them in and out of the room. My dad never voiced his theory but he looked at me differently sometimes. I wondered if he suspected, but he never asked.

EPILOGUE

In Russell County, as darkness settled on Ellen and her family, they gathered for dinner around a battery-operated lantern. They ate their meal while Ellen shared her plan for the next day. Jim's parents were not thrilled with the idea, despite Ellen's assurances. Pete and Ariel were so excited she suspected they would have a difficult time going to sleep. Moving to Jim's cave would be a lot of work, but it was the safest option she could imagine.

One mile up the road from Ellen and Jim's home, a grim cabal shared a meager dinner around a campfire in the yard of an older mobile home. A few folks had left over the past two days, hoping to find shelters or relatives who would take them in. A little more than twenty folks remained, including children. This group had no intention of leaving. For one thing, revenge burned in the hearts of some for the men who'd not come home. For another, it seemed that the family up the road had supplies. They didn't seem to be hurting like they were. At one point, they were pretty sure they heard a generator running up there. All they needed was a plan and it could all be theirs – food, house, and vengeance.

OUTSIDE THE TOWN OF CRAWFISH, an ancient man stood in a kitchen, prying the lid from a Mason jar. He poured the home-canned tomatoes overtop the green beans he'd already poured from another jar. He set the pot of beans and tomatoes on the eye of the old wood-fired cookstove that had been in this kitchen since before he was born.

While he waited for the pot to heat, he heard heavy steps on the porch. He knew the thuds that accompanied each step were the sound of his son's banjo bouncing off each rotting step as he climbed them. This was confirmed when he heard the banjo dragging across the porch. There was a creak as the screen door opened. There were more steps and the scrape of the dragging banjo on the floor.

"Mommy," moaned the man with the banjo. His voice was too loud and his word as ill-formed as he himself was.

The older man turned and faced his son. "Mommy didn't come home, Lawrence. Nobody did. I don't know what the hell happened to them."

Lawrence, middle-aged and diaper-clad, the product of a genetic abnormality, considered his father's words, his mouth agape, eyes slow to register his thoughts. A social worker once tried to get them to send Lawrence to an institution, assuring them he'd get excellent care and would be happy there, but his parents had not allowed it. Lawrence was their son and his place was at home. The man and his wife were both in their seventies now and they'd started to consider they might have to make other arrangements for Lawrence. They wouldn't be able to look after him forever. Now the man was afraid they might have waited too long.

Lawrence raised the dirty hand holding the banjo and pointed toward town. "Bubby...four-wheeler...go town," he said, his pronunciation staggered and awkward. The words were long, drawling, and atonal.

The old man set down the wooden spoon with which he was stirring the tomatoes and green beans. He turned to his son. "You saw your brother Bubby go into town on his four-wheeler?"

He knew this could not be the case because he'd seen Bubby leave with Lawrence's mother and the rest of the family this morning. They'd gone up the Parkway searching for their other missing son.

"Bubby four-wheeler," Lawrence said. "Not Bubby."

"You saw Bubby's four-wheeler going into town with someone else driving it?" the old man asked.

Lawrence grinned and nodded.

The old man returned to his beans, thinking over what his son had just said. If there was another man on his son's four-wheeler then it meant his son was probably dead. Bubby would not give up his four-wheeler without a fight. If his son was dead, they were probably *all* dead. He watched Lawrence silently strumming the string-less banjo he held across his lap. Saliva pooled in the toothless maw of his mouth and ran freely down his chin and neck. The old man knew that he could not care for his child on his own. Even at fifty-four years old, Lawrence was still his child and required every bit as much care as he had when he was a toddler.

The old man would pay town a visit tomorrow and see what he could find out. If a man went through town on his son's four-wheeler, someone would have seen something. He would start with the barber, the one who was always asking questions about the old times. The one who played music. The one who'd given Lawrence his banjo.

When he found his son's four-wheeler, he would kill the man riding it.

TO CONTINUE READING

The story of The Borrowed World continues in
Book Two, Ashes Of The Unspeakable

Available in ebook, paperback, and audio.

Made in the USA
Columbia, SC
08 April 2021